"Things don't always turn out the way we want them to, do they?" Victoria asked softly.

Something in Joseph's gaze caught and held Victoria breathless. She looked away quickly, but for an instant ten years vanished and they were back on the deck of the riverboat on the Mississippi River, with the water splashing against the shore while she memorized every inch of his face.

"This isn't the end," he'd whispered. "It can't be. I'll never stop loving you."

Then the whistle blew and the deck beneath them moved, and the years stacked atop each other once more. She blinked and shook the memory away, but not before she relived the heartbreak of loss. Not again. Never again. She couldn't bear to feel that kind of pain for a second time.

Books by Hannah Alexander

Love Inspired Historical

*Hideaway Home
Keeping Faith

Love Inspired Suspense

*Note of Peril
*Under Suspicion
*Death Benefits
Hidden Motive
Season of Danger
"Silent Night, Deadly Night"
Eye of the Storm

Steeple Hill Single Title

*Hideaway
*Safe Haven
*Last Resort
*Fair Warning
*Grave Risk
*Double Blind
A Killing Frost
**Sacred Trust
**Solemn Oath
**Silent Pledge

*Hideaway novel
**Sacred Trust series

HANNAH ALEXANDER

is the pseudonym of husband-and-wife writing team Cheryl and Mel Hodde (pronounced "Hoddee"). When they first met, Mel had just begun his new job as an E.R. doctor in Cheryl's hometown, and Cheryl was working on a novel. Cheryl's matchmaking pastor set them up on an unexpected blind date at a local restaurant. Surprised by the sneak attack, Cheryl blurted the first thing that occurred to her, "You're a doctor? Could you help me paralyze someone?" Mel was shocked. "Only temporarily, of course," she explained when she saw his expression. "And only fictitiously. I'm writing a novel."

They began brainstorming immediately. Eighteen months later they were married, and the novels they set in fictitious Ozark towns began to sell. The first novel in the Hideaway series won the prestigious Christy award for Best Romance in 2004.

Keeping Faith

HANNAH ALEXANDER

HARLEQUIN® LOVE INSPIRED® HISTORICAL

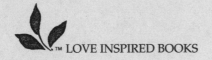 LOVE INSPIRED BOOKS

ISBN-13: 978-0-373-82980-4

KEEPING FAITH

Copyright © 2013 by Hannah Alexander

www.LoveInspiredBooks.com

Printed in U.S.A.

Trust in the Lord forever, for the Lord,
the Lord himself, is the Rock eternal.
—*Isaiah* 26:4

This story is written in loving memory
of Lorene B. Cook, Sept. 13, 1925, to Feb. 25, 2012,
whose inner strength will live on in my characters
as long as the stories exist.

Chapter One

Dr. Victoria Fenway sat beside her young assistant in the opening of her host's covered wagon, grinding herbs with mortar and pestle as she studied the tree-shrouded wilderness for a shadow, a shape or move- ment that might tell her their camp was being watched by a monster.

Broderick Thames, her husband's murderer, was in- deed a monster, and he was here in the south of Mis- souri. She had no doubt of that. For the past few days, after discovering the first unique track of the killer's fire-red horse, she'd lived on the razor edge of fear. He'd come this way for a reason, but why?

A screech of youthful male terror reached her from a distance. She jerked, startled, spilling powdered cham- omile everywhere.

Her fourteen-year-old helper, Heidi Ladue, dropped her empty teabags and caught Victoria by the arm. "Dr. Fenway, that sounds like Claude. Did you hear a splash?"

Victoria turned and tried to peer through the trees to- ward the roar of the flooded creek that had halted their journey today. "In that torrent? How could anyone hear a single splash?"

Another cry reached them from the direction of the creek. "The rope," came a familiar voice. "Help me, please! Get the rope."

Heidi scrambled from her perch on the wagon's edge, long strands of her flax-pale hair dangling over her shoulders and the calico ruffles of her sleeves. "That *is* Claude. He's in trouble!"

Victoria shoved her work aside and leaped from beneath the canvas of the Ladue wagon. "We don't have the ropes. Your mother tied the horses with them." They'd been unable to form a corral with the wagons on this narrow strip of land between cliffs and overflowing creek.

She ran toward the trees in an effort to catch sight of Claude but all she could see was muddy, churning water between giant trunks of oak and broadleaf evergreens. Heidi's younger brother was not a clumsy boy. Could Thames be nearby? Could that wicked man have pushed him?

Heidi clutched Victoria's arm and tugged. "He was with the Johnston boys earlier. Please come, Dr. Fenway. They had a rope. They were trying to make a pulley out of it to get the wagon across the water."

Victoria allowed herself to be pulled forward. "They told you this?"

"No, ma'am, I could see it with my own eyes." Heidi released her grip and turned toward the creek. "I heard them talking. I told the captain and he got on 'em, but they didn't listen. They've been up to something, and I don't see Claude, but right there's the Johnston boys."

She pointed toward Claude's constant companions, blond-haired Buster and Gray Johnston. They stood across a narrow clearing beside a huge oak tree that shaded a section of the raging water. They were struggling mightily to straighten a tangled mess of rope that connected their wagon to the tree.

Despite stern reprimands, the boys appeared determined to float their wagon to the other bank before the floodwaters died down, like children taking a dare to prove they were men. They were proving just the opposite with their careless disregard for safety.

"Buster?" Victoria called out, clutching her funereal-black skirts and hurrying through treacherous mud toward the boys, Heidi at her side. "Didn't you two hear your friend? He's in trouble."

"I know, but this here's what he needs." Buster held up an end of the rope in his hand. "It's too knotted."

Claude cried out again and Heidi turned to run toward the sound of her brother's voice. "It's the creek, Doctor. I know he fell into the creek!"

Buster tugged with more force on the rope, his face dripping with sweat. "I'm tryin', ma'am, doin' all I can, but he's got to have this to get out!"

"Heidi, be careful!" Victoria turned back to the Johnston brothers. "Boys, please hurry. What is Claude doing in the water?"

"Hangin' on for life right now," Gray said.

Victoria could imagine all sorts of awful endings to this and it made her dizzy. "To what?"

"Old stump."

"That isn't good enough. We need your help right now." Victoria wanted to stamp her foot. Did these young men have difficulty grasping the plain truth? She still couldn't see the thirteen-year-old boy. "Find something else, a plank of wood, a branch. Something!"

"Gotta get this thing unwound to reach him." Buster's fingers slid on the muddy knots. "He's way out there."

Victoria wanted to thump their heads together as she watched the detritus being shoved along at a mighty pace down the widened creek. Couldn't they get a little more excited about the threat to their friend's life? "No stump's going to protect him from being knocked to pieces if he's in that creek. You need to try something besides the rope and do it quickly."

As if he hadn't heard her, Buster gave the snarl another tug, which made it cling more tightly to the tree.

Victoria nearly growled aloud. "Buster, now!" She could hear only Claude's cries for help over the flood-stage roar of Flat Creek—which was anything but flat at the moment. It sounded as if an invisible giant rampaged through this southern Missouri valley, tearing trees from their roots to thrust them out of the racing, muddy water. And now Heidi, too, ran dangerously close to the edge of the steep bank.

Victoria turned, slid and nearly fell in the thick mud. "Heidi Ladue, you get away from the water! Help me find something long enough to reach him."

Heidi came rushing back, her dainty, even features tight with fear, pale hair flying out behind her in the breeze. "He's too far out, Doctor. We can't reach him." She grabbed Victoria's arm. "I'm scared," she said, her voice catching.

"Round up help from the camp. Now, my dear." Victoria gave her a quick hug and urged her up the hill, but as she looked over the girl's shoulder she finally caught sight of Claude. He was being flung back and forth in the water, choking and spitting, his head barely above the surface as he grasped the stump. "Get the adults quickly!"

As Heidi ran up the muddy track, Victoria raced along the side of the creek. "Hold on, Claude, we'll get you out!" She searched for a thick limb or a length of vine she might use to reach the boy, but the limb she picked up immediately broke. The vine fell apart. Everything was too soaked to hold up under Claude's weight.

She glanced over her shoulder to see if the Johnston boys were having any luck with the rope, but Buster and Gray were now in some argument she couldn't make out.

"Boys, grow up and get to work!" she called, but they didn't seem to hear her. With the sound of the water, she could barely hear herself.

She closed her eyes and screamed at the top of her lungs, "Gentlemen! Help!" Those young men should never have been allowed to leave home without their father. Instead of eighteen and sixteen, they behaved like eight and six. Why had Joseph chosen them to help build his town in Kansas?

She turned and ran toward Claude again. "We need more men on this trip," she muttered to herself. How would this group cross the state border safely into Kansas Territory if the Johnston boys kept pulling stunts like this?

With a glance uphill, she searched for the one man who claimed to always be there for help and protection, though she couldn't see proof that he practiced his assurances. "Captain Rickard?" she called at the top of her voice. "Trouble! Help us, please."

But Joseph was nowhere in sight. According to Heidi, he was helping collect wood for the fire, a job Claude and his friends were supposed to be doing. Instead of helping, Claude had hovered near the creek with Gray

Johnston, both of them in apparent awe of Buster Johnston's glowing presence.

Victoria scowled at the thought, but she realized that, deep down, she'd been as hopeful as Buster that there would be a way past the flooding so they could cross, though they each had widely divergent motivations. She knew Buster wanted a fresh start as far from home as he could get, and he was in a hurry to get there. He'd suffered deeply after knocking over a lantern where he worked and burning down the general store in their town. A man had died because of Buster's clumsiness. Anyone his age would go in search of a new life after that. What she feared was that the clumsy bear cub would leave a path of destruction behind him.

She, on the other hand, wanted to scout ahead of the others and scour the fresh mud for familiar tracks. For the first couple of weeks she'd been able to put aside her thirst for revenge as she'd settled in with the friendly people of the wagon train, especially the Ladues. Last week, however, she'd seen evidence that the killer, Thames, had been through the town where the Johnston boys had joined them. She'd seen the unique hoofprint three times along the trail they now followed—a horseshoe that had an inch of length broken off on the right front hoof of Thames's crimson-colored horse.

She owed Matthew so much; finding his killer was the least she could do to honor his memory. She knew Joseph had wanted her to come with them as their physician—though she felt herself to be a poor substitute for her late husband—but she had her own reasons for coming, and the murdering slaver was never far from her thoughts. He terrified her and he enraged her, and she couldn't tell which emotion controlled her at any given time. What she knew, however, was that she could not rely on her emotions. They could betray her as ruthlessly as Joseph had done a decade ago.

But Joseph didn't belong in the same league as Broderick Thames. A man who killed for the simple pleasure of beating his political opponent was a monster, indeed. What would he do if he knew this wagon train was filled with abolitionists set on building a slave-free community in Kansas Territory? He would find a way to destroy them all, and he had the connections to do it.

"Someone, please!" Heidi's high-pitched voice echoed down to Victoria as she searched around the camp. "Dr. Fenway, look!" The girl's voice spiraled upward in terror, echoing against the cliffs that halfway surrounded the wagon train on the eastern side of the flooded creek.

Victoria saw Heidi pointing and turned to find that Claude no longer held on to the stump. Only a lone hand stuck out of the water. It grasped upward, much farther downstream than expected. The stump floated away, roots pointing toward the sky as if they were hands grasping for a firm foundation. The water was carrying Claude.

Before she could catch up with his progress, he shoved away from the tumbling log and lunged toward the bank, at least fifty yards from where the Johnston boys continued to wrangle with their rope.

She raced toward him, stumbling over vines that had been washed ashore. The Ladue family had already lost their father. What a nightmare if Luella and Heidi were to lose Claude, as well.

Even as she ran, however, she heard solid footsteps coming up behind her. She could imagine she felt the shaking of the ground when she heard the rush of heavy breathing. She looked to find one of the older men,

Mr. Reich, racing by her, slipping and catching himself on the wet grass and mud, paunch hanging past his belt. The wagon train's scout, long-legged, raw-boned McDonald, ran barely a stride's length behind Reich. Victoria tripped over another vine and finally lost her balance for good to land in a patch of muddy grass. Others rushed to her to help her up, but she urged them to follow Reich and McDonald.

There was a sudden throng of rescuers, including Luella Ladue with her daughter. Luella surpassed all but the two first men, her light brown hair flying. She jumped into the creek with her grip on a thick vine connected to a gnarled oak tree.

Victoria sat where she was for a few seconds, glad for the rescuers but still anxious. No one should be in the water. True, it wasn't stagnant, but who knew how many stagnant pools and contaminated ponds now mingled with the running water? She'd seen too many cholera victims in her ten years of medical practice.

Mrs. Ladue locked her free arm around her son's middle. Luella was a strong woman, as she'd had to be since her husband's death last year, but Victoria feared she might not be strong enough to fight the water and the tossing logs and trees…even worse, the contamination that could lurk in the water.

"Luella, you've both got to get out of there now!" Victoria pulled herself to her feet. Despite her warning, others followed Luella's lead and jumped in to help push Claude up. "Please, stay out of the water. It could be poison!" And yet, she saw no other way for them to haul the weakened boy from the fierce rush of the creek.

Mr. Reich and Mr. McDonald had flopped onto their bellies at the edge of mud, ready with arms outstretched to pull the others to shore. Typically the first person to help out when needed, Mr. Reich had a heft about him that suggested more padding than muscle, but he was as strong as a warhorse. Mr. McDonald, wiry and tall, matched his friend's strength.

The men and women of their group stood along the bank or knelt over the side to help, and several made use of the same vine Luella had used to lower herself into the dirty creek water. It appeared to the onlookers, of course, that Claude was safe for now as his mother grasped him and their rescuers formed a chain to aid his rise from the flood.

Knowing Luella, Victoria knew Claude was in for the scolding of his life, after his mother had smothered him with kisses.

"Victoria?"

She heard the voice and turned to see the man who had, to her shame, held her heart captive for ten years. He came running through the camp with a load of wood in his arms, his strength making the load look insignificant. Captain Joseph Rickard was a title she'd never become accustomed to these past four weeks of tedious travel through unmarked hills and over rocky terrain. After the first few days of attempting to use the formal address, she'd felt so awkward she'd reverted to calling him Joseph, despite a few raised eyebrows. After all, had he not abandoned her in St. Louis with Matthew, they would be married. It was his decision, his rejection, that had helped her keep her distance from him... most of the time.

By now everyone who traveled with them knew that she and Joseph had been friends long ago. Few knew about the depth of that friendship. She was, after all, still in mourning, and women of society didn't feel it seemly for a widow of seven months to spend her available hours with an unmarried man—not that she'd ever been particularly concerned about the women of society. A female physician would always be sneered at by those women, so why waste her time?

The last time she'd seen Joseph before he left for his father's plantation in the South, she'd been sobbing in his arms, begging him not to leave, all dignity replaced by abject pain at the thought of losing him.

"I heard the shouts." He tossed the wood beside the Ladue wagon and rushed to Victoria, his attention drawn to the mud on her dress. "What happened? Are you all right?" He brushed at some of the heaviest clumps from the black cotton.

"Never mind me. I slipped while trying to get to Claude." She pointed toward the crowd, where everyone hovered around the boy, slapping his back as he choked up dirty water.

"He fell in?" He took her arm and started in the direction of the crowd.

She went with him. "I haven't decided yet. Nobody seems to know what happened."

"What do you mean?"

"At this point, considering his choice of companions and their determination to prove to the grown-ups they could cross that water—"

"The Johnston brothers. Again." Joseph looked up the creek toward the blond-haired boys, who had just managed to untangle the mess of knots in their rope and untie it from the tree. He frowned at the brothers, his dark eyes narrowing. "Claude wouldn't just fall in for no reason."

"That's my concern."

Joseph turned to her. "What concern?"

She pressed her lips together, sorry she'd been so

quick to speak her mind. "Only that he could have been pushed."

Joseph's thick, black eyebrows rose. "You can't think Buster or Gray could have pushed him."

"Of course not, Joseph. Give me credit for a little common sense. Believe it or not, those boys are the least of our troubles if my suspicions are correct." She shivered and glanced around them through the shadows of the forest once again.

"Victoria?"

There wasn't time to get into that conversation at the moment. Soon, though. "Please disregard my chatter. I'm simply overwhelmed at the moment. Those boys were supposed to be helping gather wood for a fire to dry things out, and instead they're doing what you told them not to. They need a firmer hand, Joseph, or they need to return to their father."

Joseph crossed his sun-browned arms over his chest and shook his head. "All of us were supposed to pitch in, Doctor, and I'm not their nanny."

She took umbrage at his defensive posture. "Not their nanny, but certainly their captain, and from what I understand, their father convinced you to bring them along. I thought you had nearly ten years of experience with captaining a wagon train."

She pressed her lips shut at the brusqueness of her own voice and glanced toward the rescuers, who were having success in getting everyone out of the water. She needed to check on her patients soon and let go of this petty little ten-year resentment that had been doomed to cause friction between the two of them.

"I'm sorry, Victoria." Joseph sighed, and the familiar deep voice that once whispered words of love in her ear held a note of sadness.

"Sorry?" Eyebrows raised, she turned back to him and was captured by the depth of those dark brown eyes, as she always had been. But she'd learned the hard way to look past a man's words and mesmerizing eyes to the character beneath. His behavior had taught her to beware of other men, though that lesson had come too late for her to avoid his impact on her life.

"We seem to be at odds on this trip when we're not avoiding one another," he said. "It wasn't what I'd hoped for." Gone was the typical display of golden sunlight in eyes that were often touched with humor. She missed that.

She also missed the man she'd once thought Joseph to be. "Don't lecture me about avoidance. I wasn't the one who stayed away for ten years like a sulking child. You knew where Matthew and I were anytime you came to St. Louis."

"That's right." He said the words with an emphasis that implied he'd explained it all, when in truth he hadn't explained a thing.

"Don't doubt my gratefulness, I do appreciate your arrival at the perfect time for me to escape an ugly situation, but I don't understand why you asked me to join you on this trip."

"I wanted you out of St. Louis. I worried about you all winter after word reached me about Matthew's death."

"Then where were you all winter?" She'd wondered that several times over the long, hard winter months, when neighbors became unfriendly and the sheriff tried more than once to convince himself that she had been the culprit in Matthew's death.

"I was in Kansas Territory," Joseph said, "bound in by snow."

"Of course. My apologies. I heard the snows hit the

Territory hard this past winter." She couldn't miss the fact that Joseph was studying her every expression with deep interest.

"I had hoped we could put old disagreements behind us," he said, his voice softening. "I know you're angry with me for some reason. You're brooding."

She wouldn't try to deny that. "I apologize for making you uncomfortable." She couldn't tell him the truth—that guilt combined with old resentments made her awkward around him. While she grieved for her husband, the truth was Matthew had always known she didn't love him the way a woman should love her man. Not the way he loved her. Not the way she'd loved Joseph....

"Matthew made me a top priority in his life," she said. "You did not." That was, indeed, a great deal of her problem, but it certainly didn't explain why she'd been unable to dismiss Joseph the way he'd obviously dismissed her. "Indeed, you became engaged to another woman." That, above all other things, still angered her when she allowed herself to think about it, and this was not the time to allow her temper to flare.

"I'm sorry. I don't know what made you think that, but—"

"Perhaps we could save this discussion for another time," she said. "I have patients to see." Without waiting for a reply, she strode away from him toward the crowd of wet and upset travelers. Why had she come on this trip? Now Joseph must think she would always be willing to simply drop everything and do whatever he wished.

How on earth could this situation get worse?

Chapter Two

Joseph stood staring after Victoria's enchanting, black-clad figure, and considered, as he had dozens of times in these past weeks, that this journey could be his chance to correct past blunders. Yes, she had misunderstood his actions at the worst possible times, believed some wild tales about him that were completely untrue, and yet if he was picking up on the right signals, her heart was trapped in the same position as his. After all these years. It amazed and humbled him.

In spite of all the past tensions between the two of them, his father's machinations to marry him off to another woman and whatever Matthew had convinced Victoria to believe, Joseph suspected, with growing excitement, that something within her wanted to block out all the efforts made by others to keep them apart.

Not that he would want his old friend—and perhaps foe, at least in romance—to die in order for Victoria to see the truth about their enduring love. Joseph was no romantic. Most folks married for the sake of necessity, and they had good, strong marriages. But for Joseph, there had always only been Victoria.

It mystified him still. Some people were meant to

be together; he and Victoria were two of those people.
He'd known it since their first kiss, his first desire to
marry her and take her out of St. Louis and carry her
home to meet his family.

If anyone should feel slighted about that time, it
should be him. He'd merely wanted to introduce his
soon-to-be fiancée to his family and friends at home,
take her with him as he cared for family, being the oldest son.

Yet Victoria would have nothing to do with that; she
detested slavery, and his father owned slaves in Georgia. Yet would she be gracious and allow him to prove
his convictions to her? No. She merely rejected him.
He had determined on his way back to St. Louis from
Kansas Territory that he wouldn't be so easily kow-
towed this time.

Ahead of him, the woman who occupied his thoughts
nearly slid to the ground. He caught up with her and re-
claimed her arm, because if she fell again she could end
up as a patient instead of the much-needed doctor. He
resisted the impulse to remark on what she'd just said.
She was right; this wasn't the time to debate old hurts.

Right now they had people to see to, when what he
wanted to do was gather some strands of her disabused
hair and tuck it away. He loved the color of that hair,
which matched a golden Missouri sunset. Though he
also loved the shimmering blue of her eyes, he was glad
they were walking side by side, because he didn't want
to meet her gaze.

This was not the time to explain why he'd avoided
her and Matthew when they were married or admit the
chink in his armor when it came to her. That would re-
quire a much longer conversation. Later.

As they strolled toward the others, he saw that Mc-Donald and Reich had things well in hand.

"I apologize for not responding to the news of the death of your intended." Victoria's voice could bite with such gentleness that he barely felt it until the meaning struck him across the face. "I didn't know about her for months."

He cut her a glance. "I wrote to you."

"I received nothing."

"You should have."

"And yet, somehow, I didn't." She snapped the words, as if she didn't believe him.

"Now I'm a liar?"

She cut him a look of confusion. "I don't know what to believe, Joseph, and I haven't for a very long time. I only know you're not the man I thought you were."

"Of course I'm not. Then I was barely more than a rank youngster. People do grow, you know."

She cast a glance toward the Johnston boys. "Let's hope that's true."

He wasn't going to let her take her jabs and then change the subject that easily. "I didn't get engaged." He thought about his dear childhood friend, Sara Jane. Despite Father's wishes, Joseph and Sara Jane would never have married. He'd loved her like a sister, a trusted playmate from years before, who had grown into a fine woman and who was secretly betrothed to a man from Atlanta. She'd told Joseph all about it and he'd been happy for her. Though heartbroken at her death, losing her wasn't the reason he'd turned his back on plantation life.

"That catastrophe was the result of my dying father's desire to build an empire for his oldest son using a legal bond between a neighbor's daughter and me." Joseph kept his voice low. "Neither Sara Jane nor I were complicit in that arrangement, only our fathers. We were determined to break the supposed engagement together, but she sickened and passed away before any formal announcement could be made."

There was a long silence before Victoria spoke. "I see."

"I'm not sure you do. How did you hear of my father's plans?" he asked.

Her arm stiffened in his grasp, but he held on and tried to catch a glimpse of her expression, see what she was thinking. He'd been able to do that once upon a time, but she held her own counsel as her attention focused on the crowd.

"Victoria?"

"Matthew told me of a letter you wrote to him."

"He received my letters and you did not? Don't you think that's odd?"

"Why would I think it odd? From my perspective, you had forgotten about me and found someone else."

Joseph gritted his teeth. How this woman could drive him to distraction with her stubbornness. "You didn't at least read Matthew's letter for yourself?"

"Mine and Matthew's was a business partnership. I didn't read his personal mail, nor he mine."

Joseph took a moment for those last words to sink in. As they did, he continued to doubt his own perception. "Business partnership? You and Matthew?"

She tugged her arm from his grasp, and he realized he'd stopped walking. He caught up and fell into step beside her again.

"It was a socially acceptable way to form a partnership and spend all our time together as he taught me medicine," she said. "You must have some grasp about how much there is to learn."

"Dr. Fenway?" called Audy Reich from Mrs. Ladue's side. "Hon, I think we need you over here."

After a final look at Joseph, Victoria gathered her skirts and hurried toward the group huddled beside the raging creek. Joseph watched her for a moment, stymied. The Victoria Foster he had known and loved before she'd married Matthew Fenway would never have lied. But Matthew had always been an honorable man. If Victoria didn't receive those letters, then who did?

Claude was still gagging and coughing up creek water when Victoria reached him. Luella sat on the ground beside her son. Although Victoria gave her an assuring nod, she felt ill equipped to give her friend any kind of assurance.

"Boy's swallowed lots of water." McDonald's voice was gruff as if from years of disuse in his solitary search for trails. "Luella did, too."

"No, see to Claude," Luella said. "I'll be okay."

Victoria tugged Claude onto his side as the creek continued to pour from his mouth. "We'll take care of all of you. Mr. McDonald, would you brace him for me?"

She saw Joseph watching from a distance, waiting for a signal. She nodded, and he returned it. Time to get the treatments started.

Heidi wrapped her arms around her mother, sobbing. Luella's hair was drenched with mud that covered her clothing and face. Victoria took both mother and daughter into her arms.

"This is horrible." Luella's whispered words came out staccato from her shivering body. She twisted her work-worn hands in her lap.

Victoria grabbed the blanket a man offered then wrapped it around Luella's shoulders. "I know. Take deep breaths—try to relax."

"I just lost Barnabas last year." She looked at Victoria with frightened eyes. "To think that I might've lost my Claude…." Luella's sobs came in silence, as if from long practice, and Victoria held her more tightly. "Captain Rickard and the men are gathering logs. This won't be comfortable, but we'll do what we can to keep you well."

Luella nodded, sniffing. "I'm sorry. I know you lost your Matthew last year. You know how it feels."

Victoria felt like an imposter.

Mr. Reich knelt beside them, jerking his head toward the water. "Think we're far enough from the danger, Doc?"

Victoria glanced at the creek, which, if anything, carried more refuse than before. "I believe we should find our way farther up into the forest for safety." She helped Claude and Luella onto their feet, dreading the consequences of this awful day.

McDonald walked over to Joseph. "I'll go get more logs, Captain, unless you'd rather I go knock those Johnston boys' heads together."

Joseph thought about it a moment, then shook his head. "I'll deal with them. But I think we have enough logs for now. Just don't go trying to cross the creek before morning."

McDonald nodded and turned to help the others move closer to the wagons. Joseph made his way toward the Johnston boys as they stretched out their rope and leaned crazily over the floodwaters to wash off the mud.

Buster, eighteen and full of vinegar, had a longish face and sharp features that made him look serious and much wiser than his years. Much wiser than he actually was, for sure.

"That clumsy oaf got the rope all tangled and then dropped one end into the water," Buster said. "We barely caught it before a log could get tangled in it. Then the mud just fell out from under him and we couldn't get him out."

"He isn't clumsy." Gray glared at his brother in an unspoken reprimand. "We tried to grab him." The younger brother was by far the smarter of the two, but Buster controlled him like a pet dog. "I almost had him, but then he caught that old stump. I told him to hold on and I'd get the rope."

"And you didn't think to pull him out?" Joseph demanded.

"What was he supposed to do?" Buster asked. "We needed the rope for that. Couldn't reach him any other way. He was too far out."

"His mother didn't have any trouble getting to him," Joseph said.

"He'd floated farther down by then." Buster's voice rose with youthful outrage. "I was trying to get the rope untangled so I could throw it out for him to catch."

Joseph reached for the rope in question. "I'll take that if you don't mind."

Buster refused to release it. "Hey, you can't take my dad's rope away from us! We're going to need it."

"You mind telling me why you felt it was so important to stand over here and plot to cross the creek when you'd been ordered not to?"

"We would've waited for the right time." Buster's contrary attitude had begun to irritate Joseph from the first day the boys joined them. Buster also knew how

to egg on the younger boys. He was a natural leader—
a dangerous quality in one so pigheaded.

Joseph stepped forward and loomed over Buster until
the boy released the other end of his prized rope. "You
need to think past the end of your nose, Johnston, before you get someone killed."

Buster grimaced and looked away. "Claude's fine,
isn't he?"

Joseph glanced over his shoulder, where Victoria had
moved up the hillside with her patients. "No thanks to
you, he's safe for now, but if he or any of the others get
sick from swallowing contaminated water, I'm holding you boys responsible. You could have kept half the
camp from risking their lives if you'd followed my orders in the first place." He turned and walked uphill
toward the rescue team.

"We're going to need that rope to get across the
creek," Buster called after him.

Joseph looped the item in question over his arm, ignoring Buster's protest. Instead of waiting at his brother's side, sixteen-year-old Gray followed Joseph—a
habit he'd begun to develop soon after joining the wagon
train three weeks ago. Joseph suspected it was one reason Buster acted out so often.

"You should help your brother move that wagon away
from the water," Joseph told the boy. "You never know
about flash floods."

Gray snorted. "He won't move it."

"You don't think it's in a dangerous place?"

"You think my opinion matters to him? I'm his stupid little brother."

"I need you to help me with the patients, then."

The boy looked up at Joseph, eyes brightening.

"If I find out what Dr. Fenway needs, will you gather the items and help with treatments?"

Gray ducked his head. "Sure thing."

"Don't stare at the patients while they're being treated."

"No, sir."

"Go check on Claude."

Without a word, Gray did as he was told.

Joseph watched Victoria. She moved quickly between her charges, but she had a comforting voice that obviously soothed everyone who heard it. Her eyes softened as she assured Luella she would do her best to protect everyone from any contamination, and then examined a cut on Luella's arm. She gave Heidi orders to run back to the wagon for supplies.

She finally looked over her shoulder to find Joseph watching her. He beckoned for her to join him for a quick word. She hesitated, then excused herself from the others.

"Yes, Joseph?" She looked at his hair, which he knew hung over his forehead in untidy black strands. Once upon a time she would have reached up and straightened it for him; he couldn't help hoping she would at least attempt to brush the sawdust from it.

But her hands remained at her sides as she waited for him to speak.

He cleared his throat. "What's your complete plan of action, Doctor?"

"According to a Dr. Snow I spoke with in England last year, cholera is definitely caused by bad drinking water, hence my concern, of course. As I've stressed, we have no idea how much contamination that creek is carrying with it or how far north it started. Everyone who was in the water could be in danger if they swallowed anything, and that cut on Luella's arm worries me."

"Is there no treatment to prevent them from developing the illness?"

"I wish there was. We can try to force as much water from them as possible."

"More than rolling them over the logs?"

"Yes. I wish I'd brought ipecac," she said. "But I had an order that didn't come in before we left. I've sent Heidi for some salt and pure water. If we can give them salt water to drink and then dilute what's left with clean water, it's logical we could ward off some contagion," she said. "Thank you for gathering the logs for us. I know it's a long shot, but we'll take what we can right now."

"I'll help with that."

As he turned to leave, Victoria touched his arm. "Wait, Joseph. They don't listen to me as they do to you. Some of the people are still hovering too closely to the water for my liking. That bank could collapse with them at any second. We need to move them into the forest."

He took her hand, which was still soft despite her habit of taking turns at the reins of the mules pulling the Ladue wagon these past four weeks. "Except for Buster Johnston, I think the rest are willing to listen. I'll do all I can."

"I appreciate it." She returned to her patients.

Victoria had once told him his touch gave her strength she didn't know she had. He missed her touch. He'd lain awake too many nights out on the trail during the years after his father passed, and he'd recalled her gentle touch, the feel of her lips against his, the sparkle of her tears when he'd left her for the plantation with the belief that it was his responsibility to take over the running of it as the oldest son.

Victoria hated slavery. They'd disagreed about it often, but he hadn't changed his mind until he'd arrived at the plantation. He'd felt a kick of knowledge in his gut for the first time. He'd seen slavery from her eyes, heard her voice in his head and knew he would not be able to stay. He planned to return to St. Louis and walk back into Victoria's arms a changed man. That had never happened.

Oh, he'd changed, all right. He'd been ravaged by bitterness upon arriving back in St. Louis and finding that Matthew had for sure taken care of Victoria. He'd married her.

And Joseph became a man who led others across country, and saved his money and brooded about the treachery of the friend he'd once trusted and the woman he still loved.

"My friends, it's time to start treatment." Victoria leaned over Luella and nodded to Joseph, Mr. Reich and Mr. McDonald, who held others over the logs, facedown. "This won't be comfortable, but we need to try to prevent contagion if we can." She raised her eyebrows at Joseph and they got started.

Despite all, she couldn't prevent a lingering look at Joseph. He appeared to have everything in hand, up to and including a threat that if the Johnston boys didn't move their wagon they might well lose it. Buster didn't listen.

Despite Joseph's deep, calm voice and manner, the anxiety in Victoria's belly tightened like a snake she and Matthew had once seen wrapped around a man's arm when they journeyed overseas. The man eventually lost his arm. What was this wagon train going to lose as a result of this catastrophe?

The clouds lifted as she worked with Luella, but the sunbeams didn't lighten her spirits. Too much could go wrong, and she felt the burden of responsibility for these people. Would Matthew have done this? Would he have had other options? When working with him, she'd felt confident in her abilities, but after losing her mentor she'd lost that confidence, despite the obvious approval Matthew had always shown for her skills.

Luella gagged on the cup of salted water.

"I'm sorry you have to go through this," Victoria said, holding her friend as the poor woman lost the water she'd swallowed.

Luella nodded and took another sip.

Victoria watched Joseph repeat the same actions with Claude and one of the younger men. He worked with such gentleness. What a good doctor he would have made. If she'd known ahead of time the heart break that would ensue after she refused to accompany Joseph to his parents' Georgia plantation, would she have gone? What a mystery about the fiancée, Sara Jane. She'd never forgotten that name, and she needed to know more. What would their lives have been like now if she'd given in to his pleas to go with him? They would never know.

She studied Joseph's firm-set chin, his narrowed eyes. Then she allowed her gaze to wander across the expanse of his shoulders, the corded muscles down his neck. When he'd first walked into the clinic last month, she'd nearly rushed into his arms, all dignity abandoned. It was a good thing she'd learned better self-control in her profession. Memories of her husband's murder seven months ago, however, had returned in a tempest. Seeing

Joseph had made her feel safe for the first time since her widowhood, despite old resentments from their past.

And yet, was she safe? Were any of them safe? She could still close her eyes and see that telltale hoofprint of the horse Thames had ridden the day he'd killed Matthew. She'd seen them on this very trail a couple of days ago, that distinctive print packed into mud and left to harden.

After her first sighting, she'd tried to tell herself the horse would have been reshod by now, but what if the horseshoe was shaped to the hoof? If that were so, then it would be easy to track him across the state. She just needed to make sure he didn't track them.

She would tell Joseph about the whole thing as soon as she knew for sure. Maybe she could find more tracks once they crossed the creek. Fresh tracks in the mud, perhaps?

She was just finishing with Luella and checking the others when a whoop and a loud cry reached them from the wagon camp.

"Oh, Lord, have mercy!" Audy Reich called out from her perch beside the fire where she'd been soaking beans to cook. She jumped up and ran through the trees toward them. "I hear some mighty cracklin' from up north. Captain, better get that young man away from there. Something big's coming down that creek!"

Chapter Three

Loud pops resounded through the forest like shots from a rifle. Hundreds of rifles in excruciating succession. But Victoria knew that sound. She'd heard the same several times when caught in an ice storm and the ice grew so thick on the branches that they broke. Limbs were breaking.

The creek had claimed another tree, and this one was a giant. She glanced downhill at the creek and saw a huge shadow being thrust forward by the water—for sure a giant tree uprooted. Its limbs grasped out toward everything near the swollen creek, and from the vantage point of the hill on which she stood, she saw the tree wrenching with it other trees, rocks and mud, creating a dam that blocked the motion of the water.

The creek spread and splashed far above its banks. The dam would break at any second. She could hear the creaking of wood and rumble of water under pressure. The forest blocked her sight of the place where Joseph had left Buster moping beside his wagon near the creek.

"Buster!" Gray's shout of horror bled into the roar of the water. He shot through the trees and down the hill toward his brother with the speed of a wildcat.

Joseph and Reich leaped forward and raced down the hillside behind him. Heidi started to cry, and her mother put an arm around her.

Mr. Reich's voice rang out through the valley. "Get away from the creek!"

The man's voice boomed with authority, but Victoria knew how little regard Buster had for that. She left the others and followed the men, sliding through the waterlogged forest, bracing against the trees until she reached a ledge where she could see directly down the hill. What she saw terrified her.

Joseph caught up with Reich, bracing for a wall of water to come crashing down on them at any moment. He couldn't forget his friend Johnston who'd scouted for Joseph a couple of years and once risked his own life to save Joseph from a rampaging brown bear. It would destroy Johnston if his sons never made it out of Missouri.

Gray reached Buster seconds before Joseph and Reich. He grabbed his brother's arm and gestured wildly toward the impending dam break.

Buster turned and looked up Flat Creek. "No! We have to get the wagon first. Gray, help me!"

"You can't save it now, Buster," Joseph called. "It's too late. Get out of there or you'll be killed."

Buster broke free of Gray's hold and lunged for the wagon hitch. "It's all we've got."

"You still have your life," Reich said. The big man reached for Buster's arm and dragged him from the hitch. "Now, boy. You've got to come now! Gray, get back up that hill. Go on!"

Gray hesitated. "Buster, they're risking their lives for you. Don't let more men die for you!" His expression held fury and horror as he obeyed Reich and ran.

Joseph heard another series of deafening cracks and looked up to see the water pour past the dam of debris. The fountain of water became a flood, and then the natural dam gave way with the sound of thunder. Joseph joined Reich to jerk Buster from the oncoming tempest of an evergreen with limbs the size of horses, which reached past the farthest edges of the flooded creek bank.

"My gun!" Buster shouted. "Gotta get my gun." He turned back toward the wagon.

Joseph nodded to Reich, and together they lifted the brazen young man between them and ran.

The wall of trees, uprooted shrubs, mud and rocks tumbled forward in a crash of violence. A foot-thick limb grabbed Joseph and knocked him into Buster. Water deluged them. They scrambled to keep their footing, but another limb knocked them into the mud, dragged them sideways and back toward the creek.

The water retreated, but the tree held firmly and pulled them with increasing speed toward the racing stream. Joseph dug his heels into the mud and held on to Buster. "Don't let go!" he shouted at the others. "Don't stand up." If they did, another branch would have more leverage against them. That tree was a monster they couldn't control.

"Captain! Reich, grab on!" came a voice from behind them. McDonald. Joseph looked up past the barrier of the limb and saw his scout throwing out a loop of thick rope. It was the one Joseph had taken from Buster.

"Grab it," he told the other two. "Look up and grab it, now!"

The loop came down over the limb and Joseph reached for it. Before he could grasp it, another limb tumbled over the first with another wave of water, thrusting them closer to the creek.

"Captain, hurry, try again!" McDonald tossed the rope atop them this time and Joseph caught it. He saw Reich's strong hand grip it and they jerked to a stop.

The limb scraped along Joseph's side, digging into his ribs with agonizing sharpness until the tree withdrew as suddenly as it had hit them.

They lay panting in the grip of terror for a long moment, then looked up to find a crowd of rescuers holding the other end of the rope.

Despite a bloody nose and scratches on his face, Buster scrambled to his feet and ran hollering after his wagon. With a practiced stretch of the leg, Reich tripped the demented man, then rolled forward and grabbed him by the arm.

Joseph grasped the other arm and turned to watch as the pine tree hauled off the wagon in the clutch of its green arms and strong limbs. Chunks of wood and wagon flew through the air. A loud creak and groan echoed from the cliffs behind the camp as Buster's angry cry rose to the sky.

"I could have gotten it!" Buster's face flushed with fury as he rounded on Joseph.

"No, you would have died and left your brother alone." Joseph released the scoundrel and nodded to Reich. "Let him go. If he's crazy enough to go running after it after all this, he deserves whatever he gets."

Buster fell to his knees and gave a wordless groan of frustration as the axles and wheels sank permanently into the muddy maelstrom.

"Oh, I don't believe this." Mrs. Reich came marching toward them through the mud. "You men oughta be ashamed of yourselves." She leaned over Buster. "Don't you worry, son. You're not alone here." She shot a glare over her shoulder at her husband and Joseph. "Can't you see the boy's just lost everything he owns? How would you feel if it'd happened to you?"

"Aw, woman, it wouldn't've happened to Joseph or me because we'd've never tempted the creek like that." Reich put his fists on his hips. "This boy needs to listen. At least he's still got the horses."

Audy Reich shook her head. "Don't you think you oughta have a little mercy? Why, I'd be ashamed. Come along with me, Buster, my boy," she cooed as she took Buster by the arm. "The doctor will want to get those cuts cleaned and bandaged. Can you walk okay?"

A low grumble reached Joseph, and he turned to see Mr. Reich glaring after his wife and the wayward Buster. "That woman would take any cur in off the street and treat him like a child instead of the man he needs to be."

Joseph grinned and reached a mud-caked hand out. "And her husband would risk his life to save that cur in the first place." He patted Reich on his muscular shoulder. "He'd be dead today if not for you, my friend."

"And you. See what we get ourselves into when we go meddling into the affairs of others?" He chuckled.

"Okay, you two." Victoria came down the hill toward them with her treatment bag slung over her arm. The sun had burned away the remaining clouds and touched her hair with a red-gold glow. "Heidi can see to Buster, but I reserve the right to treat our heroes first." She pulled a bottle of medicinal whiskey from her bag and held up a clean cloth. "Did either of you swallow the water?"

Joseph glanced up the hill toward the spot where they had just been treating poor Claude and his rescuers. "No ma'am, not me. I knew better than to open my mouth."

"Same here, Dr. Fenway," Reich said immediately. "Kept my jaws locked, not a drop of water passed these lips. You don't need to go rolling me around on one of those logs and forcing salt water down my gullet."

Victoria narrowed her eyes at them. "You do realize how dangerous it could be if you did."

"Sure do, ma'am." Reich rubbed some of the mud from his hands onto his muddier clothing. "And look at this, not a scratch on me. You oughta see to the captain, though. That tree walloped him good."

Before she could reply, the big man scrambled through the mud and up the hill after his wife. Joseph watched the traitor escape, then met Victoria's gaze, wincing inwardly as he anticipated the sting of her medicinal whiskey on his grazed skin.

Victoria nodded toward a fallen log farther up the hill. "We can sit up there. I need to get you cleaned up."

"Give me the medicine and I'll do it myself."

She drew the bottle close to her side. "You'll do no such thing. I'm the doctor. I'll also take a look at your ribs." With a nod toward the place where the limbs had ripped his shirt, she raised her eyebrows. "I need to see if anything's broken."

"It's not."

"Are you having any trouble breathing?"

He took a deep breath and let it out to show her he was fine, and was relieved to find that at least breathing didn't hurt. "Just a scratch." But he followed her when she turned and walked up the hill.

"Have you considered sending the Johnstons back home now?" she asked.

"I've considered it every day."

"We'd be ever so much safer without them. You can see that, can't you? At least the horses weren't hitched to the wagon," she said with a glance over her shoulder toward the creek. "Those boys are a hindrance out here, and now you're injured because of them. They can ride a lot faster by horseback than wagon."

"I'm not even sure they'd make it back home alive, and I can't spare a man to lead them."

She seemed ready to argue, but instead fell silent. Ten years ago she'd have gnawed on the subject like a dog with a bone. Instead, she led him deeper into the woods to the fallen log, where trees screened them from sight of the others.

When she turned back to him, there was a teasing smile in her eyes. "We can't have the people losing faith in their captain if you start crying like a baby."

He checked the log, kicked it and when nothing slithered or skittered out of it, he sat down. "Try me."

She unfolded her pure-white cloth, pressed the open bottle of whiskey into the material until it was soaked. "This may burn." A quick but gentle touch of the medicated cloth met the cuts and scratches on his face and the exposed skin of his hands and arms and neck. It stung a little.

"I don't recall you saying this would be such a dangerous trip." She dabbed at the dirt around the cuts. "Or such a long one."

"Difficult. I said it would be difficult. That implies danger, don't you think? It was why I wanted a doctor to join us this time. We need one in the new town that's waiting for us."

"So you've told me. Have you traveled with a doctor before?"

"One or two came with my wagon trains to California, but people went their separate ways at the end of the trail back then. This time it's different."

She set the bottle down on the log and continued to clean the rest of his face until the white disappeared beneath a coating of mud. "You have quite a bruise on your forehead. Do you recall losing consciousness?"

"I stayed awake for the whole thing."

"Why is this trip different?"

He couldn't tell her it was because it was the only way he believed he could convince her to leave St. Louis. "Why are you surprised by the hardships? You told me you and Matthew traveled."

"We never went by wagon train over rough terrain with barely a trail to follow."

"I believe I warned you we would have to take the road less followed by others for the safety of our mission. We'll encounter the wrong people on the main trails. I'm expecting more trouble the closer we come to the border of Kansas Territory."

Her whole body stiffened for an instant and he saw fear plainly in her eyes.

"Victoria? I'm sorry. I thought you understood. I didn't mean to frighten you. My plans are to take the southern route into Indian Territory, then head north once we're well past the border. I'm hoping to have less trouble with border ruffians on that route."

"You're right, of course. I knew it would be a difficult journey." She sank onto the fallen log beside him, her dress already so covered with mud that the black material appeared brown.

Something disturbed him about her posture—erect, stiff. "You were planning to make this a permanent move, weren't you?" he asked.

She nodded. "I feel safer here in the wilderness with these companions than I have felt since Matthew's... death."

A slight change in her demeanor caught his attention. "Why is that?"

"I was determined to keep the clinic open by myself, but many didn't appreciate my caring for the wounded slaves. I had my windows broken three times, someone tried to burn down the clinic and my wagon was burned."

"Then I was right to worry. I prayed for your safety all winter, but as I said, the snows made it impossible to get back."

She took a deep breath and her shoulders slumped. She met his gaze. "Thank you for caring."

He suppressed a smile. That was putting it mildly. But mild seemed to be all she could handle with him right now. Or maybe ever. Ten years was a long time to harbor the love he'd held for her. He was an oddity, he knew. How could he expect her to still care for him after all the changes in their lives? And there had been plenty. Because of her, he'd never moved on with his life, never married, had lived the life of a loner.

"You definitely had a change of heart since you left for Georgia," she said.

Yes, he'd changed, but not about her, as she seemed to think. "It took me several months, but your words struck me forcefully when I reached my father's plantation."

"And now you're leading abolitionists into Kansas Territory."

"Remember those arguments we used to have?" he asked. "As you told me, power corrupts most men. When one human being has total power over another—"

"It's too easy to become corrupt, to see the slave as nothing more than a piece of furniture or farm equipment." Victoria nodded. "You really did listen."

"Now the famous John Brown, outspoken abolitionist, is my greatest hero. Do you know of him?"

She chuckled softly. "I most certainly do. Tell me, what changed your mind?"

"My closest friend on the plantation had long ago been the son of a tribal leader in Africa. Then he was captured by men from his own continent and sold in America. My father named him Daniel. A few years ago, Daniel described the conditions of his journey."

"I've heard a great deal about them. Horrible."

"Nearly half the passengers on Daniel's ship died before they reached harbor. I always hated the thought of that, but I knew my father was different. I believed most of our neighbors were, too. I never saw brutality of the type I saw when I was in St. Louis. No one bought or sold slaves in any market near us. My father and our neighbors always traveled to purchase their slaves."

"What happened to Daniel?"

"When I returned home ten years ago, he was gone."

She caught her breath. "He'd been sold."

"You must understand," Joseph said, "my father was well respected in Georgia by a majority of the slave population because he treated his workers more kindly than most, gave them plenty of food, never broke up families—"

"But he sold Daniel."

"Another plantation owner wanted him for a young woman who was healthy."

She scowled. "Brood stock."

"That was when it hit home for me. You won the argument, Victoria."

"I never set out to win anything."

He knew that. He always had, though during their worst arguments about slavery he'd accused her of gloating whenever she proved him wrong on a point. "You were the more mature one. For me, life was a competition."

She smiled, but it was a sad expression. "Was? Isn't it still?"

"The stakes have been raised, and I've changed sides."

"Then if ours was a competition, I'm glad I won. Still, I think our conflicts had less to do with maturity and more to do with our differences." She leaned toward him slightly, enough to raise his hopes. Then she straightened. "I was passionate about slavery, and not much else at that time, if I remember correctly."

"I do believe you were passionate about one other thing."

She raised her eyebrows, held his gaze until it dawned on her. "Oh." A pretty flush stained her cheeks. "Of course, I was young and considered myself to be in love."

"Considered?"

"I'm afraid I behaved badly when I realized it was not to be."

He closed his eyes. Why did she have to say that? "It was my fault."

"Not entirely. Your father blamed you for purchasing your own ranch in a free state instead of carrying on the family tradition on the plantation with slaves."

"I should have left it at that, but I couldn't bear the thought of my father dying while holding such a grudge against me. I had to ride to the rescue of my family, as if they couldn't possibly make it on the plantation without my honored presence."

"Did your return heal old wounds?" she asked.

"No, it only caused new rifts with those I loved." He

tried to catch her gaze, but she made it obvious that she didn't want to return to their former subject.

"Did all of your family reject you?" she asked.

He appreciated the compassion in her voice, but he would have enjoyed more. "Only my father. I have a sister and several cousins who moved north. I was so angry about Daniel that my father finally realized I would never stay and run the plantation. He left it to my younger brother." The sadness of that final break with his father lingered with Joseph all these years later.

"And then you returned to St. Louis to find that Matthew and I had married." There was a catch in Victoria's voice, and Joseph saw the sorrow in her eyes. "Things don't always turn out the way we want them to, do they?" she asked softly.

Joseph's fingers tingled with the urge to reach up and touch her cheek. He could already feel the softness of it, but he squeezed his hand into a fist. She'd made it obvious she wouldn't appreciate anything so personal. *Oh, Victoria...*

Something in Joseph's gaze caught and held Victoria breathless. She looked away quickly, but for an instant ten years vanished and they were back on the deck of the riverboat on the Mississippi River, with the water splashing against the shore while she memorized every inch of his face.

"This isn't the end," he'd whispered. "It can't be. I'll never stop loving you."

Then the whistle blew and the deck beneath them moved, and the years stacked atop each other once more. She blinked and shook the memory away, but not before she relived the heartbreak of loss. Not again. Never again. She couldn't bear to feel that kind of pain for a second time.

"You mentioned your admiration of John Brown and his sons." She forced a grin. "Matthew and I became acquainted with him about five years ago."

Joseph's eyebrows rose. "*The* John Brown? Freer of slaves?"

"See what you missed when you hid out on the Oregon Trail, leading folks to gold and prosperity in California and Oregon, hiding from your friends in St. Louis?" She held on to her teasing lilt, friendly and nothing more, hiding behind it as if it were a cloak. "You could have visited from time to time. Look who you may have become friends with."

"Did you know he once moved to a town established by Africans so he could learn their ways and help them better integrate into society?"

Victoria enjoyed Joseph's admiration of the man. "He became a dear friend of Matthew's and mine. He and his sons lodged with us twice during their travels through St. Louis. We've heard many stories of their escapades."

Some of the excitement left Joseph's expression. "You're still in contact with the man, himself?"

"I received word of their condolences when Matthew died. They dared little more contact than that, considering the circumstances. Our plans to leave St. Louis were under way when Matthew was...killed."

Silence reigned for several long seconds as Joseph's frown deepened. "You can't know how shocked and saddened I was when I heard the news of Matthew's death."

"I'm still recovering."

He was silent for a moment, then said softly, "You two became quite close, didn't you?"

She looked up at him. If Joseph was implying what

she thought, he was being completely inappropriate. "We *were* married."

"You implied a marriage of convenience."

"I beg your pardon? Please tell me you aren't outright accusing me of loving my husband, as if that's a sin." What was he doing? Was he actually…jealous?

And yet, hadn't he always been? Hadn't she known that was why he'd stayed away? If Joseph had accepted her marriage to Matthew, he would have visited with them the many times she'd heard he was in St. Louis.

"Joseph, ours was a marriage of kindness and goodwill." He couldn't possibly expect an apology from her for having tender feelings toward her own husband.

"Goodwill." Joseph's voice sharpened. "You cared for him as your employer when you and I were together, but he felt more than goodwill toward you. I know he loved you. Was he satisfied with your simple human kindness?"

She stared down at her hands, feeling the sting of guilt that had haunted her for many years, yet also stinging with offense. "It wasn't Matthew I loved ten years ago." The words, and the accusatory tone, were out before she could withdraw them.

"No, but it certainly was Matthew you married, wasn't it?" He caught his breath audibly, as if he, too, had spoken without thought. "Victoria, I'm… I had no right."

"No, you didn't." She cleared her throat, swallowed, took a deep breath to fight back the hurtful words she wanted to speak. "Forgive me, Joseph, but every woman needs to feel she's the most important person in her man's life. I acknowledge that isn't often the case, but I was young enough to want that for myself. You obviously couldn't give me that." He was a different man now, however, an adult who had been tested in fire, seasoned and strong. Why should he continue to suffer for one horribly wrong decision that had ousted her from his life and shattered her heart? "As for Matthew, I was led to believe he wanted a partner for his practice. It was the way he proposed marriage. Businesslike and logical." So unlike the way she and Joseph had been together, slowly falling in love over the course of a year, unable to stay away from each other, a constant challenge for those who chaperoned them.

She'd dreamed of becoming a rancher's wife, especially after Joseph built a new room onto his ranch house and started teasing her about becoming "Mrs. Joseph Rickard."

"I knew he loved you by the way his gaze followed you wherever you went," Joseph said. "By the way his eyes lit up when he talked about you."

"So it appears I got what I wanted, after all."

"I don't think so. Matthew had priorities that took precedence over your welfare, it seems, or he wouldn't have drawn you into your present dangerous position."

"Don't speak ill of the dead."

He leaned closer to her and she caught the scent of the watercress he liked to pick along the streams, and the earth and water that had nearly killed him. He sighed and brushed at some drying mud on his sleeve. "Listen to us arguing again."

"Not everything has changed," she said.

"I didn't expect him to marry you after I left. Keep you in his employ, yes, but…you're right, I was stunned when I found out about your marriage."

She turned away, barely hearing the voices of the others near camp. "I believe you expected that I would wait for you no matter what, even after I heard of your engagement."

Joseph was silent for a long moment. She looked over her shoulder at him and saw him staring toward the flooded creek, and she recognized the lines of self-recrimination in the square frame of his face.

"Shouldering the blame can't repair the past," she said, gentling her voice. How hard she'd been on him these past weeks, avoiding him when possible. He'd been a perfect gentleman, treating her with respect and kindness while she'd remained reserved.

"I thought my father needed me."

"Your father sold your closest friend. I'm sorry you had to endure so much."

Joseph reached for her hand, and to her surprise, she allowed him to raise it to brush his lips against her knuckles. "Leaving you in St. Louis was the most painful decision I've ever made."

"Good. I wanted you to feel the same pain I did."

"But maybe it was right for you at the time. Had we stayed together, you wouldn't be a doctor now, and Matthew would never have had the wonderful experience of being your husband for those ten short years."

Victoria reminded herself to breathe. The intimate touch of Joseph's hand affected her more than any touch she had received from Matthew, and the guilt of that discovery caused her to withdraw again. Joseph released her without a word.

"Brown is planning to move later this year into Kansas Territory." She hoped he didn't hear the race of her heartbeat in her voice.

"He'll have my support. It could determine the balance of power in the whole nation."

She allowed the warm breeze from the south to dry

the perspiration from her face, and she felt the warmth from Joseph's nearness when he stepped up behind her.

"No matter how many measures you took to get out of St. Louis discreetly, someone could have followed you. Someone who knew you were friends with Brown." His deep voice, laced with concern, made her shiver.

A crow cawed deeper in the woods and she gasped, jerking so hard she nearly toppled the bottle still open on the log.

Joseph frowned. "Are you ready to tell me what's had you so frightened these past days?"

How tempting to place her faith in this man, to allow him control over her life so she wouldn't have to stand on her own, but that wasn't what she needed to do right now. She had left her parents in Pennsylvania, her husband in the ground by the Mississippi River. She was an independent woman now, and she didn't need another man to bolster her. Joseph meant well, but despite the time they had spent together he didn't know her intentions enough to direct her path.

She turned to look up into his carved-granite face and intent regard. He didn't know her most important secret, and that was something he especially needed to be aware of in order to protect his wagon train.

Steeling herself against his discomfiting attention, she took a deep breath of rain-cleansed air, closed her eyes briefly and made the decision she knew would change everything. "Matthew…" The words caught in her throat. She swallowed and looked back at Joseph. "He was murdered."

Chapter Four

Joseph might have been a copy of the wood carving outside the trading post door at the last town, where the wagon train had stopped to purchase supplies. Silence seemed to hum with the power of a beehive. The chatter of the others merged into a low echo in the distance. The wagon train had struggled through deep mud, broken wheels, lost wagons, illness and loss of livestock. Few things had disconcerted Captain Joseph Rickard these past weeks on the trail, but this definitely affected him.

She wished it hadn't been necessary to tell him, and yet he needed to know how dangerous it would be to follow the killer's trail.

"Who murdered him?" he asked at last. Was that a tremor she heard in his voice?

She hesitated, bracing herself against the pain as she relived that day. "A slaver by the name of Broderick Thames."

"How do you know?"

"I heard the shots on my way home from town, where I was purchasing medicines. I was out of sight."

"Or your life would most likely have been snuffed out, as well." Joseph glared at the ground, his jaw muscles flexing with an obvious attempt to quell the effects of his fury.

"Likely."

"Thames," he said. "I don't know the name, and I've been making an effort to learn more about our enemies."

"Oh, Joseph, believe me when I tell you that this man is an enemy."

"Are you sure he wasn't a robber?"

"He didn't rob us of goods, only of a good man with a heart of pure kindness."

"Was there laudanum missing? I've heard of doctors being attacked for their supplies." Joseph's tone was clipped with anger. She knew his ire was not directed toward her, and she was touched deeply by his outrage.

"No." Tears stung her eyes. "Matthew was a specific target. His killer rode away before I could get my rifle sights on him, or I'd have put him on the ground instead of grazing the side of his neck and staining his silvery hair."

"You're the one who did that?"

For a moment she couldn't take a deep enough breath. Joseph knew of that wound? "What do you mean? What do you know about Thames?"

"Only what I overheard at one of the trading posts." Joseph nodded as if her confession seemed to have made some puzzle pieces fall into place. "A dour man with a long, silver braid and a deep red scar along his neck and jaw was asking questions about abolitionists in the area."

"The red scar was from my weapon."

"Good. You do, however, seem to shoot squirrels better than you do retreating murderers."

"Joseph, I've seen evidence of him on this trail. He

rides a red horse shod uniquely, as if part of the right front hoof is missing."

"You've tracked him?"

"Of course. What would you expect? I know where he's headed. That much I was able to discern from Matthew's final words." How she grieved those moments. Though she'd never been able to love her husband the way she knew a woman should, Matthew Fenway's heart had been that of a true healer, kind and strong. She'd always honored him as her husband, and he'd honored her on a pedestal of his own making.

Joseph gently touched her arm. "Where did Matthew say this Silver Braid was going?"

"Kansas Territory, and if he's going the same direction we are, that might mean he's caught wind of our movements, possibly of the town you're building. You've been through here several times, and I don't care how cautious you are, people talk."

"Then we'll have to change our route. I'll talk to McDonald, but I still worry that Thames will know what you look like, Victoria."

"He couldn't have seen my face that day. I was wearing a kerchief over my nose and mouth because the road was dusty. My hair was braided behind me and I wore a hat."

"But wouldn't he have known who you were, especially if Matthew was a target already? He may well have observed you when you weren't aware. He likely discovered your connection with John Brown."

Victoria nodded. "Matthew and Thames went head-to-head in public debate about slavery versus abolition a few days before Matthew was killed. You know how well-spoken Matthew was. He managed to enrage

Thames, and he received much applause from crowds who'd crossed the river from Illinois."

The muscles of Joseph's jaw flexed as his eyes darkened. "Then you can count on Thames knowing everything there is to know about you, Victoria. Did your husband not give a thought to his wife when he did such a thing?"

She looked down at her hands. "You knew Matthew had a calling that, to him, was more vital than any other."

"What about caring for his wife, as a man is supposed to do? I thought he gave you a place of highest honor."

"Would you choose one woman's safety over the lives and freedom of millions?"

"Had he felt that way, he should never have married." The gruffness of Joseph's voice somehow warmed her.

She blinked up at him and was touched more deeply than she would have expected. "I willingly joined Matthew in his quest. I felt as he did. Be honest, Joseph, you feel the same. Your whole life right now is focused on helping millions of captives."

"Not at the cost of your life."

"I'm with you now, in the middle of dangerous territory."

He reached up and touched the back of his fingers against her chin. She nearly gasped at the instinctive caress.

He straightened and dropped his hand. "Forgive me. It isn't my wish to speak ill of the dead, but I believe a man should protect his wife above all else."

"Which is why you remain single."

He swallowed and took a long, slow breath. "Perhaps it's why I've remained single to this point. I'd had no cause to give it thought until…" He looked into her eyes and for a moment she barely allowed herself to breathe. "Please," he said at last, "tell me more about Matthew's killer."

Why she felt such a strange mixture of elation and disappointment she refused to consider. "Thames is a member of a newly formed group of men from Louisville, Kentucky, who call themselves the Knights of the Golden Circle."

"I've heard of them. Their goal is to expand slavery into nearby southern nations. I'm talking about whole countries, Victoria," Joseph said. "I believe if men of good conscience allow that to happen, we may see anarchy rule the world."

She met his gaze, and she couldn't look away for a moment. Some things about him had definitely changed, and she liked those changes. "John Brown believes there's a connection between the knights and the border ruffians of Missouri."

"Of course there is."

And of course, throughout this journey, he'd known more than he'd let on to her. "My presence could be a danger to this wagon train if you're right about Thames knowing me." Why hadn't she considered this? And Sadie, her mare…Matthew's mare…why hadn't she traded in St. Louis?

"I believe this is where you need to be."

The gentleness of his words and the affection in his eyes settled something that had nagged at her since his first arrival in St. Louis this spring. She could relax a little. Not completely, of course. What would he do if he knew she continued to carry some dangerous secrets?

Joseph was in trouble and he knew it—had known it since first arriving in St. Louis. How was he supposed to think straight when his thoughts and attention automatically sent him looking for Victoria first thing every morning, when he had to force himself several times a day not to ride past the wagon she often reined or the horse she rode?

He needed his wits about him, for sure, now that she had confirmed for him that the most dangerous men in the country might be focusing on his little group of trusting, good-hearted people.

"John sent word to us about a conspiracy," Victoria said. "This was only a few days before Matthew was killed."

Though the lilt of her Pennsylvania accent and the soft, musical quality of her voice could draw him to her through the most threatening of battlefields, her words were like a splash of ice water in his face. "How did he send word?"

"Through a mutual friend. He needed our medical aid in Kansas Territory." She placed the muddy cloth on the log and pulled another from her bag. She dampened it with a splash of whiskey and dabbed at his chin again. "He told Matthew that the Missouri slave owners traveled en masse to Kansas to vote illegally to make Kansas a slave state."

"There's going to be a deadly battle over that territory as voting time draws near." Joseph took a moment to digest the reality that Victoria's safety could well lie in his hands. "Do you think that's why Matthew was killed? Could your contact have been followed?" He reached up and stilled her hand for a moment, relishing the feel of her skin.

"It makes sense, doesn't it? Men risked their lives to infiltrate the coalition of slavers and to pass this information on to Washington, D.C. Many died." Gently but firmly, she pulled away.

"I wish I'd known about your precarious situation sooner, Victoria, though I suppose I should have guessed." Joseph would have hacked his way through head-high drifts of snow to reach her and protect her.

"John also sent some friends of ours, Francine and Buck Frasier, to the Village of Jollification." Victoria reached up as if to sweep the hair from his forehead, but she stopped herself. "Have you been there?"

"Often. Locals call it Jolly Mill. It's on a main road from Springfield to Kansas and Indian Territories."

"Francine and Buck traveled there last autumn with their so-called slaves, John's adoptive son and daughter-in-law."

Joseph looked at her in surprise. "I heard he'd adopted a freed slave."

"Yes. He's fully invested in helping the slaves in every way. I hear we'll be passing by Jolly Mill in a few days."

"No," Joseph said. "Not after what you've told me. It's sure to be overrun by border ruffians."

Victoria gave a soft sigh. "Yes, I know, but someone needs to help them get past the border."

"Tell me Matthew didn't drag you into the middle of that situation, as well."

Victoria didn't meet Joseph's gaze. "Matthew and I were planning to travel this way."

"Do you think Thames knows about the Frasiers and their charges?"

She picked up the whiskey again and soaked the cloth more thoroughly. "Word is that he is leading a group tasked to kill off the influential Brown family one by one, and that would especially include the adopted son."

Joseph knew by the darkening of her eyes and her fidgeting hands that there was more she wasn't saying. "Victoria, you realize we must lie low."

She nodded. "I won't do anything to endanger these people."

"Or yourself."

She didn't reply.

He hated this. "I've seen you ride ahead of the rest several times until you were out of sight."

"It does no harm to have an extra scout." She reached for his hand and pulled it toward her, then began to dab at more scrapes on his forearm.

"I saw you once when we came riding around a stand of trees. You had dismounted from Sadie and were studying something on the trail. I had supposed you were hunting for mushrooms."

She looked down at the cloth in her hands, dabbed at another spot on his neck then discarded this cloth, as well. "Tracks. I need to see your ribs."

He blinked at her. "What?"

"Your ribs. Pull up your shirt so I can check your ribs. You'll need to have medicine on them, too."

"So you did see tracks that day?"

"Not what I was looking for. Not Thames. Now, shirt, please?"

He sighed and glanced toward camp. "This might be misconstrued."

"Then so be it. I'm a doctor. Right now you're my patient. If you'd rather I call Heidi to come—"

"No." He tugged out the left side of his formerly blue plaid shirt, which was now thick with drying mud. He could already feel his face flushing.

Victoria busied herself soaking another cloth, then visibly winced at the sight of Joseph's bruised and scraped ribs. She pressed the cloth against them. "They must hurt a great deal."

He gritted his teeth against the sting of the whiskey. "To be honest, I haven't had time to think about it." Until now. He'd been too distracted by Victoria's bracing presence and the shock of her news.

"I gathered some wild onions yesterday," she said. "I know it isn't the science I've learned under Matthew's tutelage, but I learned a lot from a tribe of Cherokee who lived near us when I was growing up. If you would allow me to make a poultice—"

"I would be grateful."

"Good. It'll take the soreness out much more quickly." She dabbed again at his ribs until the mud that had leaked through his shirt had been cleaned away. She had the most gentle touch, and a caring spirit with a strong thread of heroism that he admired.

"I'm frustrated by the hard rains," she said as she wrapped a long cloth around his rib cage and fastened it to itself with a knot, deftly woven. "It would have removed any tracks we might have used to warn us."

"I'd prefer you didn't track this man." He knew she probably wouldn't listen. "You can tell McDonald what to look for. And Reich. In fact, I'd prefer anyone else in the wagon train be on the lookout for the tracks, just not you."

She tugged his shirt back down. "Come with me and we can get the onions. I can pound them and then slide them beneath the cloth. It's true we'd best not start tongues wagging. If we stay closer to camp everyone will realize I'm simply treating a wound."

He suspected she was using his wound and the onion poultice as a ruse to prevent him from pressing her further about her tracking plans.

She turned and gathered up her bag and supplies. "Speaking of camp, Joseph, despite all we've tried to do, some of our people may have contracted cholera. I wish to play it safe and separate those who were in the water from the rest of the travelers for a couple of days."

"That means you and Heidi will have to remain separate from her mother and brother," he said. "She won't like that."

"She'll do as I ask," Victoria said. "She can ride her mule and camp with the Reichs until we know for sure our friends are out of danger. I will stay behind the train with the patients and keep watch over them.

"Placing yourself in harm's way." He fell into step beside her.

"Believe me, Joseph, I know how to avoid illness. I've done well for ten years. This may be all for nothing, but the moment I see signs of illness I'll be able to start treatment immediately. We have seven who were in the water." She stopped and turned, placing a hand on his shoulder. "You were telling me the truth earlier about not swallowing the water? You didn't inhale any, obviously, or you'd have choked."

"I was telling you the truth. I'd like for you to make a drawing for me of the track you've been searching for. I want to show the adults so all can be on the lookout for it, just in case."

She raised her eyebrows. "You don't think you'll start a panic?"

"These people know how dangerous this trip could be. They don't panic easily."

"True." She continued ahead of him and stepped from the shadows of the forest into the churned mud of the trail. The dried mud had begun to cake and fall in clods from her dress. Her hair had all but fallen from its binding, and he could do nothing but stare at her; to him, she was the most beautiful woman in the world, and always would be.

"I need to have Heidi collect some rabbit-ear leaves to go with the onion compress," she said as she crossed the trail. "I'll use some of the tea bags we just filled to make a batch of comfrey and chamomile tea for everyone, including you." She glanced over her shoulder at him. "You're going to be sore if we don't get those ribs taken care of, and that won't help when you're on horseback."

He caught up with her to steady her in case she slipped. "I'll do whatever you say, Doc. You obviously know what you're doing."

Her steps slowed and she looked up at him, her blue eyes glowing with gentle appraisal. "Why, thank you, Captain Rickard."

Welcoming the warmth in her voice and eyes, he took her arm. "I don't recall Matthew using the plants you've been utilizing on this trip."

She shook her head. "As I said, I learned a lot from the Cherokee back East."

"Did that ever cause discord between you and Matthew?" As soon as he asked, Joseph knew he was being too intrusive. Still, he couldn't help wondering if Victoria's natural skill and unique intelligence had ever caused her difficulty in her marriage. Most men were too proud to walk in the shadow of a wife with superior talents, and Joseph had to admit to himself that he had a selfish reason for the question.

Joseph's old friend had never seemed to hold grudges or experience the typical human emotions others grappled with—such as the jealousy Joseph had fought within himself for ten years.

"At first," Victoria said. "He even tried to order me not to use them on the women who came to me."

Joseph chuckled. "I'm sure he learned his lesson quickly enough."

"He did." She cast him a mischievous grin. "I eventually managed to teach Matthew a few herbal treatments, and once he realized I knew what I was doing, he swallowed his pride and learned all he could from me."

"And now you're teaching Heidi."

"She seems eager to learn." Victoria slipped on a muddy rock.

Joseph held her firmly. "You're good with her and the other children." He paused, judging to see if his next remark might generate an uncomfortable answer. But he needed to know. "I always thought you would make a wonderful mother."

She tightened her grip on his arm as she continued to walk toward camp. "I would have loved children."

They reached camp as Joseph suffered shame for pressing her. "I'm sorry, Victoria."

She released her grip from his and looked up at him. "You've done nothing for which to be sorry, and as for children, I wouldn't have wanted them to endure what I have, to be in danger. Maybe someday...."

"Captain?" Mrs. Reich called to him from a bonfire the men had built. "You think we're safe here? Maybe we oughta move farther away from the water."

"We'll make camp where we are," Joseph announced for everyone to hear. "If we don't have any more rain tonight, the water should be low enough for us to make a safe crossing at dawn, but if we do have rain, we're high enough up that nothing should touch us." He looked over his shoulder toward Buster and Gray, where some of the ladies were already sharing blankets and utensils, food and clothing with the Johnstons. At least the young men would be mothered on this trip. Not that being mothered would help them grow up and meet the hardships of life head-on.

Victoria glanced up at him over her shoulder. "You don't expect more rain?"

He shook his head, and for a moment held her gaze and tried to study the thoughts taking place behind those deep blue eyes. After a few seconds her eyelids fluttered and the shadow of dread lined her face. His stomach grew taut with tension.

He'd seen it twice before—ten years ago, when he received the missive from his family to return to the plantation where his father struggled for his life. He'd also seen that look a month ago in St. Louis when he stepped into Victoria's office for the first time since he'd left—perhaps as if refining their former relationship might bring still more heartbreak if she were to allow it.

"And now," she said, "time to prepare that plaster for your ribs."

Four people met him with questions, and as he answered them, he watched her work. He marveled that the two of them were together in this place after all this time. He made a promise to himself and to God that he would do all he could to keep her safe, no matter what it took, but would that be enough? Would the rogue searching this trail for abolitionists find her? Had he already?

Chapter Five

Five days later, the killer struck. It wasn't Broderick Thames who destroyed two of their own but the cholera Victoria and the others had fought hard to prevent. She stood in a valley near Shoal Creek, observing the hideous handiwork of the illness that had stalked them to this place. Perhaps the measures she'd taken had only delayed it for a day or two; typically, cholera started its damage within a day. No amount of chamomile tea, mashed black walnut hulls or yarrow root had made any difference for Luella and Claude Ladue in the end. Though the illness had not spread, those two dear people had died.

Victoria's body jerked every time Joseph's shovel tossed dirt onto Luella's grave. Watching his steady movements as he handled the shovel, she sought a sense of comfort despite the events this afternoon. There would be time later for self-admonition. For now, she wanted to escape the pain of the moment and settle on the image of the man so familiar to her. She needed a break from this awful sense of failure and loss. And so she studied him, lost herself in memories, comforted herself by looking at him.

In the ten years that had kept them apart, he'd aged twenty—not in appearance but in maturity—and it looked good on him. It wasn't so much the evidence of his physical strength that drew her, but his demeanor reflected an inner core of power that she recalled with clarity. The fact that he looked better to her than he ever had was a distraction she welcomed, but at the same time it brought her overwhelming guilt.

Tendrils of Joseph's straight black hair blew across his tanned forehead at the impetus of a spring breeze. How she appreciated the way his shoulders worked with effortless strength.

She inhaled a silent breath and exhaled deeply. Joseph looked up at her and caught her gaze, his dark eyes shadowed as he paused, barely breathing hard. Along with the powerful build and inner strength came a keen wit. She shivered, though the breeze wasn't cold. She admired much about him, and her admiration had experienced a recent growth, especially with his tenderness toward her these past days.

But the quality she respected the most was his ability to look at reality head-on. He attacked hardship with all his might and never held back, never waited for someone else to take the lead. He made it clear he was in command of his own heart and mind. How could she not be drawn to such a man?

She nodded to him and then looked at the ground, studying the mud that clung to the hem of her black dress. Heat rose to her face. A widow of seven months did not share long glances with a handsome man while he was burying two of their friends, especially while the only remaining family member grieved in stunned silence, intentionally isolated from the others.

If Victoria wished to continue calling herself a doctor she would need to toe the line of propriety more than any other woman on the wagon train. She could no longer bask in the shadow of her physician husband.

She cast a glance about them toward the trees that darkened the edges of the creek-fed valley. What other disasters would they encounter in this forest-shrouded, water-poisoned Missouri wilderness?

"Nobody blames you, sweetheart." It was the warm, sisterly voice of Audy Reich from behind her.

Audy stepped to Victoria's side and placed an arm around her. The woman was stout muscled from years of hard work and childbearing, but she had a smile that was as warm and genuine as the earth beneath their feet. She smelled of sage and fresh perspiration, and Victoria drew comfort from the woman's reassuring regard.

"I've never been more proud of someone as I have of you these past days," Audy said. "Tending the sick, bringing them back from the jaws of death itself."

"Not all."

"Five of them, my friend, and you prevented more illness."

"Your husband's the one who risked his life for others. He helped, exposing himself to the same risk."

"I do believe you're the most modest doctor I know."

Victoria shrugged. "My family warned me I would never be accepted into a medical society. I was always told no woman could be a doctor."

"There's no medical society out here on the trail, just grateful patients." Audy shook her head. "That husband of yours, he must've been a special man. I'm glad he taught you so well. The way you and the captain wrenched those others from the cholera was nothing less exciting than the rescue from the flood."

Victoria glanced toward the graves and mourned.

"Those were not your fault, and you know it," Audy said. "Luella would have jumped in to save her son even if she'd known it meant death."

Victoria winced. She'd been thinking all day that if Joseph hadn't agreed to bring the Johnstons along, there'd have been no illnesses or death. Audy tightened her hold around Victoria's shoulders. "You two worked wonders as you fought to save lives." She patted Victoria's shoulder firmly. "Seems to me you soaked in some of your husband's teaching instincts."

Victoria appreciated her friend's ability to distract. "How's that?"

"Oh, I don't know, it may have something to do with the way our Captain Rickard hovers over you." Audy gave an exaggerated wink and a grin. "I'm sure that's so he can catch your every word about doctoring, don't you think?"

Victoria's face heated again. "I believe that's exactly what he's doing."

"I heard he learned a lot about doctoring from your husband, and was called upon to treat many a patient out on the Oregon Trail."

"He continues to learn, though. As does Heidi." Time for a change of subject. "The girl's a natural healer. I'm hoping Kansas will be more open to women practicing medicine, so when she's grown there'll be a place for her."

Audy shook her head, the smile lines gone from her eyes. "I've already told her she has a place in our family, though she's not listening. Right now she can't even hear it."

Victoria linked arms with her steadfast friend and took a few steps with her from the burial site. "Thank you for hunting the herbs and roots we needed. You kept Heidi distracted from the worst of it."

Audy's hazel eyes welled with sorrow. She puffed loose strands of graying brown hair from her face. "My six boys did the distracting. When Heidi wasn't helping William herd those wild younger brothers of his, that sweet gal was on my heels looking for those plants even if she had to tromp through the weeds and risk stepping on copperheads and poison ivy."

"She's brave," Victoria cast a glance around for her young assistant and caught a flash of long, pale hair in the clearing before Audy leaned close to her ear.

"Mind you, William hasn't been able to keep his attention on his chores since the Ladues joined our train. After all, it's definitely springtime." She paused. "Love seems to hover in the air no matter the circumstances. I think you might be aware of a little of that yourself."

Victoria refused to glance toward Joseph.

Audy gave Victoria another squeeze of the arm and let her go. "Now, honey, don't you act all innocent with me. Even my crusty ol' husband can see a good match when it's right there under his nose."

"Are you hinting that the captain and I—"

"Hinting? Not me. I'm saying it straight. You and our good captain seem to be more than friends. Don't you think it's only natural? You're a young woman alone. Luella mentioned a time or two that you and the captain were alike in so many ways."

Victoria took a deep breath. Physicians weren't supposed to weep over the deaths of their patients. "Luella knew that…that Joseph and I are old friends." This physician likely had swollen eyes and a red nose from all her tears.

"That would make sense, knowing he and your Matthew were friends." Audy's voice was gentle as she said, "Luella would be touched that you grieved her so, but we knew her deep faith. She and her boy are past suffering."

Victoria hesitated, choosing her words. "There are many things I don't know anymore."

"That happens as we grow older and wiser. It don't hurt to question the Lord every so often, because He already knows what's in your heart."

"But Heidi's alone. How could God—"

"He'll see to her. She'll be loved to pieces amongst our brood. Who wouldn't adore such a thoughtful child?"

Victoria nodded as her attention wandered back to Joseph—her anchor today amidst the loss.

"Remember what the Good Book says," Audy murmured in Victoria's ear. "In heaven there is no marriage. In spite of what some folks think in high society, you're not tied to any rules out here in this wild land."

Victoria wanted to hug Audy Reich and thank her for utilizing her skills for distraction. She knew how deeply the death of the Ladues affected everyone.

"A man and a woman don't linger talkin' late into the night if they don't have something to say to each other," Audy said.

Victoria swallowed as the heat warmed her face once more. What a temptation to give in and tell her friend about her struggles with Joseph. "Audy Reich, must I remind you my husband has been gone barely seven months?"

"Nobody needs reminding of anything out here. One does the necessary thing when times are difficult."

But what was necessary? Taking care of each other and making it safely to their new home was vital right now. Romance was not.

Victoria glanced toward those who hovered near the burial site. No one was looking their way. The oldest Reich boy, William, stood over by one of the two family wagons, casting shy glances in Heidi's direction.

The young girl, nearing her fifteenth birthday, seemed unaware of anything at the moment. To be alone in the world at such a young age would be a horrible thing. She didn't yet realize that she would be smothered with love, mothered by each woman in every wagon. After all, they'd taken Buster and Gray in after the wagon debacle; how much more would they care for her?

Victoria knew, however, that no one could take the place of family.

"I think your Matthew would understand," Audy said.

Victoria returned her attention to her friend, and at the mention of her late husband's name tears prickled her eyes. "Understand?"

"He just wouldn't want you struggling alone."

"But I'm not alone. I'm surrounded by good people. Joseph knew what kind of community he was building when he chose these folks."

"Aw, now you're just trying to distract me. Guess Reich didn't tell you what a matchmaker I was back in St. Louis."

"It wouldn't take much of an imagination."

Audy gave a soft chuckle. "You're right, I'm afraid. I'm an interfering old biddy."

"No, you're a kindhearted friend." Victoria glanced toward Joseph again and saw him bowing his head for a final farewell over the mounds of the graves. They'd all had their prayers over the bodies and honored their memories. She doubted so many tears had ever been shed in this beautiful valley filled with birdsong and flowers and rushing water. Did anyone else know this place as a valley of death?

When Joseph raised his head, he looked straight at her. She gave him a brief nod and turned away. She had other duties to perform, and though he didn't know it yet, her direction and his wouldn't coincide. Though Victoria had no choice but to leave the wagon train, she couldn't bear the thought of Heidi feeling totally abandoned by her family and her mentor all in the same few days.

Victoria closed her eyes and took a deep breath. She had already hinted to some of her friends that she had to leave the wagon train for a while, and now that was going to be more difficult. "You know, Audy, I have a stop to make before I continue my journey, so I may not arrive right along with you to that promised land in Kansas."

Audy caught her breath and drew back, the sun-streaked lines of her face more pronounced. "A stop?" Her voice, always robust, grew louder, and some from the huddle of mourners turned to cast a glance.

Victoria quietly shushed her.

"Has the captain been told?" Audy asked more softly.

"I've made some medical calls along the route before when we've heard of illness and injuries. You know that's my way."

"Yes, and none of those have slowed you down, so what is it about this stop that would keep you from traveling on with us?"

"I recently discovered that this one's out of the way of the wagon train, since we've changed our route to avoid the border ruffians."

"Ah, yes. The captain told us about your husband's

dastardly killer. You think he'd have the nerve to show up on the trail, then?"

"I believe he would. I planned this stop before Matthew's death." Victoria looked toward Heidi's slight figure—she stood a good stone's throw from the rest of the group. "You will watch after her while I'm gone."

"But, honey, a woman alone in this wilderness? What on earth would you do out there?"

"I can protect myself in the wild. What I can't do is risk taking the rest of the wagon train with me." An image of Broderick Thames, with his hulking shoulders and long, silver braid down his back, had haunted Victoria for months. "I have no choice. I made a promise. Audy, Heidi nearly fell apart when her brother passed on yesterday afternoon. She's going to need a tender hand for quite some time."

For a moment, Audy didn't say anything, simply watched Heidi and shook her head. She sighed. "The captain won't let you do it, my dear."

"I know." And she did. It wasn't difficult to see how protective Joseph was of her.

"He's quite smitten, I believe."

Victoria nodded, for once allowing herself to enjoy the warmth of that knowledge for a few seconds. She loved how he sought her company. "But he doesn't need any distractions on this journey, and I've had enough heartbreak to last me a lifetime." She studied the graves. She'd been married to a man whose passion she couldn't return. Could she even love again as she once had loved Joseph?

Matthew had deserved a woman's whole heart, but he'd settled for her broken one. As he'd worded it the day he'd asked her to marry him, he believed this was the closest a man like him was going to come to true happiness. They'd had a full marriage in every way, and Victoria knew he'd been content. If he ever wondered about her heart, however, he'd never spoken of it. For that she was grateful.

"Those two children were close, what with their poor papa passing on last year." Audy's voice wobbled with emotion. "I noticed she couldn't seem to shed more tears with her mother's passing. It was too much for her."

Victoria was far too familiar with the pathway tears made down one's cheeks and through one's soul, and when they ended, one fought hard to keep them from returning, even if it meant not weeping over the burial of another loved one. "She'll revisit her grief when she's ready."

As if in one accord, they both turned to look at the young subject of their conversation. Heidi's fair hair hung in limp strands over her shoulders and down her back, and her neck appeared permanently curved downward, like a broken woman carrying too heavy a load in her thoughts.

She had done nothing this past hour except stare into the deepest shadows of the forest, as if she wished to enter them and lose herself there. She had spoken to no one, not Audy, nor William, nor any of the other dozen or so friends and neighbors who had tried to draw her back into the fold. Not even to Victoria.

"That poor child doesn't need to be alone right now," Audy murmured. "I'm going to see if I can get her to talk."

"I've tried several times. Check her hands to see if they're cold. I tried to get her to drink something warm, but she simply shook her head. I don't want her to fall into a fugue."

Audy patted Victoria's shoulder and turned to march

across the close-cropped field of grass the livestock had munched down. If any mother could manage to get Heidi to talk, it would be Audy.

Southwest Missouri's blanket of spring grass made a bright contrast against upturned soil tamped down over the graves with stones from Shoal Creek. The evidence of life in this teeming valley hinted at hope despite the scars of loss on the wagon train's journey toward Kansas, and despite the looming forest that surrounded the sunshine.

Giant oak, pine and fir trees hovered over the camp of the stalled wagon train, crowding closely, their billowing tops intertwined like heads pressed together to better observe the petty struggle of mere mortal travelers. Heidi stood at the foot of those trees, soaking in the gloom of their shade. Audy dodged the spots of horse, mule and oxen manure that would grow yet a thicker yield the next time the blades of grass pressed upward.

Victoria gazed into the forest and shivered. She'd seen no more tracks. Perhaps their wagon train would indeed manage to avoid an encounter with the silver-braided killer. Or maybe he was now behind them instead of riding ahead in search of them. If he knew of their presence, he might be lingering to see which way they went.

What if he was perched in the eerie gloom even now, watching with a rifle slung over his shoulder? Worse, what if he'd brought friends?

She shuddered and turned toward Joseph, where he was settling yet another stone into the dirt over Luella Ladue's grave.

Perspiration beaded his forehead. "May she rest with her son in God's mercy."

A certain pique spun through Victoria, though she

knew he meant the words kindly. "God's mercy," she muttered under her breath. "I've yet to see a sign of it."

Where was God's mercy in Matthew's death last year? He was a physician who could have helped so many. She glanced over her shoulder and studied the sad expressions of those who had become familiar to her these past weeks on the trail. Mr. and Mrs. Reich talked together every evening over the fire about their hopes for Kansas. Mr. and Mrs. Delaney, though dour of expression and typically silent, were quick to help out when a wagon wheel broke or an injured animal needed tending. Deacon and Ellen Fritz sometimes rode with McDonald and allowed their two half-grown boys— black-haired, the opposite images to the Johnstons in every way—to manage the oxen pulling their wagon.

Victoria had marveled many times at her good fortune to end up in such a good company of folk, but she knew Joseph had handpicked these people. How she admired his astute perception of human character. She allowed her gaze to return to Joseph's tall figure and wasn't surprised to find him watching her with an expression of…what? Concern? Regret? Though perspiration beaded his brow, he was barely breathing hard when he stepped from the graves and crossed the recently worn pathway toward her.

Her irritation at God slid back into its hiding place. This was where mercy existed, in the tender heart of a leader who buried his own, and who still honored God with his words. Yet another discrepancy stood between them. She could never be as faithful to the Lord as this man. How would she ever reconcile evidence of God's power and goodness with such pain and heartbreak? She lacked the faith of Captain Joseph Rickard.

"I have no doubt they're in heaven, you know," came

Joseph's deep and mellow voice as his shadow loomed over her. "I knew them. So did you."

She looked up at him and blinked when a beam of sunlight found its way past his shoulder. "My concern is for Heidi. She's lost everything important in her life."

"Not everything. She hasn't lost you."

"She needs a more solid family from which to choose."

"You're saying she can't carry on with your help in her family wagon?"

Victoria flashed him a look of displeasure.

"Forgive me," he said. "It isn't my intent to make you feel guilty."

"No? It sounds as if that's exactly your intent."

"I merely felt that, since you had been traveling with the family and sharing space in their wagon, you would continue to do so. You've done nothing for which to feel guilty. We have five healthy people who would likely have been sharing those graves if not for your talents and knowledge." There was admiration in his voice that spread warmth through her. Even Matthew had never shown such approval. But then, Matthew had been the teacher, she the student. He'd had twenty years on her in knowledge and experience. And age.

And that thought reminded her to place some distance between Joseph and herself, because no matter how Audy might want to word it, Victoria knew her own hidden desires. Part of her wanted to renew a lost love, but a larger part wanted protection from further loss. Hadn't she endured enough? How could she even contemplate more?

"If you'll excuse me," she said, "I think it best I check on the drying roots and supplies."

"Would you like some help? I've learned much from

you since the outbreak. It wouldn't hurt me to know a little more about all those plants you've had Heidi and Mrs. Reich collecting."

Victoria hesitated. She would love to have him by her side as she sorted through the herbs her friends had brought her, but propriety gave her pause. "Joseph," she said quietly, "not only are you the physical leader of this group, but you're the spiritual leader, as well. No one comforts people better after a loss, and there are people upset by this tragedy."

She thought she heard him give a quiet sigh as she turned away from him. Frustration? Despite all, his desire to be near her gave her pleasure. Close on the heels of that pleasure came dismay. "Oh, Matthew," she whispered, "I'm so sorry."

What kind of a wife developed a wayward heart only seven months after the loss of her husband? Though she and Matthew had endured their differences, she would never be sorry for any of it; in spite of Joseph's words to the contrary, Matthew had left her well prepared for the future. She might not have been able to make a livable income without him by her side, but he'd left her enough wealth to keep her supported for years to come. Many physicians had to work other jobs to follow their true calling, but thanks to Matthew, she wouldn't have to.

She washed her hands and arms in the nearby creek and glanced over her shoulder to find Joseph commiserating with one of the patients she had just checked— the young husband who had endured a bout of the cholera and recovered. She smiled to herself. Joseph was, indeed, doing as she'd asked. It felt good to have a man trust her word, to actually listen to her. To respect her. That was something she'd missed since Matthew's death.

Tired from a weekend of short snatches of sleep, she settled for a moment on the front bench seat of the Ladue wagon and closed her eyes. The sunshine warmed her face as the chatter of her traveling companions burgeoned over her. The distraction of treating patients and talking with Joseph, worrying about Heidi and fretting over the future, had blocked out her ability to focus on her fellow travelers until now.

"…poor, poor child. We must do all we can…"

"…captain knows what he's doing, but isn't there a shorter route?

"…safer to pass through Indian Territory than risk the border attacks…"

"…be a good match if you ask me. I don't care if it hasn't been a full year of mourning…"

"Perfect couple, I agree. Every wagon train needs a doc, even if she is a woman."

A meadowlark's song echoed across the valley, its beautiful minor-key notes sinking into her mind. Victoria kept her eyes closed and suppressed a sigh of satisfaction as she basked in the words of her companions. Soon she would be parting from these people. Thanks to the danger Broderick Thames posed, this wagon train could not follow the trail Matthew had marked out on his map last year, as she'd hoped. She would follow Shoal Creek to Capps Creek and reach the Village of Jollification between dawn and dusk tomorrow; speed was vital now, especially after their long delay.

Danger in the form of a silver-braided man might be somewhere in the vicinity, and she had no way of knowing where. If she parted from the group, would she be drawing him away from them? If so, she must catch that danger and contain it if she could.

"Victoria." Joseph's voice, familiar, warm and deep, reached her from behind.

She straightened, shaking off her weariness, and leaned across the seat to see him approaching her, his black hair and beard recently trimmed, hat still in his hand in respect for the departed. "I'm sorry I didn't consider that this must be renewing your own memories."

She nodded, unable to voice a reply, touched by the sympathy in his night-dark eyes and his effort to see to it that the bodies of the dead were well protected from the teeth of hungry wild animals when the wagon train went on without them. She was also touched by his efforts to speak with her again. These past days he'd gone out of his way to spend time with her, to ride beside her, and she had to admit his company meant a great deal to her.

"I've made my rounds," he said. "As you asked. Now would you like some help with your medicines?"

She clenched her hands until her nails dug into the flesh of her palms. She must tell him the truth about her plans now. And yet, what would it matter? Whatever she said, she had no doubt he would take the news poorly.

She steeled herself for an argument. "No, thank you, Joseph. I do need to speak with you, however." And yet, the words wouldn't come.

Chapter Six

Joseph fingered the stiff canvas brim of his hat and waited as he studied Victoria's expression. In the past five weeks on the trail, he'd prided himself in relearning those expressions well. Right now, however, he couldn't even fathom what was on her mind.

"You aren't feeling ill?" he asked with alarm.

"No, I'm well."

"Victoria, I know you're taking these deaths awfully hard, but we'll all get through it together."

"I appreciate what you're saying, but I've lost patients before. I've lost friends. It's just that… Oh, dear." She folded her hands together and looked down at them as her face grew pale and then pink again. "I have patients to attend to up the creek a ways."

"Patients? Did I miss seeing someone come through?"

"I wouldn't know. I've been busy."

He shook his head, confused. "If you have patients, you must have spoken to someone."

"Not…recently. This was a prior appointment."

He couldn't help focusing on Victoria's clear blue eyes. The expression there disturbed him. She was avoiding his gaze, squeezing her hands into fists, and her breaths came more quickly than normal.

"When did you plan to see them?"

Her gaze returned to his. She didn't reply. One look from her could send shivers down to his toes, but he didn't let on. Something was certainly affecting her, and it was beginning to concern him a great deal.

He glanced around as others passed them. "Something's wrong. You haven't seen another sign of Thames, have you?"

"Not yet, and we've all been on the lookout for signs of that silver-tailed jackal."

Joseph let out a breath of relief. He couldn't imagine anything worse at the moment than to have Broderick Thames call in his slaving buddies to help destroy this wagon train.

"But there's something else," he said more softly, so that no one passing by them could hear.

She looked away, sighed and reached up to rub the back of her neck, as if it had tightened from being held too stiffly. "Do you remember the Frasiers, my friends who traveled to the Village of Jollification? Matthew and I promised them last year that we would see them when we could make it through this way. I can't let them down. I'm sorry, but I should have been clearer about this last week. We just had too many things going on, what with the flood and the cholera scare, and now this." She gestured to the graves. "And Heidi."

He felt a sting of alarm. "I'm sure the Frasiers would understand that you're in danger and can't make it to Jolly Mill."

"How could I make them understand if I have no contact with them?"

"I'd planned to take that route until you told me about Thames's track. You know we can't risk it now."

"I understand perfectly. You can't risk the lives of all these people for a promise I made last year. I believe I can still help them, however."

He held his hand out. "Please walk with me. We need to talk."

She gave a quiet sigh, paused then pushed herself up from the lip of the wagon.

He smiled at her. Finally, perhaps they could clear the air a bit. It had been a tense few days, and he felt sure he could show her the wisdom of staying with the wagon train.

She turned toward the far western end of the valley, and he strolled beside her.

"I was furious with Buster Johnston and his bull-headedness," she said. "I still am, and it doesn't matter how many buckets of water he and Gray haul, or how much firewood they cut, or how many hours they spend searching for tracks, I blame Buster for these lost lives. At the risk of making you think less of me, I resent that Heidi's family is no longer here to care for her, leaving it to others to take their place."

Joseph waited for her to continue. Buster wasn't the subject of her disquiet.

"He doesn't listen to wiser heads. It's why he and Gray are with us in the first place, because he caused the fire in his own hometown that killed a man."

"I agree," Joseph said, "but he seems to be taking things a lot more seriously this past week."

"If he hadn't drawn Claude into his rebellious ways, he might be in one of those graves right now, not the Ladues."

"Is that what you wish?" Joseph asked.

Her steps slowed. She took a deep breath and let it out. "I wish there was no such thing as illness. I wish there was never a need for a doctor. I don't understand how God can allow such suffering, and I don't understand why half-grown young men can't listen to their elders, especially orders from their captain."

"You've apparently been brooding about many things for quite some time. But these aren't what's causing your concern now, are they, Victoria?"

He noted her stiff shoulders. She was angry and frustrated, of course, but she was also braced for something. He took her elbow to guide her over a rocky hillock and felt the tension in her arm. "You haven't traveled with a wagon train before, have you?"

She looked up at him. "Matthew planned for us to ride west to Kansas, but we had no chance before…" She sighed. "We had no time."

After the hillock was far behind them he released her elbow, but he did so with reluctance; despite the rough conditions of their travel, she had the softest skin he'd ever felt. Being in her presence was like a special bit of extra grace from God, even if she was trying to divert his attention from her main concern. She was stalling, and he couldn't help wondering what she hadn't told him.

"I learned early on as a wagon-train captain that we exist to give suggestions, not necessarily instructions, and definitely not orders," he said. "We work with the scout to consider the best route forward, help with broken wheels, guide and advise. It's a democratic form of travel." From the corner of his eye he could tell she was studying him again.

"That's fine." She slowed her steps. "I'm sorry to be going on so. I'm only trying to figure everything out."

"I understand." And she was deftly keeping their main subject at bay. This was something else he remembered about her—this dogged determination to control a conversation.

"Victoria, are you going to tell me what it is you're so afraid to speak to me about?"

She looked down at her clasped hands. "I don't wish to get into an argument with you. I have a long memory, and those arguments have caused us both a lot of pain in the past."

"Tell me anyway," he said, threading his words with a hint of steel.

She didn't move. Strands of golden hair blew across her face. She didn't speak; she only waited.

He could see by the surprise on her face that the hardness in his voice had startled her. He'd never spoken to her like that before, not even when they were younger and she'd refused to go with him to Georgia. They were so in love then that they barely noticed the world around them until it stopped turning.

It wasn't his habit to treat ladies with anything but gentleness. That was part of his heritage he refused to unlearn. He had never forgotten to show proper manners toward the milder gender. Not that he recalled Victoria being particularly mild when he'd decided to leave without her. Quite the contrary.

Had Matthew been instrumental in quenching some of the fire from her, or had years of maturity and her hard loss done that?

He inhaled the scent of her skin—rosemary and sage with a hint of smoke from the fire. "Please don't ride off into that wilderness alone."

Victoria's healthy pink lips parted in surprise, showing a flash of those perfect white teeth. She did meet his gaze then, and he could see the dismay. That was the subject she'd been trying to avoid. Joseph restrained a sigh and braced himself for the argument that he'd known would come the moment they spoke of this.

"I know how to make my way through a forest, Joseph." Victoria had softened her voice. It was a cajoling sound that nearly undid him. She knew him well enough to get past his defenses.

This time, however, he couldn't allow her to do that. "I know you think you do, but you grew up in the eastern side of the Appalachians, not here in the west. The land where you lived was more inhabited, not so wild."

She gave him one of her saucy half grins, placing her fists on her hips. "Other than floods and cholera, I haven't noticed a lot of danger across Missouri, and believe me, I can avoid the cholera, Joseph." She said his name with more of a teasing lilt. "My travel will be like riding through a children's park." She spared a glance toward the giant trees that hovered over Heidi and Audy in the distance, and he followed her gaze. Those trees were like sentinels overlooking the wagon train.

"It's been a few years since your childhood." He spoke the words, then grimaced. A gentleman didn't say such things to a lady. And Dr. Victoria Fenway was every bit a lady. More than a lady, in fact. She didn't just care for the well-being of others, she went out of her way to put her fellow travelers at ease as she tended to their wounds and illnesses.

Though her eyes widened in surprise at his comment, she quickly hid it behind a grin. "Are you commenting on my age, Joseph? Twenty-seven isn't ancient. It's barely been ten years since our last…conflict." Her grin faltered. Her eyes lost a little of their luster, and it pricked at him that he was the cause of that remembered pain. His overly developed regard for his father's wrong-headed rules had caused him to lose her. She still obviously felt that loss as well, though she couldn't feel it more than he did.

"This land is dangerous for a lady," Joseph said.

"I daresay I could match you in a shooting contest. And few would call a female doctor a lady."

"I would definitely be one of the few, and I wouldn't argue with your shooting skills." He nodded toward her waistline. He wasn't always a Southern gentleman. "I've noticed you never go anywhere without your weapon."

The humor remained in her eyes as she patted the Colt revolver he'd seen her pull from her skirt pocket when danger loomed. She even glanced back toward camp again, where he knew her rifle rested against her saddle in the Ladue wagon.

"But you're no rival against me in a contest of survival in this wilderness," he said. "Big cats, wolves and bears roam this land."

"As they did where I grew up." There was a challenge in her voice. She'd always loved a dare.

"Sometimes I've seen poisonous snakes on the forest floor as thick as bees in a hive," he said, knowing he could meet that dare but fearing she still wouldn't listen. "Your horse could fall into a wolf trap—deep holes dug into the ground and covered by brush, with deadly spikes aimed upward to impale the unwary." He noted that her cheeks lost some of their color. "That'd be the end of you both," he said. "This isn't the settled land you knew."

She closed her eyes briefly, but when she opened them again the resolve in her expression remained. "What my father and brothers didn't teach me, Matthew did."

"I don't think you understand what it can mean for a woman such as yourself to be alone out in the wilderness. You won't be able to help anyone if you're dead."

The battle against fear was obvious in her eyes. "I...I know. Joseph, you're making this more difficult." Her voice had gone hoarse, as if she could barely get her words through her tight throat.

He hesitated for a long moment. His first priority was to the wagon train. Their safety was of utmost importance, but she was part of that wagon train. And part of his heart. "I'm telling you that you don't have to go alone, Victoria."

She broke the tension with a brief smile up at him. "Spoken like a true gentleman. I have to say it's not easy to resist that Southern drawl of yours. It charms the challenge right out of me. But this time it's different. I can't drag someone else into the consequences of my choices."

"Were those your choices, or were they Matthew's?" Never in his life had he wanted so badly to reach out an arm of comfort and tell her everything would be okay, but she couldn't do this, and it wouldn't be okay if she tried.

"I chose to follow through for him."

"Then you have friends who will help you make good on that promise," he said.

"Who do you think I should drag along with me? One of the Johnston boys? Who else's life should I risk for my personal convictions?"

"Now you're telling me you know your life could be at risk?"

The parted lips, fingers quickly covering them, told him she'd said more than she'd intended to. Now he was getting somewhere.

* * *

Victoria stepped away from Joseph, irritated that she'd betrayed herself so thoroughly. Hadn't she suspected this could happen?

"Have I explained the name of Jolly Mill?" Joseph asked.

She frowned. She hated being caught off guard. Now what was he up to? "Only that the name was shortened to make it easier to say."

"That's because when the men have had their fill of the hard liquor so abundant in the mill town, the longer name is as hard for them to pronounce as it is for them to walk," he told her. "That's what one of the drunks came up with when he came tumbling out of the dram shop one night. Not a pretty sight for a lady such as you." His voice deepened, grew softer and gentler, and his last few words felt like a caress.

"Do you think Thames went to the mill town?"

"Last time I rode through it was crawling with border ruffians, and you saw from his tracks that he was headed in this direction. It's likely that's where he would wait for us if he's aware we're on the trail. I've seen two or three wagon trains camped there at a time, and that will draw the troublemakers."

Victoria paused to breathe. "You never mentioned that."

"I'm telling you now. It's why we're keeping to the south."

"I understand what you're saying, but all I have to do is treat my patients and pick up a couple of travelers along the way before Thames can catch wind of their whereabouts."

"Hold on." Joseph pressed his hand against her arm,

and that touch was a definite distraction. "What did you say?"

All she could focus on was the firm feel of his hand. "About what?"

"About a couple of travelers you plan to take with you. Did you mention this to me earlier?"

She paused, then withdrew from his touch so she could think straight. "Perhaps not, but with God on my side, what could go wrong?" She spared a hesitant glance at him and found him staring her down. Had he caught the sarcasm she'd been unable to keep from her voice? Or how his nearness was affecting her?

"When did you and God suddenly start speaking again?" he asked.

"Mine is a righteous cause, so why wouldn't the Almighty be on my side?"

"Maybe because you're not on His?"

"But if I'm completing my husband's plan—and Matthew did know what was right—"

"For you?" Joseph gave a soft sigh. "Victoria, you can't know God's will for you without being led by God, Himself, not the intentions of a man who no longer walks this earth."

Victoria pressed her lips together. Now Joseph had taken to preaching to her.

"How long have you been this angry?" Joseph asked more gently. "This blaming God for Matthew's death. How long?"

The presence of this man so close to her, his warm strength, his insistence on protecting her... She should have known better than to allow him so close in the first place. She turned away.

"Victoria—"

"He could have stopped it." Long-held anger streaked through her as if lightning had flashed.

"Do you claim to know the mind of God?"

She stepped away from him, needing a chance to breathe properly. "I know that if He's the Almighty, Matthew could still be alive."

Joseph followed. "You're speaking as if God turns His head from evil on a whim, but you know your Savior better than that. He doesn't work that way."

"I'm afraid we're doomed to opposite sides of that argument."

"I disagree."

Despite her wish to remain serious, Victoria turned and looked up into Joseph's earnest face at last. She chuckled, and then she watched his expression as he realized what he'd said. She enjoyed his sheepish grin.

"Maybe you have a point," he said. "For now."

When she thought of her laughter reaching the others, she was glad they'd walked so far from the burial site. Her fellow travelers were grieving. This was no time for frivolity.

"I'm sorry," she said. "Despite all, I find it charming that you're this concerned about my welfare."

He gazed at her for a moment and, though he didn't take a step, it seemed as if they were nearly touching. "It's good to hear I'm charming you," he murmured. "I'll continue the debate if you wish, for the sake of charming—"

"No need." She felt her face flush. "It feels good to have a man…someone…." She sighed. "It's good to feel less alone."

"I'm glad. I understand loneliness."

"Sometimes we pay dearly for our convictions. Had I known the trials I would encounter after Matthew's murder—had we known he would be murdered for his fight to free the slaves—would we have backed away from the fight?"

Joseph touched her chin and lifted it until she had to meet his gaze. The fire of his touch trailed a path down her neck, though his fingers remained where they were. "I've never known you to back away from any fight."

She could so easily lose herself in those dark eyes and the tender passion she saw in them. Everything within her faltered as she considered giving in to the temptation to cede their debate.

Even so, how could she place any more people from this wagon train at risk?

She couldn't. Buck and Francine needed to be warned. John Brown's adopted son, Naaman, and his wife, Josetta, had to be moved away from danger. There was no other way to do it.

"I should warn you." Joseph released her, and once again her mind cleared. "If you take justice into your own hands against Matthew's killer, you'll be surprised how difficult it is."

She met Joseph's gaze. She'd never doubted that he knew her well, but they were venturing into new territory, and still he could read her thoughts. She had considered the prospect of dark revenge more than once. Often, when tracking Thames, she'd questioned her inner motives. But a man like that needed to be stopped from hurting others. If she had the opportunity to be the one who stopped him, she could do it.

She pressed her lips together to keep from smiling again, then paused, unable to resist riling Joseph. "I don't believe it's as bad as you say."

She glanced up and winced at his glower. Despite the seriousness of this whole conversation, she felt warmth throughout her body. More was at work here than simple friendly concern for her welfare. The powerful attraction that sparked between them could become addictive.

Though she and Matthew had used whiskey as medicine over the ten years of their practice together, she had seen the power the alcohol could exert over some of their patients. For that reason, she had attempted to use alternative medicines whenever possible and avoided the brew herself, lest she turn out to be one of the unfortunate who became dependent. She grinned up at Joseph. Perhaps it would be a good idea to avoid her growing addiction to this man, as well.

But first, just a few more things to discuss. "Captain," she said, using his title intentionally, "how much would you be willing to give up to be sure that Kansas will be a free state?"

"My life, of course." He said it without hesitation, as if she should know that. And she did. He frowned and took a step closer. "I would risk my life to ensure Kansas becomes a free state, just as I believe you've decided to risk yours. Isn't that what you're planning to do?"

"Most definitely. I've learned from the best. You're an excellent teacher. You've portrayed your true character in every wise move you've made, every person with whom you've spoken, every patient whose forehead you've cooled." She enjoyed watching the skin flush around his beard and mustache. The ways he had impressed her were too abundant to mention, some of them even too private to mention.

She felt heat prickle her own face.

He quietly cleared his throat. "The admiration is mutual, I assure you, though I do wish you would trust me with your plans for Jolly Mill."

Time for a bit more distraction. "Perhaps I'm simply following the example you set years ago."

"What do you mean?"

"When you returned home to take your father's place at the plantation. I thought you were gone for good, especially when you sent word to Matthew—and not to me, by the way—that your father wanted you to marry a childhood friend."

He straightened. Obviously, the technique worked. "Tell me, was that before or after you and Matthew married?"

"Before, of course. Until then I held out hope that you might change your mind and return. I had heard you were engaged to Miss Sara Jane many months before I was willing to consider a partnership with Matthew." She boldly held his gaze. "I was going to travel with my brother to California when I decided you weren't returning to St. Louis. Matthew offered to make me his partner if I would stay. Of course, you hadn't told us your plans." She was surprised by the sudden testiness in her voice.

Joseph frowned, but he didn't reply immediately. Instead, he gazed across the valley, his jaw muscles flexing, eyes brooding. He pulled off his hat and looked down at it as he rubbed his fingers over the brim. "I never intended to marry anyone else."

"You didn't see fit to tell me that and you left me behind. What was I supposed to think?"

"My letters should have told you everything."

"And as I've told you, I never received a single letter from you."

"I can't help wondering why. Where could those letters have been stopped, and why didn't you receive them?"

"Please don't tell me you're placing the blame for that on a dead man."

"No." He sighed. "Maybe. I have no reason to believe Matthew would hurt us this way."

"You were the one who left, Joseph. You can't blame Matthew for hurting us."

"I came to my senses not long after arriving home, and I did write to you about my change of heart." Joseph put his hat back on and caught her gently by the shoulders.

She shook her head, aware only of the warmth of his hands. "Even then, when you were barely twenty, you were a man who knew what he wanted," she said softly. "Why would I have expected you to change your mind?"

As if just then realizing he was holding her, instead of releasing her, he drew her closer. "You know about honor, don't you? That's why you're here, isn't it? To honor your dead husband's memory."

She bit her tongue. Joseph could always bring the subject back to where he wanted it. And yet she'd never felt safer than right now, in the circle of his arms. Times like this she didn't want to let him go. She wanted to think something could work between them, and she wanted his support in her endeavor.

"You know others have gone before us into Kansas for the same reason, not only from Missouri but from the rest of the country, migrating there with family and friends." She hesitated. "Francine and Buck Frasier also believe in our cause."

"I don't expect you'd be so intent on this visit if you thought they didn't." Again, that see-all gaze, and then his expression changed and realization struck. "And this valuable cargo you mentioned?"

She held his gaze. "What do you think John Brown would call precious cargo?"

"His sons."

"What could be more precious than a son, and possibly his wife?"

He hesitated, let out a heavy breath and looked away, his dark eyes intent on the horizon, his strong jaw muscles still working beneath the neat beard.

For a moment her own breath refused to come and she realized how badly she wanted this man on her side. Maybe even more than that. Maybe she simply wanted him beside her. Guilt once again prickled along her arms as she thought of Matthew. She'd never experienced this kind of powerful awareness of Matthew even after their marriage metamorphosed into something more than a business arrangement.

Overcome by a sudden wave of sadness, she turned to walk away from Joseph—the man who had once rejected her. Matthew never had. The very direction of her heart betrayed her. Was she also betraying Matthew?

Chapter Seven

Joseph watched the woman he loved strolling slightly ahead of him, her golden-red hair glowing in the sunshine, the scent of honeysuckle scattering in her wake. "I've realized I can't hog-tie you to a wagon and force you to continue with us," he said.

She walked in silence for a moment, her shoulders drooping, her head bowed. What had he said wrong? Why was she so downcast now?

"Of course not," she said after an uncomfortable hesitation. "Matthew learned after our first week of marriage that I don't take kindly to commands."

"Haven't I respected your wishes to this point of our trip?" he asked. "Try me, Victoria. If I interfere, you can shoot me with that little pistol of yours."

He thought he heard her sigh, but she continued walking and her speed increased as if she didn't want him to catch up with her. So naturally, he did. She had entered the shade of a giant pine when he reached out for her hand, grasped it and held it. He heard her catch her breath, but she didn't pull away. He thought he could sense her wavering, and then she stopped and turned to look up at him.

What was it that made her eyes shine even in the shadows? Or maybe it wasn't her eyes but something in her expression, her thoughts, her heart, in the feel of her hand in his. He raised her hand and kissed it, never taking his gaze from hers. She held it with characteristic boldness.

As if the touch of his lips on her skin drew her, she stepped forward until he could smell the subtle fragrance of the herbs she collected and turned into healing balms. She had always been the healing balm in his life. It was why he'd wandered alone for so many years.

She reached up and pressed the back of her hand against the side of his face, sending warmth through him. "I want to tell you a story."

"I love stories." And he wanted this moment, this touch, to last forever. He could listen to her stories all day long.

"Our friends Francine and Buck Frasier were attacked one evening last year by a drunk outside a saloon in St. Louis. A slave came to their rescue and was shot by a black-hearted hate monger for his kindness. They came to our clinic for help. That's how we became acquainted. We found we had similar interests."

Joseph no longer winced at her references to Matthew and herself as "we." She often spoke of Matthew, and Joseph no longer experienced the sharp sting of jealousy that had attacked him at first. He knew that if he loved her he was going to have to love everything about her, including her past, her memories and the fact that she was no longer the young, inexperienced woman who had wound herself around his heart.

Would that be a challenge for him? Would he be willing to wait until she was ready to love again?

"Joseph? Am I boring you?"

Hannah Alexander 97

He glanced at her. "Of course not. You could never bore me. Please continue."

She seemed mollified. "Among other things, Francine and I both wished for children. She taught me how to knit and crochet, and Matthew taught Buck several things medical."

"Who was this blackheart who shot their rescuer?"

"A plantation owner by the name of Otto Duncan."

Joseph knew that name, and it gave him a chill. "He has a lot of productive land in the Missouri River Valley."

"He defended himself later with the excuse that no slave should ever be allowed to attack a white man, no matter the reason." She looked up at Joseph. "What else do you know of him?"

"He has a prosperous plantation, which enables him to make the money to get by with inhumane activities." Joseph took Victoria by the elbow, and though he wanted to take her into his arms and kiss her, he knew better than to push her too far. He guided her forward and out of the shadows into the sunlight again. "I've heard fellow trappers report that the man treats his captives like grasshoppers in a field, and he has enough income through extortion that he can afford to lose a slave or two every month. He does it for the sport, sets them free in a forest and chases them down with his dogs, promising freedom if they can reach the edge of the plantation before he catches them."

Victoria gasped. Her steps slowed. "The law allows this?"

"He owns the law in that area."

"I believe he's connected to Thames."

"More reason for you to avoid that silver-tailed skunk. I'm not excusing Southern plantation owners for using slaves, but he could at least have the good sense to keep his slaves cared for in order to yield good crops."

"Spoken like the son of a plantation man." She touched Joseph's arm. "Before you arrived in St. Louis last month, one of Duncan's neighbors was mysteriously killed and his crops burned."

"You suspect Duncan?" Joseph asked.

"Everyone does."

"Was the neighbor an abolitionist?"

"No, he had slaves of his own." She dropped her hand to her side and gave a soft sigh. "Everyone around us seems so corrupt. Do you think we even have a chance to make a change toward integrity in this country?"

He knew what she was thinking. Had he been the one planning to break away from the wagon train and travel north to help protect the innocents, he wouldn't allow anyone to talk him out of it, either.

Joseph caught the scent of smoke and looked up to see the camp as they drew closer to it. "Do you think the Reichs are the kind of people to make a difference?"

"With all those smart young boys? Most definitely."

"Deacon and Mrs. Fritz?"

"Oh, yes. You made good choices, Joseph. Except maybe for that young blond-haired scoundrel who refuses to respect the wisdom of older men."

"Buster's father was once as wild as his son is now, wouldn't listen to a word of advice, so he had to learn the hard way. But what he learned toughened him up for life. Buster's already learned some awfully painful lessons. If I didn't think he had a future I would never have taken him on."

"I would think one troublemaker per wagon train would be enough for you." She shrugged. "Though I realize I can also stir things up from time to time."

He grinned and shook his head. "I'm not going to argue, but you do make up for it." She obviously didn't take offense. "You get enough clear-thinking folk together and you'll have a chance for change," he continued. "Those clear-thinking folk will have a good influence on that one wild young man."

"How many wagon trains did you say you'd led to Kansas Territory?" she asked.

"This one makes five," Joseph said.

"So the town is already a good size."

"We started work on it the day my first wagon train camped on the chosen ground." He recalled the pride and sense of excitement he'd felt then. "We settled far enough east that we have trees for wood to build, so no one is living in a sod house. Every family has a home built by the community. We have over five hundred souls living there now, and we're growing every day with young families and wiser folk to guide the way." How he would love to have his own family someday with this beautiful, determined, compassionate woman by his side.

"Are you far enough away from the border to avoid ruffians?"

"I hope so. When we settled that land, the political climate wasn't as hostile as it is now. We can pray we'll be overlooked by troublemakers, but the people are building a border of our own around the town property, as well as a protected tower should we need to keep watch."

"Like a fort?"

"Exactly. A fort in a protected valley." He thought about Otto Duncan's murdered neighbor. "What happened to the slaves of the murdered plantation owner?"

"They were hidden away."

"By whom?"

"Francine and Buck Frasier may have had something to do with leading them away from harm," she said. "They have a lot of friends in Missouri. If I know them, they did all they could to help the homeless find shelter."

"No wonder you became friends with them. You're an amazing woman, Victoria Fenway."

She stopped walking and looked up at him. Moisture filmed those priceless blue eyes. "You approve?"

"How could I not approve of what's in your heart? It's pure and good. If you were to manage to help John's son and daughter-in-law escape, what if the free-soil vote doesn't go our way in Kansas?"

"Then we'll continue west until we find a place of safety. When this is over they will have their freedom."

Joseph removed his hat and brushed at his forehead with the sleeve of his shirt. He sighed and replaced the hat as he gazed around at the people tending the wagons and livestock, the men placing more large chunks of freshly dressed venison over the bonfire. It would be hours before dinner, but the scent of roasting meat made him hungry now.

He glanced down at Victoria and could guess her thoughts by the direction of her gaze and the way she nibbled at her lower lips. What would happen to all these good folk if someone like Duncan or the border ruffians got hold of them, especially if they found out she was working against the ruffians?

"Victoria, do you have any way to fake slave ownership should you be stopped with John's family in your company?"

"I'll have what I need. Buck and Francine don't have papers, which is why they're in a dangerous situation. I brought a stack of blank sale bills for livestock and slaves that Matthew had printed by a friend of his in the newspaper office. Until I can provide those, however, Jolly Mill, with those roving ruffians, is a bad place for all."

The thought gave him a chill.

Victoria looked up at Joseph in time to see him grimace. She loved the fact that he was too much of a gentleman to remark often on her bullheadedness.

"We could send scouts with you to check out the town," Joseph said. "See what kind of activity is taking place there now. It is, after all, a good place to stop and resupply. It's our usual passage, with a good route straight into the Kansas Territory."

She gave a soft sigh. Why had she allowed herself to be convinced he would let her follow through on her plans? "Joseph, no. You can't get our people involved in a border skirmish."

He nodded as if in agreement, and she relaxed. For a moment she'd thought he was serious. Taking everyone that direction would add days to her travel—and she could not afford the time. After spotting Thames's track, she'd grown more restless as time went on. Though she'd feel ever so much safer riding into town with the knowledge that backup was on the way, that would be selfish.

Joseph gave her a sidewise grin. "I could send McDonald down around Elk River to meet with the other wagons due to join up with us there. They can meet the rest of us in Neosho."

"Isn't it just as dangerous there?"

"We have a field above town where we meet. It's surrounded by thick forests and the land that's there is farmed by other abolitionists."

She bit the tip of her tongue. He'd been thinking

things through for a while, apparently. "When you and McDonald were redoing our route, you decided not to go as far north as Neosho."

"That was days ago. We're staying off the busiest trails, but see that creek over there? Shoal Creek goes all the way to Neosho."

"How do you know? Have you followed it?"

"My scout has. That's where a good scout earns his keep. So don't go telling me how to captain my wagon train." He said the words lightly, as if teasing.

"I won't, if you won't try telling me which way to guide my horse." Her tone matched his.

He paused, his steps slowing. "But that's my job."

She looked away. Better to back down than to dare him to get drastic.

Though she prided herself in her ability to keep a professional facade with her patients, she'd been unable to maintain that same countenance with Joseph these past few days. Could he feel her fear? These insights of his must change, and quickly. So must her weakness when it came to men with equal measures of strength and kindness in their hearts.

She had a task to perform that trumped any other, and as an overwhelming desire grew in her to accept his aid, she rejected it. Joseph was the last person she would ever wish to endanger. "Excuse me, Joseph, but I have packing to do. I'd best get to it."

Joseph watched and appreciated the beautiful Dr. Victoria Fenway as she marched away, head high, hair the color of a golden sunrise that continued to escape her chignon. It drifted across the black material that covered her shoulders, and he noted that those shoulders had begun to slump once more. Her head slowly bowed and the starch left her almost as quickly as it had stiffened her spine not a moment ago.

Dr. Matthew Fenway had been a blessed man to have a woman like her who was faithful to his memory long after his body had been planted in the earth. She remained the picture of despondency as she walked to the wagon she shared with the Ladues—now with only Heidi.

Her determination to save her patients this past week would have earned Joseph's unceasing respect if she hadn't already done so. He knew it took a stubborn spirit to fight death and win, and she needed that strong spirit to keep her going, particularly since she had some obvious qualms with the Almighty.

What concerned him was where her strong spirit might take her and how much danger she might find there.

He watched as she climbed into the back of the wagon, her hair finally falling completely from its twist and waving in the brilliant afternoon sunlight—a lovely vision of the sunrise encircling her shoulders right here in the middle of the afternoon. She disappeared beneath the oiled canvas of the wagon cover.

"We could make a few miles this afternoon," Zeke McDonald's voice rattled from behind.

Joseph turned and raised his eyebrows at his red-headed, scruffy-faced scout.

"There's an easy crossing in the shallows only about fifteen feet up from the old trail," the tall man continued. "We can be on our way, collect our other wagons down along the Arkansas border, and be riding across the wild prairie in a couple of weeks. Kansas is gettin' closer all the time."

"Any word of the ruffians in these parts?" Joseph asked.

"Not so much through Indian Territory right now. That's our plan." McDonald squinted at Joseph. "Isn't it?"

Joseph kicked at a rock. "What's along the trail from Springfield these days?"

McDonald shook his head and grunted. He glanced toward the Ladue wagon. "Got to you, has she?"

"Did she mention to you she was leaving the wagon train?"

"Luella Ladue said something to me about it a few days back, but since our doc's made a few calls along the trail, I figured she'd just catch up with us the way she has before." There was heaviness in McDonald's voice when he said Luella's name. He and the widow had formed a friendship these past couple of weeks.

Joseph felt badly for him. As his thoughts once again rested on Victoria, she stepped from the wagon and glanced in his direction, then toward Heidi.

"I think we'll wait until morning," Joseph said. "Give the girl some time to say goodbye."

McDonald released a quick breath. "Thought you'd see it that way. Looks like we'll have some clear weather for at least a couple of days. If you want, I can ride up to see what kind of travel we might have to the Jolly Trail. It'd be easier for the rest of you to go there and rest while I round up the others—that is, if there's no troublemakers around."

Joseph nodded. "Ask folks in the area, but be careful. There are likely to be problems."

"Not a lot of slave owners in these parts. Not a lot of anything, what with the rocky farmland."

"You know as well as I do that the ruffians are watching for anyone who might be headed toward the state line."

"You're right. Indian Territory has the safest route." McDonald grunted. "Plan to leave the doctor behind, do you?"

Joseph inhaled a lungful of bonfire smoke, choked, and coughed it away.

The scout chuckled. "I could trail behind her, let you go on without me."

"We need you more than ever right now."

"I've never seen you have trouble with a decision."

Joseph mulled. "Last time was ten years ago."

"The doc's got a mind of her own." McDonald lifted his hat and scratched his head. "There's good folk in Jolly. They've got a church with regular services. We could resupply there and give our sick ones more time to heal. If it's safe, that is."

"If it's safe. Probably isn't."

"And if it ain't?"

"Then I'll have a harder decision to make."

McDonald grunted, his eyes matching the calm water that reflected the clear Missouri sky. "I'd better ride up a ways and see if there's a chance we'll get across without being spotted, then."

"Thanks, my friend." Joseph was grateful for a good scout to depend on, who even seemed to understand this sudden wish to change all their plans for the sake of one woman.

But Joseph did have a responsibility to many more than one woman.

He shook his head as Victoria stepped down from the Ladue wagon, hair now drawn behind her in a braid. The women who traveled this route were brave, strong and determined, or they often didn't survive. Their courage paled in comparison to Victoria's. Or perhaps that was his heart talking.

As McDonald rode away, the soft ground muffled the sound of horse hooves. Joseph looked around for Buster and Gray Johnston. Victoria was right about Buster being a nuisance, maybe even a menace at his age. He was headstrong and seldom thought before he acted, but if his younger brother could corral him, the two boys may become more than water carriers and weight bearers.

Despite their efforts to make amends for their earlier actions, Victoria still trusted neither of them, and many of the others with the wagon train had followed her lead now that the much-loved Ladue mother and son were buried. If not for the fact that Buster would probably get himself killed if left in the wilderness alone, Joseph would have sent him back home and let his daddy work some sense into him. The boys were hard workers, for sure, but Buster's muscles didn't extend to his brains. Yet.

At the moment, sixteen-year-old Gray stood near the graves with his hat in his hands, head bowed. Gray was wise enough to be aware of his older brother's failings. The younger brother was the more intelligent and discerning by far, but he obviously admired his elder brother and had little control over Buster's unreserved personality.

Buster stood beside the bonfire, poking a stick into the wood to stir up a better flame. Every few seconds he gawked toward the Ladue wagon. The young man had obviously caught sight of Victoria. He'd accidentally allowed a fire to burn nearly out of control one day because his attention was drawn to the good doctor.

For that reason alone, Joseph was tempted even now to send the young rooster back to his papa.

Joseph caught Gray's attention and gestured to him. The young man immediately put his hat on and came forward. "Yessir?"

"You realize, don't you, that secrecy on this trip is one of the many things that will keep the people safe?"

"Yes, I do, Captain. I haven't spoke to no strangers, and I've made sure Buster hasn't, either."

"You couldn't have been with your brother every second."

"I stay pretty close when we're around others, but he's kind of shy around new people, anyways."

Though Joseph had once trusted their father, Walter, with his life, he wouldn't trust a feral pig to Buster Johnston. Not yet, anyway. Still, he'd promised Walter he'd watch out for them. Time to put a bit of a scare into the one with a brain.

"Son, we're getting closer to the border between Missouri and the Kansas Territory. I hope you know what that means."

Gray glanced over his shoulder toward his brother. "Yessir. We both know. Angry slavers ready to stop us from crossing. Our daddy drilled it into us. We lost our rifles in the creek, which is a shame, because Buster's the best shot in the county."

"We're not in your county anymore."

Gray sighed. "You know I can't do much with him, Captain. Papa said Ma always pampered him too much while Papa was out trapping or scouting. Then Ma died and something in Buster kind of went wild."

Joseph knew all this. He knew Walter had hoped they'd toughen up in Kansas. "We'll see. Time's always the great separator between the men and the boys, and if boys stay boys, they may never make it to manhood." Joseph leaned closer so Gray would hear him well. "That means they could do something foolish and die."

Gray winced. "Yessir."

"Now, you and Buster stop making eyes at Miss Ladue and Dr. Fenway and get serious about rustling up some weapons next time we come to a trading post. You can work a little harder and maybe earn some money to pay for them. You say Buster's a good shot."

Gray's expression lightened. "A deadeye."

"He'd better be. And so had you. I chose our traveling companions for their wisdom and abilities. You and Buster are hanging by a half-torn spiderweb."

"Yessir." Gray's face reddened until it clashed against the lightest blond strands of his hair. "But I'm not moonin' over Heidi Ladue. I just feel she's…well…my responsibility, seein' as it was me who listened to my brother and believed the water was safe to cross. She needs someone to take care of her."

"Heidi is going to be cared for by others. You attend to your chores." Joseph turned with a nod, dismissing him. At least the water west of here was pure, and McDonald didn't report any bad weather brewing. Still, Joseph felt in his bones that there were more storms of another kind heading their way.

His focus changed when he walked across the clearing to where Heidi sat staring into the deep woods. Mrs. Reich stood with an arm around her. Both were silent until he reached them, and then Heidi's eyes brightened.

"Captain, I've searched the edge of the woods and from right here I've seen four different plants Dr. Fenway can use for medicines."

Mrs. Reich turned a startled look up at him, then

shrugged and shook her head. This was apparently the first time Heidi had spoken today.

"There'll be more even deeper in the woods, I know," Heidi continued. "I've learned all the medicinal plants and drawn pictures of those she's picked along the way. I know how to dry them, too. I've watched."

"You hope to become a doctor just like Dr. Fenway someday?" he asked.

"Oh, yes. She knows everything about all kinds of plants, and she told me someday I could do the same thing if I wanted to. I hope she teaches me everything I want to know it all."

"I think she's taught you a lot already."

Heidi nodded. There was an unnerving brightness in her eyes, as if she had no memory of the loss of her family—or as if she was intentionally suppressing it. "You know, folks think women can't be doctors, and boys think we're stupid. Most men do, too, according to…" Her lips hovered open and her eyes widened.

"According to your mother?" he asked gently.

She looked up at him, and then her attention drifted away as if they hadn't just spoken.

Mrs. Reich returned to patting and soothing her, and Joseph excused himself quietly. Gently. As if one word spoken with too much force would shatter whatever hold Heidi had on herself.

Buster Johnston was stirring a kettle of greens and roots that had been collected around the field while teasing William Reich about his crush on Heidi. William, of course, took it with good humor, but his gaze seldom wavered from the direction of his mother and his friend in the clearing.

After seeing to it that all was well enough with the rest of the wagon train and telling the people they would be leaving in the morning, Joseph wandered once more in the direction of the Ladue wagon, where Victoria stood working in the sun that had just peered out from behind a passing cloud. He needed her help once again.

Chapter Eight

The aroma of roasting venison filled the air, making Victoria's stomach grumble. No one had been hungry for breakfast this morning, and her lack of nutrition was making itself known as she examined the medical supplies distributed across the white square of linen along the back edge of the Ladue wagon. She would have to temporarily abandon so many of her herbs and medicines, and even some of her bandages.

Not that she knew for sure she would need anything at the Frasiers' home, but one always needed to be prepared. Many of the herbs and roots, however, she would be able to find in the forests, or in the fields, even along the stream. When she and Matthew had traveled, she'd learned to pack lightly and make do.

She rubbed some of her utensils with what was left of her whiskey and wrapped them securely. These were the surgery utensils Matthew had given her, and she cherished them more than she'd have cherished the expensive wedding ring he'd wanted to give her two years after their wedding—soon after making his true affection for her evident.

A glance at Sadie reassured her that the mare was

eager for a ride. One more night of rest and the sweet girl would have her wish.

Satisfied that most of the group was occupied around the bonfire several yards away—with Heidi and Audy still lingering at the edge of the forest—Victoria left the remainder of the utensils for later and pulled back the sheet of linen to study the map she'd slid beneath it. She knew the route by heart because she'd studied it so many times, but during their passage through Missouri she had marked down the small towns and trading posts along the way that Matthew had dismissed as trivial. It wouldn't hurt to draw a rough map of places she'd covered and study once again the route she would have to follow to avoid detection. She marked down the places where she'd seen the track proving Thames had been on their trail before they traveled it, and studied the drawing of the track. Could she have been wrong? Could there be more than one horse with a right front shoe broken at the far tip?

A shadow moved behind her and she caught the familiar scent of wild mint—another of Joseph's favorite edibles. Even as a tingle of pleasure warmed her, she instinctively covered the map with a casual unfolding of the linen. She laid her rifle atop it so the corner wouldn't blow up and kept a smile to herself. The man seemed to keep popping up today, as he had been doing a lot recently. Her inner delight battled an equal measure of inner guilt; the man she'd once loved was obviously still attracted to her and she was enjoying it far too much, like a giddy young girl.

In some ways it seemed a lifetime had passed since their painful parting, but when they were together she couldn't help feeling that some invisible force had brought them back together now, as if time had folded in on itself. What was that invisible force? Would she ever have seen him again if not for Matthew's death?

That thought helped her keep the smile away.

"Victoria, I'm afraid you haven't finished your work with us, as Gray Johnston just reminded me."

She swung around, lips parted as all her private thoughts scattered like the bonfire's smoke. "What are you talking about? You're now allowing a boy to tell you what I should and should not be doing?"

He grimaced and raised his hands. "Hear me out,"

She crossed her arms. "I'm listening."

"Gray seems to think it's his responsibility to take care of Heidi, since he couldn't stop the shenanigans that took her family from her."

"I'm sure you disabused him of that notion. Does he think he can do a better job than Mrs. Reich is doing right now?" She jerked her head toward Heidi and Audy. The older lady hovered closely with a sturdy arm around the lone girl standing in the cusp between the menace of the forest and the brightly colored spring meadow.

Joseph glanced over his shoulder toward the work that had consumed the men this morning, then he turned from the two graves, as if satisfied no wild animals would breach the hold of the dead. "I happen to believe that girl may have an important career in her future. She has an unusual acuity for so young a woman, intelligent, wise beyond her years, a lot like you were ten years ago. She needs someone to guide her and keep her mind occupied after her losses, and right now I fear for her mind, especially after what I just witnessed. She's not herself at all."

Victoria wilted, overwhelmed by the crush of responsibility she felt toward too many people at once. How could she leave Heidi after so great a loss? And yet, she must reach Buck and Francine as soon as possible.

"I know you're worried about your friends," Joseph said, as if reading her mind, "but we can help them, too, even get them out of Jolly Mill if they need to come."

"Joseph," she warned, "that wasn't part of your plan, and the safety of all these people hinges on that plan."

"I know, but don't you realize yet that your dreams are mine? We both want freedom for all in this country. So do our fellow travelers. We're all in this together, and together we're stronger than we are alone."

"You were talking about Heidi, so let's talk about Heidi." Victoria fought back a wave of panic. "Of course the girl isn't herself. She just lost the last of her family. She's not going to be herself for quite some time. It will take her years to recover. As for changing your plans, the change you made last week was a good one. You need to stick with it and let me deal with Buck and Francine. They're my responsibility, not yours." She turned her back to him and reached for the lid to her medicinal whiskey.

"I've been thinking about Naaman, John Brown's son," Joseph said. "If the Knights of the Golden Circle have discovered their whereabouts, then there could already be trouble for the Frasiers. This whole corner of Missouri could be crawling with dangerous men in search of him. Do you know what they would do to him in an effort to cut at John Brown's heart, stop his crusade for abolition?"

She stared down at the pure white of the linen. "I'll do my part. I'll take Naaman Brown and his wife, Josetta, with me to Kansas. I'll do the best I can. It's all I can do. Matthew thought this was a righteous task, a God-honoring task. God will either protect us all, or some will die. From what I've seen on this trip, either could happen."

Joseph winced outwardly at her words, then his attention was drawn toward the linen cloth, beneath which she had slid the map. He looked back at her. "You're willing to die serving a God you're not sure you believe in."

"Haven't you found it harder to believe after witnessing the deaths of such good people? Don't you find it harder to believe that our powerful, Almighty Lord loves us enough to keep us from harm? He didn't rescue Luella or Matthew—"

"He did rescue them from permanent harm," Joseph said, his voice gentle again. "You have to also believe in heaven."

"And the other, of course, which is where poor Heidi must be dwelling right now."

He shook his head. "The story hasn't ended yet."

"Don't drag this wagon train into danger for my solitary commitment," she said. "I never made any promise to you or anyone else that I was going all the way to Kansas with this wagon train."

"I told you we needed a doctor, and you agreed to come with us in that capacity."

"You had one when you needed it, and if I succeed in Jolly Mill you'll have one again." She realized the camp had fallen silent, and that her voice seemed to echo against the wagons. Probably startling the animals. "I'll be back to mentor Heidi," she said softly. "All will be well if that's God's plan."

Joseph leaned closer to her. "We haven't reached Kansas yet. We'll need you all the way."

"I'll only be away from the wagon train for a few days at most."

"With ruffians beating the bushes? Do you know how badly they'll want Naaman Brown?"

"If they even know he's there."

"And do you know what those beasts will do to him and his wife, anyone coming to their aid?" Joseph's voice deepened with frustration.

"More reason for me to get to them quickly and get them out of the state. Don't forget, I have the bills of sale. All I have to do is fill them out."

"And if people like Broderick Thames and Otto Duncan are hovering in Jolly Mill, expecting your arrival? Thames must know who you are. He must have studied you and Matthew long before killing him. He'll know what you're up to."

The sound of Joseph's voice echoed, and the silence of the others remained. He and Victoria stood looking at each other until the chatter picked up and continued amongst their travel mates.

"Naaman and Josetta will trust only me because they know me," Victoria said. "They won't place their lives into your hands no matter what you say, not even if you tell them about me. They must be frightened, Joseph. You don't understand the kind of fear they endure every day."

"I have an idea."

"Then you must understand why I'm so determined about this."

There was another long silence, and Victoria could almost see the thoughts flitting across his grave face. She could guess at the questions that must be occurring to him, as they had occurred to her so many times these past weeks.

"Would they be frightened if you brought a friend with you?"

Her fingernails found their familiar spot on the palms of her hands and dug in. Persistence was his nature. She'd always known that. What had made her think, ten years ago, that she had the patience to endure that kind of determination for a lifetime? She'd changed. Loving a man of such boldness and strong will would wear a woman out.

She still grieved Matthew's death, but she was beginning to think single women had freedom they could treasure. She could afford to remain single, free from having a man try to run her life—a man who might well praise her one moment for a job well done and then in the next moment grow angry with her for the very thing he had previously admired.

"Trying to reason with you is like pounding my head against a giant boulder," she muttered without rancor.

Joseph looked down at her—he was one of the few men tall enough to do so. There was a challenge in his obsidian eyes. "Whatever you do, please don't forget the young woman who needs you to treat a wound greater than your own."

"You're talking about Heidi again?" Hands on hips, she leaned forward until she caught another whiff of his wild-mint breath. "I don't think you understand me, Joseph. I have taken Heidi under my wing. She is strong enough to endure my absence for a day or two until I complete my task and am able to settle back with the train. She is surrounded by friends who have become like family."

"How can you be so sure you'll return from such a dangerous situation?"

Victoria spread her hands in the air in exasperation. "This is another of your personality quirks I'd forgotten over the years. You become so focused on a plan you think will work that you don't even hear me. You didn't before, and you don't now. That hasn't changed at all."

He took off his hat and scraped his fingers through the thick black hair. "I do listen, Victoria. What I hear you saying is that you're planning an action that could get you killed just so you can carry out your husband's last wishes." He paced restlessly away from her, his broad shoulders flexing beneath the heavy blue shirt. "I should have known," he muttered.

"What's that?"

He turned to look at her, and he wore all his thoughts in his expression. She suppressed a gasp at the deep longing and love she saw in those dark eyes.

"I should have known that if we discussed this plan of yours, I would lose control. We're talking about your life. Matthew would never place a load such as this on his wife's shoulders. He loved you, Victoria."

Oh, dear. She stood staring at him, aware her mouth was open but unable to focus on closing it, especially when he walked back toward her slowly, deliberately holding her gaze.

"You have a lot of courage," he said, his voice softening, "but don't allow that courage to lead you to make a huge mistake. Matthew would be outraged if I allowed it."

A warm flush traveled up Victoria's neck. A sudden sting of tears surprised her. She tried to blink them away. Now, hearing Joseph speak of him, she couldn't help recalling her husband's expression when he looked at her, the way he'd spoken to her as he lay dying on that hideous day.

Joseph took her hands in his and held them, seeming not to care what others thought but instinctively knowing what she needed at the moment. "Let's be honest,

Victoria, shall we? Had I not left for Georgia in search of the truth, I'd have stayed in St. Louis and married you instead of leaving you to Matthew. I would never, as your husband, have sent you out here on such a dangerous journey by yourself."

"But it was his dying wish. By then he was convinced I could be in more danger in St. Louis than I would be coming West."

Joseph closed his eyes, and she could see the thoughts flitting across his face. His expression changed and he looked down at her again. "I can think of no woman more capable than you. If anyone could pull off this plan, it would be you. Matthew knew his wife well." Joseph cleared his throat. "He was a wise and blessed man."

Victoria closed her mouth. She knew when Joseph Rickard was up to something. She recalled from years ago when they had argued in just this way, Joseph's tendency had always been to disarm her with flattery.

What he didn't know was that she'd willingly learned from the master. The man whose eyes seemed to suddenly devour her had taught her how to play that game well.

With an intentional turnabout, she swallowed her surprise and graced Joseph with her most dimpled smile. She reached out and caressed his hands with hers. This widened his eyes and appeared to drive him back a half step.

"Why, Joseph Rickard," she said, imitating his drawl, "you can't possibly know how a handsome man like yourself could turn a lonely widow's head if she were to allow it."

"But I wasn't trying to turn any—"

"And you can't possibly know how fine a figure

you are when you're saddled up and leading all these people who depend on you." She nodded and widened her smile. "A very fine leader. And that's why a leader cannot have his head turned by one stubborn, lonely widow when so many others need you, both here and in Kansas."

Joseph's thick, straight brows drew together, but she could see the color rise above his trimmed beard, and that was a satisfying sight. It was the second time she'd made him blush today. It could be done. He cleared his throat, but said nothing.

"I had noticed you never talk much about your up-bringing." Victoria gazed around the large clearing that had once held stumps of long-ago trees. "I know about your family's plantation, of course, and the slaves your family owned, because that was the subject of our very first argument."

"Correction, my father owned them. Wives are often treated much like slaves and work nearly as hard, so my mother didn't consider herself to be an owner at all. Since she came from Ohio, she was opposed to the idea of one human owning another."

"So that's why you were so open to my point of view."

An amused smile tugged at his lips and sparked from his eyes. "Oh, there were other reasons."

A trickle of perspiration tickled Victoria's neck, and she realized the sun had warmed the air considerably today. Surely that was all that caused her to be so heated. "And what were those reasons?"

"You realize, of course, that you can be persuasive when you feel passionate about something."

She bowed her head in gracious acknowledgment. "Thank you. Did you wish to help me with the remainder of my utensils?"

Light suddenly filled his eyes and he stepped forward like an eager boy. "Tell me what you want me to do."

Her heart softened. Little did he know that she would soon be done with her persuasive tactics and take things totally into her own hands. The thought of his anger made her shiver, but he wasn't giving her a choice.

Joseph watched Victoria wrap boiled cloths around her cleaned utensils, amazed anew by her beauty and strength. She was as dazzling to him as the noonday sun.

"You haven't spoken much about your friendship with John Brown," he said.

She looked up at him. "I told you plenty of things. We've hardly been silent throughout Missouri. Remember the night Deacon Fritz came out looking for us to make sure you'd make it to bed in time to get up to taste his wife's Dutch-style pancakes for breakfast?"

"He didn't care what we ate. He has taken it upon himself to see to the moral aspects of our younger set."

"Younger set? He thinks you and I are youngsters?"

Joseph sighed. "Are you changing the subject? Why did you keep your friendship with John Brown a secret for so long?"

"A lady doesn't brag about the famous heroes she's met in her life. I didn't tell you until it was vital for you to know."

Joseph thought about that. It made sense if one saw things from her perspective. "What bothers me is that in all these weeks we've traveled together you haven't told me some of the most important things."

Her movements slowed and she gently laid down her utensil. "Are we still arguing?" Her voice drifted with dangerous softness through the air. She didn't turn to look up at him. "Because if we are, and I'm distracted enough to pack these utensils poorly, you could be liable for the lives of my patients. Would you wish that on some hapless woman or child?" She turned and looked up at him, her eyes not exactly fiery, but inquisitively intense.

"Forgive me. I've wanted to ask you more about John Brown on several occasions."

"He's a man who believes in the awfulness of slavery—the kind of slavery we practice here in America—with a fierce desperation."

"Much like you, then."

"And you."

Suddenly feeling slightly off balance, Joseph wanted to pelt her with questions, ask her all about the man, what he was like, if his wife ever traveled with him, how he and his dozen or so sons traveled without being killed.

But Joseph must admit to himself that he'd continued to withhold secrets from Victoria, so he had no reason to be put out because she withheld her own. For instance, how precise was the map she'd so quickly covered when he approached? Did she know exactly how to get to Jolly Mill?

She returned to her work.

He cleared his throat. "Victoria," he said softly, so that the closest neighbor had no chance of hearing him. Her shoulders stiffened, but otherwise she gave no hint that she'd heard.

He placed his hand on her right shoulder and gently urged her to turn and face him.

"Careful." She held up a scalpel as she wrapped it. "These may not be one of those dangerous wolf traps you're so eager to warn me about, but they are sharp, nonetheless."

From recent practice, he knew where her utensils went, so he took the scalpel from her and completed the wrapping. "I did ask you to join me in Georgia." He still wanted to figure out the mystery of the missing letters, but right now there were more important subjects to discuss.

"And you knew, before even asking me to go with you, how I felt about living on a plantation shouldered by slave labor."

He set the scalpel down. For several years while traveling across the country, he'd bitterly blamed her for ignoring his pleas for her to wait for him. And to discover only recently that she'd never received the pleas…that she'd believed he'd deserted her for another woman… It continued to gouge something deep inside.

And now, today, he had already pushed the subject too far, but he couldn't help himself.

"I admired your decision." Bowing her head, she traced a finger on the cloth. "Or at least part of me did. The other part hated what you were doing, but I was young and heartbroken."

"I knew you were angry."

"You never knew how much."

"My heart never went back with me to Georgia."

Her slender neck curved as she looked at him. He wanted to kiss that neck, the delicate ear behind which she had corralled the hair that was filled with the lightness of morning sunshine. He wanted to trail kisses across her blushing cheekbone and across her chin to dominate her mouth and stop them both from arguing, at least for a few moments.

"Victoria, I love you." The words came out before he

could stop them, though he knew better. "I loved you then, and nothing has changed. Nothing ever changed."

Her eyes grew large at the gentle announcement, and he wondered how often she had been angry with him. How many times had she doubted him after he left her?

"Until you married Matthew, I believed you were the kind of woman whose heart would remain faithful to one man forever. After what I've discovered, I believe you still care."

To his dismay, he felt her withdraw without moving a muscle. As if she were still angry with him. But that couldn't be it. Hadn't they somehow reconnected on the day of the flood? She'd shown true friendship to him since then, and though they'd argued, there was a good reason for that argument.

"Victoria?"

She slowly stepped backward. He couldn't believe it. He held on to her, reluctant to let go, but she firmly withdrew.

"Please tell me you aren't still angry with me after all these years."

"No, Joseph, but this is not the time for making declarations of love and promises that may not be kept, and I know you too well, my friend. Don't you dare use words of love to coerce me from my mission."

"Coerce?" He released her with such abruptness that she reached out to catch the smoothed wood of the wagon tailgate. "You think I'm saying these things to manipulate you?"

"I know you can speak with charming words when you want something badly enough."

She might have slapped him without causing as much harm as her words did. "You think I'm speaking of love to change your mind?"

"Even if you aren't, now is not the time. I suggest you give up trying to convince me to do your bidding and get to work." She pressed her long, slim fingers against his chest and gave him a gentle shove. He didn't leave, but watched her in silence as she finished with her utensils and began on her pistol. Tiny black strips of cloth soon littered her workspace, and the pleasant scent of gun oil reached him.

His declaration of love had obviously affected her, but she'd held fast. Nothing would stop this woman from following her mission. For a moment he was struck speechless by the thought that it was possible, if she got her way, that he would never see her again. She could die.

Chapter Nine

"You're following creeks," he said from behind her, still hovering. Would she never get him to leave?

"That's right."

"This country is a maze. What if you follow the wrong creek?"

"I have a map." How many questions could this man ask? Was this just another ruse to stop her from going?

"Is that what you hid from me earlier?"

"I didn't exactly hide it. I only wanted to place it out of the way of your attention."

"Even if Thames doesn't recognize you, he would recognize Sadie when he sees her. A man'll remember horseflesh."

She braced herself. He was approaching a delicate subject. "Sadie was Matthew's horse."

Joseph was silent for a moment.

She glanced at him over her shoulder and caught him glaring.

"I beg your pardon, Victoria, but why would you ride a horse this killer would be sure to recognize?"

She turned, put her things away and strolled from him, knowing he would follow. The crux of the matter would disturb him. That was why she'd hoped to avoid this conversation. More secrets. "My own horse was lame when I left for this trip. Sadie is the best horse we ever had. She's a part of Matthew I can keep with me."

As expected, Joseph caught up and stepped in front of her. "I doubt she's as good as my Boaz."

"This isn't a competition."

"My gelding's as good as horses get," he said. "You don't want to risk your husband's murderer recognizing you before you see him."

"That won't happen." She relaxed a little. Was she hearing him right? "So you're agreeing that I should go to Jolly Mill now?"

"No. I'm saying you should get rid of the mare no matter what else you do. I don't care how good she is. Trade with me. You won't be sorry, and I'll rest easier."

Joseph's concern softened her, but she had a good reason to keep Sadie, and it wasn't a reason she wanted to discuss. "I'm afraid I must decline."

"Why?"

"I'm accustomed to her. I don't want to set off with a strange animal."

"I can guarantee you that Boaz is more experienced with that unforgiving forest than Sadie. He has saved me from a fall into a wolf trap and an attack from a pack of wolves."

Victoria crossed her arms and stared down at the ground beneath her feet.

"I see," Joseph drawled. "It was no accident that you're riding Sadie on this trip."

He knew. "I told you why."

He placed a hand on her arm. "You're a smart lady. You'd have thought this through. If you wanted to keep a low profile, you'd have sold Sadie and bought a horse this silver-braided killer wouldn't recognize. You *want* this man to notice you. You want him to come after you, give you a reason to avenge Matthew's murder."

She winced at the forthrightness of his words. He certainly made her motives sound less than ladylike. Brutal, even. "Seeking justice for the murder of my husband is not wicked."

"I want justice, too, Victoria. Matthew was my friend. I understand exactly what you want."

"He deserved better."

"Matthew wouldn't want you to risk your life for anything, especially not for revenge. Do you have enough confidence in your skills that you know you'll be able to kill him and gain retribution?"

Her mouth opened to protest, but she closed it. For the first time, she was hearing her heart's desire being stated as cold facts, and it made her shudder.

"You wish to face your husband's killer alone," Joseph said gently. "No matter the outcome. Sort of like the kinsmen redeemer of the Bible."

She looked at him helplessly, unable to protest the truth. "You, Captain Rickard, are more insightful than I realized." It seemed at the moment that he could see more deeply into her heart than she could, herself. This was not comfortable. "It would be self-defense if I were to kill him."

"Revenge now belongs to God."

"What about justice? Don't humans still have a responsibility for that? Or has all the world gone mad with anarchy?"

"Who's to say you would win in a shoot-out? This man's a killer, and you're a doctor—"

"You've seen me shoot. You've seen the amount of ammunition I've brought with me. And I've used that

OFFICIAL OPINION POLL

Dear Reader,

Since you are a book enthusiast, we would like to know what you think.

Inside you will find a short Opinion Poll. Please participate in our Poll by sharing your opinion on 3 subjects that are very important to all of us.

To thank you for your participation, we would like to send you **2 FREE BOOKS** and **2 FREE GIFTS!**

Please enjoy them with our compliments.

Sincerely,

Pam Powers

For Your Reading Pleasure...

Get 2 FREE BOOKS from the series of historical love stories that will lift your spirits and warm your soul!

Free

Your **2 FREE BOOKS** have a combined cover price of $11.98 in the U.S. and $13.50 in Canada.

◄— Peel off sticker and place by your completed Poll on the right page and you'll automatically receive **2 FREE BOOKS** and **2 FREE GIFTS** with no obligation to purchase anything!

We'll send you two wonderful surprise gifts, (worth about $10), absolutely FREE, just for trying our Love Inspired® Historical books! Don't miss out — **MAIL THE REPLY CARD TODAY!**

Visit us at:
www.ReaderService.com

YOUR OPINION POLL
THANK-YOU FREE GIFTS INCLUDE:

▶ **2 LOVE INSPIRED® HISTORICAL BOOKS**

▶ **2 LOVELY SURPRISE GIFTS**

OFFICIAL OPINION POLL

YOUR OPINION COUNTS!
Please check TRUE or FALSE
below to express your opinion about the
following statements:

Q1 Do you believe in "true love"?

"TRUE LOVE HAPPENS ONLY ONCE IN A LIFETIME."
○ TRUE
○ FALSE

Q2 Do you think marriage has any value in today's world?

"YOU CAN BE TOTALLY COMMITTED TO SOMEONE WITHOUT BEING MARRIED."
○ TRUE
○ FALSE

Q3 What kind of books do you enjoy?

"A GREAT NOVEL MUST HAVE A HAPPY ENDING."
○ TRUE
○ FALSE

YES! I have placed my sticker in the space provided below. Please send me the 2 FREE books and 2 FREE gifts for which I qualify. I understand that I am under no obligation to purchase anything further, as explained on the back of this card.

102/302 IDL F5JN

FIRST NAME	LAST NAME

ADDRESS

APT.#	CITY

STATE/PROV.	ZIP/POSTAL CODE

Offer limited to one per household and not applicable to series that subscriber is currently receiving.

Your Privacy—The Harlequin® Reader Service is committed to protecting your privacy. Our Privacy Policy is available online at www.ReaderService.com or upon request from the Harlequin Reader Service. We make a portion of our mailing list available to reputable third parties that offer products we believe may interest you. If you prefer that we not exchange your name with third parties, or if you wish to clarify or modify your communication preferences, please visit us at www.ReaderService.com/consumerschoice or write to us at Harlequin Reader Service Preference Service, P.O. Box 9062, Buffalo, NY 14269. Include your complete name and address.

HARLEQUIN® READER SERVICE—Here's How It Works:

Accepting your 2 free books and 2 free gifts (gifts valued at approximately $10.00) places you under no obligation to buy anything. You may keep the books and gifts and return the shipping statement marked "cancel." If you do not cancel, about a month later we'll send you 4 additional books and bill you just $4.74 each in the U.S. or $5.24 each in Canada. That is a savings of at least 21% off the cover price. It's quite a bargain! Shipping and handling is just 50¢ per book in the U.S. and 75¢ per book in Canada.* You may cancel at any time, but if you choose to continue, every month we'll send you 4 more books, which you may either purchase at the discount price or return to us and cancel your subscription.

*Terms and prices subject to change without notice. Prices do not include applicable taxes. Sales tax applicable in N.Y. Canadian residents will be charged applicable taxes. Offer not valid in Quebec. Books received may not be as shown. All orders subject to credit approval. Credit or debit balances in a customer's account(s) may be offset by any other outstanding balance owed by or to the customer. Please allow 4 to 6 weeks for delivery. Offer available while quantities last.

If offer card is missing write to: Harlequin Reader Service, P.O. Box 1867, Buffalo NY 14240-1867 or visit: www.ReaderService.com

BUSINESS REPLY MAIL
FIRST-CLASS MAIL   PERMIT NO. 717   BUFFALO, NY

POSTAGE WILL BE PAID BY ADDRESSEE

HARLEQUIN READER SERVICE
PO BOX 1341
BUFFALO NY 14240-8571

NO POSTAGE
NECESSARY
IF MAILED
IN THE
UNITED STATES

ammunition to provide plenty of meat for the kettle on our trip. You know I can protect myself if need be."

"As well as Matthew did the day Thames caught him unaware?"

Victoria couldn't tell if she was merely dismayed that Joseph could see into her heart better than she could or if she resented that his argument was beginning to make her second guess her readiness to go to Jolly Mill. "Unlike Matthew, I will be on the alert at all times."

"Thames must have surprised Matthew. He could just as easily surprise you."

"Joseph, please don't get in my way." She could practically see her own reflection in his deep, dark eyes.

"May I at least see your map?" he asked. "I know the land. I can help you."

She hesitated, gauging the words he spoke. There could be no harm in getting his opinion. She didn't need to agree, but he was well acquainted with this land, and she was not. "It's beneath the medical equipment. I've been studying it." She had to swallow hard to ward off the tears that seemed determined to attack her. This day was a nightmare. The image of her husband's white face, the sound of his dying breath, was never far from her thoughts, and talking about it made everything fresh and raw.

"You've been delayed all these months," Joseph said, "and we've been delayed many days with illness and accidents. What would a few more days hurt, if it means you'll be safe with us?"

"Two or three days could mean the difference between life and death for Naaman and Josetta, maybe even the Frasiers if they're caught with no papers of ownership. Besides that, if I don't rush in now, I may not be able to find out what he's up to."

"Which is more reason for you to trade horses with me. Lie low. I still—"

"No."

"It's unlikely he's by hims—"

"He's a loner."

"Not in Jolly Mill. These men are joined together solidly in their selfish cause."

She wanted to scream. Instead, she just glared, gripping the handle of a knife and squeezing so hard her fingers whitened. "I do want the man dead." She felt the power of her words. Her own intense hatred of Matthew's murderer frightened her almost as badly as the man did. It was as if she'd become a stranger to herself. No girl of fourteen needed to be under her influence now.

Joseph's face twisted in frustration. He nodded. "Think about what I'm telling you, Victoria. I can help you if you'll let me."

"I'll accept your advice, if you wish to give it."

He nodded, then gestured toward Heidi Ladue. "I still won't allow you to steal away without speaking to her. Meanwhile, let me study your map."

Victoria's right hand fisted to keep from smacking him a good one. Now he was implying she was a coward? She whirled from him. Steal away, indeed! "There it is. Study it to your heart's content, but the map, and the quest, are mine." Unable to resist, she shot him a hard glare over her shoulder and stepped into a rabbit hole.

Stumbling to right herself, she was sure she heard Joseph's soft chuckle, and it made her even angrier. He'd spoken of how they'd both changed over the years, but until now she hadn't understood the breadth of that change. She didn't have too much pride to admit to herself that he was right. They were two different people, transformed from the young couple so in love ten years ago. So why, when they'd changed considerably, did so much seem to be the same? Why was there still this connection that she felt with him every time she came within twenty feet of him?

Again unable to prevent herself, she shot another glance over her shoulder. He was still watching her. The bold, amused expression in his eyes brought an unwilling smile to her face.

He raised his eyebrows and spread his hands, as if portraying himself as a man helpless against the wiles of a woman. Indeed.

In spite of the danger that seemed to hover ever closer, Joseph found himself watching Victoria with such helplessness he could only stare. She marched toward Heidi, shoulders stiff, head erect, and this time those strong but delicate shoulders did not slump.

Despite the tragedies of the past days and the deadly circumstances in which she was placing herself, Joseph craved her company, and no matter what, he was glad he'd told her of his love for her. If, by chance, something went wrong, he needed to have that clarified between them.

The woman had ignited a fire in him that he hadn't felt in many years. And something had deepened in her. The compassion she had always shown toward her patients and the treatment of the slaves had developed into so much more. She was a grown woman now, no longer an impulsive girl, and despite the danger she was placing herself in, he was now in awe of who she had become.

Startled by the direction of his thoughts, Joseph turned his attention to another fire—the one in the center of the wagon circle, where venison had been slowly roasting. McDonald had delivered the plump young buck earlier this morning from his hunting foray, skinned and dressed and ready for cooking. The venison fat continued to drip and sizzle, spreading the aroma throughout the creek-fed valley.

Deacon Fritz, another able hunter who had joined the wagon train halfway across Missouri with his wife and crew of four boys and three girls, sauntered up to Joseph, nodding toward the roasting meat.

"Saw some cougar and coyote tracks about a mile down the creek." He pulled out a long-necked pipe and stuck it between his teeth.

"How fresh?" Joseph asked.

"Saw 'em last night. So fresh I felt my neck hairs go straight."

"Guess we'll have to toss our leavings into the creek, let them wash away from camp."

Deacon nodded as he tamped tobacco into the pipe bowl. "That might keep the animals away."

"Did you see which way the tracks were headed?" The coyotes weren't worrisome, but Joseph didn't like the sound of the cougar. Though food was plentiful in the woods, the big cats had been known to attack humans without warning.

Deacon picked up a few lengths of straw, stuck the ends into the fire then pressed the resulting flame to his pipe. "Headed away from us. I might keep watch tonight, just in case."

"That would be good. Find a couple of others to spell you so you can get some rest."

"Made some visits to folks along the creek this afternoon." Deacon puffed smoke. "Mr. McDonald thought we might have a change of plans, head north?"

"I'm still thinking on it."

Deacon gave Joseph a sideways glance. "The wife tells me Dr. Fenway plans to leave us and head north. Don't suppose that'd be part of the reason for your change of plans." He grinned, smoke billowing from his nostrils. His ruddy complexion had grown deeper in the weeks he and his family had been with the train.

Joseph knew from that moment that if he changed directions and followed Victoria north, he'd be teased without mercy for the remainder of their journey. Not that it would bother him. After their prolonged, public conversations today, he doubted he would be allowed to live it down, anyway. "I'd hate to lose the doctor who just saved five lives."

Deacon shook his head. "Headstrong women make the best wives."

"Having never been married, I wouldn't know."

"Believe me, Mrs. Fritz wouldn't've survived our own seven wild ones if she wasn't headstrong." He grunted. "Good wife. Yes, indeed. Helen took right up with Dr. Fenway, too. Kindred spirits."

Joseph cleared his throat. "What did you discover on your visits this afternoon?"

"All I hear is that the ruffians are on the prowl. There's been some trouble in the area in the past week, since most folks in these parts aren't slavers. Don't matter to the troublemakers that there's no reason to own slaves in this tree-laden backside of the world, they want to take their spite out on somebody."

"That is my concern." Joseph's heart dropped more and more deeply into his chest. "We can't risk all these lives."

"Well, that's one way of looking at it, of course, but we're not sure how we'll fare once we get to the Territory, either. Maybe all our fightin' men would do better to take out some of the bullies now, before we cross the border."

"We have women and children to protect, Deacon."

"We all came for a fight, men, women and children, any way you look at it, and maybe some of those young bucks of ours can get some experience under their belts. There's fightin' on both sides of the border. I hear say that older Johnston kid's a deadeye. If so, it's the only thing he's good at 'cept eatin' and wood choppin'. Every time he opens his mouth something stupid comes out of it or he's shoveling something into it. What say we have us a little shootin' contest?"

"You mean now?"

"Sure thing. Out here in the wilderness where the trees will muffle the shots and there are few to hear."

"Tonight, then."

Deacon nodded as he puffed on his pipe.

"We do need to get to Kansas," Joseph said.

"Which means we need to know each other's strengths and weaknesses. I could set us up a little shootin' range down by the creek. If nothing else, it'll scare away the cougars and such."

Deacon Fritz was a bright man, but Joseph didn't like the idea of drawing attention to their wagon train. "Shots will echo a long way off. If there's a troublemaker in the area, we'd be inviting him to bring that trouble to us."

"What're you getting at?"

"I suggest we have our target practice a couple of miles away. Draw any bushwhackers away from the direction of the camp."

Deacon raised his eyebrows, nodded and grinned.

"I know just the place," Joseph said. "It's a small

area surrounded by deeper woods than this. Women should practice their shooting, too—anyone who can handle a weapon."

Deacon's smile died and sadness swept across his heavy face. "Everyone on this journey expects trouble when we get to the border, but I don't see another way."

"Guess we'll do a lot of praying in the days to come," Joseph said. "The remainder of our wagon train will join us at Elk River. Dr. Fenway hopes to meet up with us in Neosho," Joseph said, "We're going to need a doctor for our new village."

"That we are, Captain."

"It might help if she made it there in one piece."

Deacon tapped the ashes from his pipe and sniffed the air. "That it would. Let me know how I can help." He gestured toward the campfire. "It appears we're to have a handsome meal this evening. The wife baked a huge pot of molasses beans and several of the other ladies are making corncakes. With the venison and Mrs. Reich's dried-apple crumble, we'll have enough to feed everyone through lunch tomorrow."

"Then we'll be well fed for our trip."

"You reckon the doc will make it to Jollification safely? I could ride along with her. So could the missus. She's a mean shot, herself."

Joseph thought about the idea. He liked it. After target practice tonight, he'd know for sure if they could shoot as well as he thought they could.

"I'll speak with Dr. Fenway about it." Joseph tipped his hat to his friend and strode toward the edge of the camp.

By the time this wagon train reached their destination in Kansas Territory, there would most likely be at least twenty-five wagons with more than a hundred people, including the children. Barring trouble, they should arrive in time to get well settled before winter set in. The oxen and draft horses would also eat well for the rest of the trip, and if he watched out for the troublemakers perhaps they would all make it to their destination without another spill into a river or a breakout of illness.

He looked up from the sizzling meat to see Victoria standing at the edge of the field with her arms crossed as she gazed toward Heidi and Mrs. Reich—a woman so sturdy she could whip an angry bull—leaning with her head close to Heidi's. Victoria was right about Mrs. Reich; the woman would take Heidi in as one of her own and shower love on her. Heidi, however, might have other ideas.

Though Victoria wouldn't admit it to Joseph, he could see that she had become attached to the Ladue family, and especially loved Heidi. She and the girl had spent many an hour riding side by side as Mrs. Ladue drove the wagon. Heidi's friendship with Victoria had just begun to draw the girl out of her brooding over her father's death when this next catastrophe threatened to destroy her heart completely.

As if aware he was watching, Victoria turned her head to look at Joseph. He nodded toward her. Fascinating woman.

Victoria frowned at Joseph, not sure if the warmth on her skin came from frustration with the man for his constant nagging today or if it lingered from the words he'd spoken to her. He loved her.

She knew he had not used those words lightly, and it took every ounce of strength within her to not run back across the field and throw herself into his arms, give way to his command for her to remain with the wagon train and let someone else do her job for her. The last thing on this earth she wanted to do was ride into that lion's den. If not for the friends depending on her, she would never follow those creeks to the mill town.

She returned her attention across the field where Audy Reich stood comforting Heidi and then gazed into the eternal twilight beneath the looming trees. She had been so focused on her patients since setting up camp here that she had taken little time to observe her surroundings. This place was like another world, uncultivated and wild. So beautiful.

Many of the forests around St. Louis had been cleared by farmers who knew how to wield their axes. However, the rivers and hills, gulches and valleys through which the wagon train had recently passed, and that continued to reach out across the countryside with its tentacles of ridges, had not yet been tamed.

Joseph was right; she had reason to be concerned. If she had an accident or was attacked and missed her mark with her weapon, there would be no one to bear witness except Sadie or, if she were to take up Joseph's offer of a horse trade, Boaz. If she died, there would be no one to take word to her family.

But if not for justice, what reason did she have to live? Revenge was an ugly thing, but there was much more to this journey than revenge.

And here she was, excusing herself to the empty air about why she could not possibly stay with Heidi at this time. Later, yes, she would meet up with the rest, but now she had a dangerous job to do, and Heidi needed a place of safety in which to heal.

As Victoria neared the edge of the clearing where Heidi and Audy had stood for such a long time this afternoon, the sound of her own footsteps rustled through the thick grass. Audy turned and glanced over her shoulder. Their gazes met in understanding. Audy nodded, patted Heidi's back and left the girl.

She scrunched her face and shook her head as she leaned close to Victoria in passing. "Poor thing ain't talkin' about it. She acts like nothin's wrong. It's like she's somewhere else."

Victoria nodded, studying the bright blue-and-yellow calico of Heidi's dress. The girl had no black to wear; her mother had told Victoria that she didn't want her young, vibrant daughter to waste away in mourning clothes throughout the journey. Here on the trail there was no room for extra material for a dress.

The child—no, Heidi was not a child, though Victoria persisted in thinking of her in that way—would now be forced to grow up more quickly. She had, however, already assumed a great deal of responsibility, with no father this past year. Claude had shouldered a man's load on this trip. If only he'd used the wisdom taught to him by his mother.

Growing up with twelve brothers and sisters had meant a crowded house and meager means for Victoria, but it had supplied her with family. Heidi had none.

When Victoria touched her shoulder, Heidi turned to look at her, blue eyes clear and smiling as if no tragedy had taken place this day. It was an unnerving look, and for a moment Victoria feared the loss might have unhinged her mind permanently, as Joseph had suggested.

"I saw you and the captain together a lot today, watching out of the corner of my eye. He's sweet on you, you know," Heidi said, her voice a little forced.

Victoria swallowed and held the fragile gaze.

Heidi sighed like a doe-eyed dreamer. "Don't I wish a handsome man like that was sweet on me."

"Please tell me you're not talking about Captain Rickard."

"See there? Even you can tell he likes you, and you never notice when the men watch you."

"My darling, you're too young to be concerned about such things."

Heidi shrugged. "I'll be fifteen in three weeks. I've heard tell that girls here in southern Missouri marry young, and they marry old men."

Victoria bit her lip. "You'll be in Kansas in three weeks. And are you saying Captain Rickard is old?"

Heidi looked up at her with such innocence. "He must be at least thirty."

Victoria suppressed a smile, wondering how Joseph would react to hearing someone call him old. "I have to admit, my late husband was twenty years older than I."

"Pa was younger than Ma by three months. She said he always behaved like a youngster."

"Behaving young makes one feel young. You'll understand it when you're married with children."

"You think he'd ever settle down somewhere?" Heidi nodded toward the captain and winked at Victoria. "You know, for the right woman?"

"I believe he might."

"For someone like you, I think he would. I can tell. Even Ma said…" Heidi's voice caught, and the agony of loss welled in her eyes for less than a second before she swallowed and inhaled slowly and deeply.

"What did your mother say?"

Heidi shook her head.

"She was a wise and good woman," Victoria said. "We were blessed to have her in our lives, and I can't imagine how much we are going to miss her. I will never forget her generosity or her loving spirit, because I know those qualities will live on in you."

The facade on the pretty girl's face cracked further. Victoria couldn't forget the despair that had taken hold of Heidi two days ago. This recent, forced lightness was a thin coating of ice on a deep pool. Until now, Victoria had not heard the naturally garrulous young lady say a word since her mother had breathed her last early this morning. As Audy had said, it was as if her spirit had contracted into some hidden place.

"I must tell you something." Victoria's hand tightened on her young friend's shoulder. "I have to take my leave of the wagon train for a few days. I…wish to help you settle before I go." The words sounded horrid in her own ears, crass and hard in comparison to Heidi's loss, but this could not be helped.

There was no comfort Victoria could give her. "Heidi, I'm so sorry. I wish there was something I could do to make this easier on you."

For a moment, she thought Heidi might attempt to reject the impending subject once again.

"Ma and Claude lived in the Truth." Heidi's voice quivered as she returned to her study of the trees.

"Yes, my dear."

"I know where they went," Heidi said. "It's not to this rotten ol' soil."

Victoria drew the girl closer to her side. Heidi had a faith as strong as Matthew's had been, almost as strong as Joseph's, but that faith would not protect her from the hard grief that would overtake her.

For a moment all was silent save for the multiple birdsongs echoing across the meadow, the whisper of wind, the rustling leaves and the splash of water along Shoal Creek, which divided the meadow.

"You have twelve families to choose from, Heidi Ladue," Victoria said. "I know any of them would welcome you into their lives and homes when they settle in Kansas Territory, and I will likely be with you there."

Heidi stiffened and pulled away. "I'm not part of a family anymore. Ma told me to stay with you if something happened to her." She looked up at Victoria. "I bet you're not even planning to go to Kansas Territory, are you?"

"I do plan to go there. I promise. But I have responsibilities to see to beforehand." Victoria turned her gaze to the needles of the pine tree above them. The lowest branch was far above their heads. That was how she felt right now—buried in a crisis that reached far above her head. She could not even imagine the dangers her journey would entail. Joseph was right, of course. He knew this country. He just didn't know how terrified she was of it.

For another moment the two lingered together in silence while Victoria identified keenly with her young friend's loss.

The memory was still so vivid that, closing her eyes, Victoria could see the man in black with a long braid down his back that blended gray with white into a silvery sheen. She saw him jump astride his red horse and race away when she shot him with her husband's rifle. She saw the image of Matthew bravely fighting to stay alive until he could warn her.

She had fallen to her knees beside him and felt for his pulse. He was alive! She pressed her ear to his chest. She heard a rattle, looked down and saw the blood. Too much blood.

"My darling, please," she cried. "It's me. I'm home. Open your eyes!" She held her cheek above his mouth and felt his warm breath. "Matthew." The death rattle. She'd heard it before. "Please don't do this, God. Please!"

"Victoria." Matthew's voice was barely a whisper. His eyes opened. "You're safe?"

"The man's getting away. I mean to catch him."

"No." His hand grasped hers and he groaned.

"Sweetheart, I have to go get my bag."

"No." He was shivering.

"I must stop the blood."

His eyes closed again, and the rattle grew louder. "I'm lost, Victoria. But make me a promise."

"I'll promise to try to keep you alive if you'll let me—"

"No." He ground out the word as his hand tightened on hers. "The letter…did you…find it?"

"What letter? I've not been inside. Please let me get my case."

"L-listen to me. Must hurry. Leave this place when spring comes. Never return…so much wickedness. Do what we'd planned. Follow the trail. Find the Frasiers. Whatever—" He grimaced and his grip loosened from hers. "You must heal the wounded, lead the helpless to safety."

"This is madness, Matthew! You talk as if you're dying, and I won't let you do that! You can't leave me."

"I have to go. You're strong…shrewd. Protect yourself…. There is…conspiracy. The map in our office… follow it. Letter from John. Don't trust anyone else…." His eyes closed. His breathing stopped.

Victoria fell across him with a cry of anguish. "Matthew, no!"

A soft, feminine voice recalled her from the nightmare of her memories. "Dr. Fenway, stay tonight with me in the wagon? Please."

Victoria opened her eyes to see Heidi's face shimmering with tears. She didn't need to spend her first night as an orphan grieving in that lonely wagon.

"I'll stay and help you get situated with another family this evening, and then I will leave at first light. But, Heidi, I must be on my way. We will meet again soon."

"Why must you leave?"

"To carry out my husband's final request, and I've recently discovered I must hurry. I have no choice, and the route I'm taking is too dangerous to take you with me."

Heidi looked down. Her shoulders began to tremble. Victoria pulled her close and let her cry. Eventually their tears blended together. Those mingled tears would help lead toward healing for both of them.

As soon as the girl slept, Victoria would once more study the map Matthew had told her to follow, and she would consult with Joseph. He had wisdom and experience beyond his years and would have good advice for her travels. She had no choice but to chance crossing paths with the killer. It was possible she would catch up to him before he could reach the mill village.

Victoria could close her eyes at night and picture Thames—but in the darkness he appeared as a rabid wolf set out across the country to steal and destroy. What would be wrong with stopping a man like that? She wouldn't shoot him in the back, but if they faced one another she would be forced to stop him from killing others. What kind of a sin would it be to hope she *was* forced to shoot?

Maybe he had other places to visit. Maybe he had orders to kill. What would be wrong with her stopping a man from killing other innocents like Matthew? She could see no sin in it. But she was often reminded that her thoughts were not the thoughts of God. She had no right to question God.

She did so, anyway. How much longer could she get away with questioning Him the way she did?

Chapter Ten

Victoria was well away from the wagon-train camp on Tuesday morning when the gloom of the Missouri forest lightened in increments. She heard splashing water as she neared a clearing where the creek had carved a cave beneath a sheer rock as tall as the trees around it.

Three hours after leaving camp, she imagined she could still feel Joseph watching her, gripping her hands as he begged her not to leave. But in the end she'd given him no options. By now he would have his company of travelers well down the trail, and Victoria hoped Heidi was tucked safely amongst the friendly brood of Reich children, healing from her loss. She may well meet up with them in Neosho, since Joseph had drawn the map for her late last night. If she got lost, all she had to do was follow Shoal Creek.

Victoria hated to admit it to herself, but she discovered that she missed Joseph's badgering; his warnings continued to sound through her head. Every splash in the water, every birdcall had made her jump for the first hour of her ride. How her brothers would tease her if they knew she was being so skittish.

She hadn't realized how alone she would feel, attacked by thoughts and haunted by memories, with only Boaz for company. She had allowed Joseph to talk her into trading horses, but now she missed Sadie, and Boaz didn't yet know how to anticipate his new rider's touch on the reins.

A battle raged inside her heart, the same battle she and Joseph had engaged in last night. It was a sin to out-and-out shoot the man she followed. It would have been much easier to kill him in self-defense, but as the captain had told her when she'd collected Boaz, quiet and discreet observation would go much further toward discovering whether he rode with others and what their plans were for the near future; whether or not the wagon train would be safe.

Joseph had the kind of maturity she had always admired in Matthew...and perhaps a little more. A wisp of a breeze reached her as she recalled her husband's voice. She closed her eyes, though she knew what would come....

His white skin glistened with her tears in the afternoon sunlight. She traced the strong outline of his face and pressed her fingers to his still-warm lips. She couldn't tell how long her sobs echoed, how long she raged at God, screamed at Him in fury.

"How could You do this to him?" she'd spat, her gaze jabbing the sky. "You're supposed to be all-powerful and just? Is this what You see as justice? Allowing murderers to kill Your servant before he even gets started?"

Boaz jerked and Victoria opened her eyes, still reeling at her own audacity on the day of Matthew's death, to challenge God with such boldness.

Boaz stepped sideways, his hooves grinding into creek gravel. He nickered softly, and Victoria froze, studying the lay of the land. She pulled the leather hat lower over her face, glad she'd dressed in Matthew's riding clothes, though oversized on her. She was grateful for the cowhide chaps.

She heard nothing save the splash of the creek beside her, saw nothing out of place in the primeval forest. Oak and sassafras, ash and birch hovered over the spreading branches of fir and pine. A narrow trail, barely discernible, wound westward through the woods, past tree trunks as thick as Conestoga wagons. What had made that trail? Human? Animal? At any rate, she suspected she wasn't alone in this place. Joseph's description of the dangers continued to cause her disquiet.

She guided Boaz away from the water and was preparing to adjust one set of the saddlebags behind her when the gelding's chest rumbled. The sound of multiple hoofbeats echoed from the cliff. Victoria turned. Someone was closing in.

Reaching for the rifle beneath her right saddle skirt, she guided her horse away from the brightness of the clearing. There were two animals, at least, coming toward her, their movements louder with each step.

Heart hammering, breaths uneven, Victoria fought the fear that had pursued her on this journey. She could not let it stop her, but there were times, like now, when she could barely force herself to move forward and focus on her task. As if finally in tune with his rider's thoughts, Boaz backed more deeply into the shadows.

The hoofbeats became a threatening rumble as the animals reached the solid stone surface that edged the creek for about twelve feet. She had crossed it only moments ago. Boaz whinnied before she could think to silence him with the tap on the ears Joseph had taught her. Whoever was coming now knew she was here.

"Victoria!"

The sound of her name echoed along the cliff side, and she was at once relieved and greatly alarmed. Heidi Ladue! Had something happened at the wagon train? Had more travelers fallen ill?

"Dr. Fenway!" Again, Heidi.

Victoria rode out into the open and back along the creek. Multiple hoofbeats meant multiple riders, didn't they? Who was with Heidi?

But as the first animal emerged from the trees— Heidi's mule, Bacon, with Heidi astride, followed by her pet donkey, Pudding—Victoria saw that the second animal was riderless, loaded down with bags and a clanking cook pot.

Heidi's eyes lit with obvious relief as she raised her hand in greeting. "I thought I wouldn't catch you, but I knew you were staying close to the creek, so I kept riding."

Her cheeks were flushed, her hair was tangled with pine needles and she had a scrape across her chin that told of a run-in with brambles. Her blue eyes held concern that she was obviously trying not to reveal.

"Where is the rest of the wagon train?" Victoria asked.

"Along the wagon trail apiece by now, I'd imagine." Heidi didn't stop when she reached Victoria but guided her animals down to the water. "We've been goin' so fast, I didn't want to take time for a drink."

Victoria followed her and gave Boaz some rein so he could drink his fill, as well. "I know Captain Rickard didn't allow you to come out here by yourself." To be honest, however, Victoria had given Joseph no further details about what she had planned. When he'd approached her last night about sending others with her, she'd shut down the conversation and bid him good-night. Even he would not have expected her to leave hours before first light. Now she wished she hadn't taken his horse.

Heidi slipped from her saddle and knelt by the flowing stream. "Think this is clean enough to drink, Dr. Fenway?"

"I saw a spring back a few yards. Drink from there, and then you're coming with me. I'm taking you back to the train."

Heidi's shoulders stiffened. "I'm not goin'."

"It's too dangerous for you out here, my dear."

"I made it this far, didn't I? And if it's so chancy, you shouldn't be here, either." Heidi straightened and turned toward Victoria.

"I have other responsibilities to attend to."

"How far've you got to go?"

Victoria fought her rising irritation. Despite her loneliness, she couldn't take the girl on this dangerous path, and catching up with the wagon train would cost a day's travel. This shortcut was turning out not to be nearly so short. "For me alone, it would be only one day's hard riding. I could have been there late this evening." Her only hope was that Joseph would realize where Heidi had come and would send someone after her. Lives could be at stake.

"I'm not afraid of hard riding. I'm comin' with you."

Victoria felt an unwelcome rush of the anger that had become familiar to her since Matthew's murder. "No!" She sank her teeth into her lower lip for a few seconds to calm herself. Easy irritability was yet another symptom of the change that had taken place in her heart since Matthew's death. "I must make this trip alone," she said more gently.

Heidi dabbed at the water on her face with her sleeve.

"That don't make sense. Since I aim to head the same direction, we might as well do it together. Besides, I brought more of your things on Pudding, medicines and such. You said you'd teach me your skills." She gestured toward her pet donkey, and Victoria recognized her medical supplies.

"When did you do all that packing?" Victoria asked.

"Soon as you left. Then I put a note on the wagon for Captain Rickard and hightailed after you."

The anger returned, and again Victoria repressed it. The girl had suffered enough; one must be gentle.

And yet, for most of Victoria's life, she had been told what to do and with whom she would do it. Though these past months had been unnerving and difficult, she'd learned to be stronger and more independent. Neither Joseph Rickard nor this child would take that away from her.

"Heidi Ladue, we will meet again, and I will be prepared to apprentice you, but this is not that time."

"I'm ready now."

"I have other things—"

"I'm not going back to that wagon train."

"You are *not* taking this journey with me." Victoria nudged Boaz in the side and reined him away from the water, hands shaking with frustration as she turned her back on the willful girl. "I will take you to Captain Rickard, who will no doubt be on his way after you." Perhaps this day would be salvaged, after all, if they met up with him soon enough.

Victoria was leaning forward to avoid a low-hanging willow branch when a deep-voiced shriek from across the water on the hillside froze her with terror and sent Boaz shooting up the creek's steep bank.

That scream didn't come from Heidi. The gelding

mingled his own scream with the unseen presence and scrambled sideways, nearly unseating Victoria. She looked over her shoulder at Heidi to find the girl gaping with horror at the top of a rocky promontory that hung over the creek.

A sleek cat crouched above them. Blacker than night, it appeared to be twice Heidi's size.

Boaz fought the reins and neighed with fear. Victoria struggled to control him while reaching once more for the rifle she'd shoved back into its brace.

The mule and the donkey lunged up the bank and galloped into the forest, cook pot clanging. Heidi turned to run after them.

"Don't!" Victoria cried. "It'll give chase!"

The huge cat flew from the rock and landed on their side of the creek with a scatter of gravel. One more leap brought it to Heidi's heels. Victoria leaped from Boaz, rifle in hand, but Boaz swerved to escape, knocking the weapon from her grip.

She launched herself forward and landed between Heidi and the panther, shouting in her deepest voice, reaching into her pocket for her pistol.

Before she could draw out her gun, claws like a surgeon's blade sliced into her right thigh. With a cry of agony, Victoria lost her grip on the pistol. The animal jerked her forward, ripping flesh. She couldn't fight. Pain slashed through her.

The cat released her leg and leaped forward to straddle her torso, fangs inches from her face. Victoria could only close her eyes, her heart threatening to explode inside her from pain and terror as she awaited death.

A crack of thunder echoed against the cliff. For one peculiar moment, as if all time and movement had slowed, Victoria stared at the break in the treetops above the creek and wondered why she saw no rain clouds. Then time resumed, and the cat collapsed, crushing the breath from her. Its eyes glazed over, with blood fresh and dripping on the dying animal's claws.

"Victoria!" Heidi screamed, crumpling to the ground beside her. She dropped the rifle and shoved at the heavy animal.

Each movement sent streaks of pain up and down Victoria's right leg, but she helped Heidi push as the smell of spent gunpowder mingled with the smell of blood.

"You shot it." Victoria's voice wavered from lack of oxygen.

"What did you think I'd do, let it eat you?"

There'd been no time to think.

"I'm sorry, I'm so sorry." Heidi burst into sobs. "I didn't know this place was so savage. Never thought something like this could happen. I thought I'd be your helper, so you wouldn't be alone."

Too absorbed in her own pain to reply, Victoria fought to pull herself from beneath the dead weight. As she did so, the amount of blood that covered the right leg of her chaps alarmed her. The tough hide had protected her to a point, but it had been no match for the panther's claws.

Heidi finished pushing the animal free, then turned back and saw the blood. She gasped. "Victoria!"

"Keep your wits, young lady! Where's your knife?"

"But you're bleeding!"

"Listen to me, Heidi." Victoria's mind swam with inertia for a moment. She forced herself to breathe through the overwhelming power of the pain. "I need your help. Stop looking at the blood and look into my eyes!"

Heidi's face grew pale.

"No! Heidi, this is no time for a swoon." Victoria slapped the girl's face only hard enough to make it sting. "Look at me! Keep your wits about you, Heidi Ladue, because I'm not sure how much longer I can!"

The girl swallowed and blinked, and then placed her hand against the place where Victoria had slapped her. She took a long, even breath and let it out slowly, as she'd been taught when working with injured animals or patients. She finally looked Victoria in the eyes. "I'm so sorry. T-tell me what to d-do."

"Help me with my coat. Rip the sleeve from my shirt and tie it around the wound until we can find some yarrow root to help staunch the flow. Where is your knife?"

Heidi blinked at tears as they flooded her eyes.

"Straighten up and listen to me! Pay attention." Victoria allowed all of the fury she'd suppressed earlier to explode through her voice. "Are you going to let your patient die because you're too weak to handle the case? Was I wrong to choose you as my assistant?"

Heidi jerked and looked again into Victoria's eyes. "No, ma'am." She swallowed and took a deep breath.

"Get a knife."

"Mine's on Bacon. He ran off." Her face scrunched with another wave of tears.

"My life's in your hands, Heidi! Save those tears for later. You've got to see what you're doing."

Heidi bit her lip and nodded. "Keep a level head, don't give in to imagination," she murmured by rote.

Victoria glanced over her shoulder in the direction the animals had run. "Bacon hasn't gone far."

"He'll run back to the wagon train."

"Not if Boaz is the animal our captain has told me about. Help me with this, and then I want you to catch your mule and get the knife. Find Boaz and get the whis-

key out of my saddlebag. I want to wash these wounds."
Victoria needed to slap her own face as well, but she
had long ago learned to keep the blackness away by focusing her attention on the one single need at hand, not
the complications surrounding her. She had to stop the
bleeding. "I'll be glad when Captain Rickard catches
up."

Heidi paused as she tugged on the right sleeve of
Victoria's coat. "He ain't comin'."

"Hurry, get this off me. Of course he'll come. He
won't leave you out alone in this wilderness with no one
but me to protect you. He doesn't even want me here."

"Doc, he doesn't know we're alone!"

The coat came off, and Victoria jerked at the right
sleeve of her shirt until it ripped. It was sewn well, with
strong cloth, and she tugged again. She didn't want to
hear what Heidi had done, but there was no choice.
"Tell me."

"The letter I left him was from you," Heidi said.

Strength waning, Victoria ripped the sleeve length-
wise and made a bandage. "What do you mean?"

"I can copy your handwriting." Heidi's voice was so
low Victoria had to strain to hear it. "I learned watching you write in your journal, and I always try to write
like you when I make labels for the medicines."

No. Oh, no. What had this girl done? "Okay, then,
what did *I* tell Captain Rickard?"

"That you met with some other riders going your
way, and so you were taking me with you since it'd be
safe, after all."

"Safe!" Victoria gasped as she wrapped the bandage
around her thigh and pulled it tight. She could think of
nothing more to say, and the pain distracted her from
her initial reaction to the girl's dangerous manipulations.

"I'll catch the animals." Heidi straightened and rushed away, obviously afraid Victoria would grab her and strangle her.

Seldom given to panic, Victoria watched the fourteen-year-old running into this forest of death and felt gripped by a terror such as she had never felt before. She was alone, in danger, and she didn't know from which direction an attack would come next. She suddenly had to become mother to a willful orphan. Heidi Ladue had the heart of a warrior, but she was obviously still a child, after all, considering this latest stunt. Victoria must protect this child.

Joseph crumpled the note in his hand as he controlled his breathing and wished he could control the thumping of his heart, the betrayal of nerves in his voice. "Where's McDonald?" he growled.

"Checkin' the south trail," Buster said. "What you need him for?"

"Get him and bring him back, and if you can't find him yourself, get that brother of yours to go with you." At least Gray had a sense of direction.

The person Joseph needed he had already sent into the woods to follow the creek that marked Victoria's route—and Heidi's, including that strong, noisy little donkey, which could quickly call attention to their presence if anyone was there to listen. And there would be. McDonald had come in at early dawn this morning with word of churned-up mud at least two miles up the trail. Looked to have come through last night—and the riders hadn't taken Victoria's route; they'd taken a main route in the direction of the mill town.

Deacon had a swift horse and was tracking Victoria and Heidi now—if there were, indeed, tracks to be found. What if this note had been left behind to throw off any rescue? Border ruffians were on the march, apparently toward Jolly Mill, where too many travelers took refuge. Even if Victoria and Heidi were safe on their own trail, they might be riding into trouble once they reached their destination.

If Joseph ever caught up with Victoria, he was going to break the promise he'd made to her yesterday. He was going to hog-tie her and toss her into the back of the Ladue wagon until they reached their final destination. At this moment, he doubted anyone would argue with him except for Heidi, who was likely to receive the same treatment.

He flattened the note and studied it. His first thought was that the ruffians had grabbed Victoria and Heidi after the two had left on the other trail and somehow forced the note. But that wasn't possible. This was not Victoria's writing, it was Heidi's. He could always tell because Heidi tried too hard to fake the beautiful swirls of Victoria's script when she marked labels for the medicinal herbs they collected. But a man in love memorized everything about his woman, including her every line of communication. Besides the overdone swirls, the spelling wasn't perfect. Almost, but it didn't match Victoria's.

After this trip was ended and they were settled in Kansas, Joseph would settle, too. He was no longer capable of risking the lives of those he loved in order to lead his country to a deadly war. What he wanted to do was keep his people safe, particularly the woman who meant more to him than life—the woman whom he hoped would no longer deny him.

A distant cry of an eagle reached him from the direction Victoria and Heidi would have ridden. Deacon had found their tracks and was following them. He was the best bird and animal impressionist Joseph knew. Now it was up to Joseph and some fast riders to take a few wagons from the train to the mill. He might not beat Victoria there, but if there were no breakdowns, he could count on arriving sometime in the early morning hours.

Chapter Eleven

Warm droplets scattered across Victoria's bare arm, waking her. She looked up to see Heidi hovering close, eyes red, face wet and dripping. "No yarrow root." She sniffed and hiccupped. "I'm so sorry, Dr. Fenway. I can't find it anywhere. I found some sassafras and chopped it up, put some whiskey in it to make a poultice, but it's gonna feel like you been set on fire."

"A little pain's better than bleeding to death." Victoria had managed to remove the damaged chaps from her legs and rip the wool material from around her wound before passing out to the sound of Heidi's footsteps racing after the animals.

Sometime while Victoria had been fighting the effects of blood loss, Boaz had returned and nosed her to let her know he was there; true to Joseph's promise, Boaz would never leave a wounded rider. Even the man's animal was of excellent quality, and was a natural leader, it seemed; the bray of Pudding's irritation came from somewhere nearby.

Heidi brought up her carefully prepared medicine and hesitated. "What if I don't do this right?"

"Heidi Ladue, you just hush and do your job." Victoria winced when she tried to move. "A real doctor would never say that in front of a patient."

Despair crossed her young charge's face.

"Do your job, Doctor," Victoria snapped, resisting the urge to comfort the girl. If she wasn't firm, they could both be in trouble in this wilderness.

Heidi's blue eyes widened. Grasping her handful of medical mash as if it were gold, she leaned forward and gently placed it into the gash on Victoria's thigh.

The fibers dug into open flesh and the whiskey dripped into the wound, sending fire throughout Victoria's body. She grabbed her jacket and bundled it against her face to smother the sound as she cried out against the pain.

Then came the sound of ripping fabric and gentle hands lifting her leg as Heidi ignored Victoria's cries and did what she knew to do. Victoria knew she had taught the girl well when she felt the bandage tighten just enough, but not too much, when she heard a soft sob, and felt again the gentle drips of warm tears on her skin that somehow soothed the streaks of hot fire deeper beneath her flesh.

"Tie it firmly, several knots." But there was no need to give directions. And that was good, because Victoria thought she might be sick. Her vision darkened around her, and she couldn't tell if clouds had covered the sky or if she was losing consciousness.

Sometime later—Victoria couldn't tell how much time had passed—the cold tip of a bottle touched her lips. When she tasted whiskey she closed her mouth against it, shaking her head.

"I brought extra on Bacon, and you need it now to kill the pain. There's no laudanum." Heidi sounded self-assured all of a sudden. "Ma always said pain could be the best killer, and I can't lose you. I don't know where we're going, and we can't go back now."

The girl was right, of course, if a little less diplomatic than Victoria would have wished. If this wound went bad and Heidi was forced to find their way, she would need to know where to go.

"Not yet," she told Heidi gently, once again thinking of the people she had seen in St. Louis addicted to opium, laudanum and alcohol. Later, if the wound became infected, she would need the alcohol for pain. But not yet.

"I know it's hurting you."

"Did you bring the clove or turpentine oils?"

"Yes, they're on Pudding."

"Good. We can try those first if it gets too painful. Keep a watch for the big, broad comfrey leaves. You know what they look like. I need my wits about me, and we can treat the pain topically before we get drastic."

Heidi slumped and capped the bottle, obviously still traumatized by the attack.

"You'll have to find the map." Victoria reached for the chest pockets of her coat and suppressed a gasp. One of the claws of the great cat had ripped open the pocket that held the directions and all of Joseph's words of wisdom Victoria had written down.

"Where's the map, Heidi? You've got to look for a folded map. It has to be around here somewhere. Tie the animals and help me look." With Heidi's help she dragged herself to Boaz and searched through the saddlebags, but found nothing. Only one small corner of a page with lines showed her the evidence of the missing directions.

"It's okay," Heidi said. "You have to rest now."

Victoria insisted on climbing onto Boaz without help,

but the ground spun and she stumbled to her knees with yet another cry of pain, this one unmuffled.

Boaz nosed her, fluttering his lips against her cheek, and nudged her back to her jacket on the ground. While Heidi searched, the big gelding lay down, saddle and all, alongside Victoria, his warm body breaking a cool wind that had blown down from the north. It was almost as if the horse embodied his master's very spirit.

They couldn't stay here. But if Heidi couldn't find the map, and Victoria somehow became confused with her injury or had complications, they could easily be lost soon and have a run-in with the ruffians of Missouri.

"We have to get going, make use of the day," Victoria said.

"You're in no shape to travel unless I build a litter for Boaz to drag behind him, and it'll take a long time to build."

"Then I'll just have to ride. We can stop and camp and see to this wound later in the day, but right now we need to make time along this route."

"And that map you're needing?" Heidi asked. "It's nowhere to be seen."

"Then I'll have to stay awake. I know the way. I know the markers for where we need to turn."

"Maybe you should recite them to me after we get you onto Boaz. If we do," Heidi muttered.

Victoria closed her eyes. *Oh, Joseph, why didn't I listen to you?*

"You need a warm meal in your stomach first," Heidi said. "You can think better that way. I've got vittles on Pudding."

Victoria winced at the sound of the braying of the animal. "We could cook him if he doesn't stop his complaining."

"Donkey meat is tough, and it don't taste too good, either."

"It can make good jerky," Victoria grumbled.

"No time." Heidi had always loved her pet donkey.

Victoria grinned to herself, and Heidi caught the look and blew out a huge breath of air. "For a minute there I thought you meant it."

"Not yet, but I might. Gather the things Pudding scattered along his newly made trail and let's get going before I change my mind and decide to sleep forever."

Heidi nudged Boaz to his feet. The big horse made sure he didn't accidentally kick Victoria. More pain shot through her leg when she mounted, and Victoria laid her head forward, barely able to stay astride while Heidi collected everything she could and bound her donkey to her mule.

Their slow beginning did not bode well for a fast trip to the mill village. Victoria longed for Joseph to come racing through the trees right now, red faced with fury and ready to haul her back to the wagon train over his shoulder if he was of a mind to. Anything but this.

"Why didn't I listen to him?" she mumbled.

"Because you're a woman who knows her own mind. That's what Ma always said about you. And you didn't expect to get attacked by some crazy giant cat."

Victoria hadn't meant to bring Heidi into this private conversation with herself, but it was better than being alone; if Heidi was going to pretend to be an adult, it was about time she was treated like one. "The captain warned me about the dangers out here."

"Well, then, maybe you *should've* listened to him. But if I hadn't come along, you'd've been dead by now."

Victoria didn't have the strength to argue. "You've got a good eye."

"Yeah, Pa taught me."

"My father and brothers taught me."

"And your husband?"

"Yes, and Matthew."

They rode in silence for a few moments except for the pot that clanged once again on Pudding's pack. Victoria wished she hadn't run out of laudanum, but as it was she could barely stay astride. She'd keep the whiskey nearby in case the pain became too much to bear, but she wouldn't use it internally unless the need became dire.

"What's it like?" Heidi asked.

Victoria realized her eyelids had eased shut. She fluttered them and took a deep breath. "You mean, being attacked by a panther?"

"No, I can see what that's like. It makes a person grumpy. What's marriage like?"

Victoria scowled at her young friend, who had ridden up beside her, bringing with her the clang of the cook pot. "I'm sure you've had this kind of talk with your mother."

For a moment, the silence beneath the hovering trees reflected the pain of yesterday's loss, but after a short hesitation, Heidi shook her head. "Ma always said she'd tell me all about it when the time came, which I always figured meant on my wedding night. Well, if I have to wait that long I might as well give up."

"Have you ever been sweet on a boy?"

"How'm I supposed to know what sweet is? Nobody's ever told me. And if I never know what to look for, how'm I ever going to get married? Weren't you sweet on your Matthew before you married him?"

"Two people don't have to be all mushy with each other in order to have an excellent marriage."

"That's not what I heard."

"I thought you just said you didn't know what it was like."

"Well, my folks argued kind of the way you sometimes argue with the captain, but they also talked a lot after we'd gone to bed. I could hear their voices up in the loft, sometimes serious, sometimes...well...anyway, that's why I wondered. Married folks can be confusing."

Victoria's headache was getting worse. "Many a good marriage is built out of a solid friendship. Matthew was a good man."

"But he didn't turn your insides to mashed goose liver."

Despite her pain, Victoria grinned at her friend's innocence. "Goose liver never had anything to do with it, no."

"How about the captain? Any goose liver there?"

Victoria groaned. "Can we discuss this later?"

"Not if you want to make some time today and stay on Boaz. I've got to keep you awake somehow. How's your leg feel?"

"Like it's been ripped to the bone and soaked with fire water."

"Oh."

"Keep looking for comfrey." This was going to be a long trip.

Midmorning the day after Victoria and Heidi took off into the wilderness, Joseph saw the tall wood roof of the grain mill, heard the rattle-squeak of the huge wheel and the splash of water from the pond dam. A carved sign announced proudly that they'd reached the Village of Jollification.

He knew the place well and had once considered putting down stakes nearby. Had it not been for the border battles and the dangerous location of the town, where travelers and wagon trains regularly stopped on their way West and were often accosted by ruffians, he might already be planted here for good.

But then he thought of Victoria and knew he wouldn't be.

He glanced over his shoulder through the dust to study those behind him. The train was shorter by several wagons after McDonald had taken seven of them south with him. It had made for a faster ride by a day, especially since Joseph had chosen those with horses instead of oxen or mules. Horses provided speed, and there was plenty of food and water for them to snatch along the way. If he could have made them fly, he would have.

Recalling yesterday still braced his anger. He'd been forced to resist entering the woods to find the two willful women. Victoria knew his responsibilities, and he could not leave the others stranded on a trail that might be dangerous. He'd at least expected to find Deacon here to greet him, but the man's piebald horse was nowhere to be found.

Mr. and Mrs. Reich had Heidi's wagon well in hand with a team of fresh horses from another wagon instead of the mules that typically pulled it. Mrs. Reich continued to fret about the safety of Victoria and Heidi out in the wilderness. Her first task was to question the women in town about Victoria and Heidi, and she had her posse of friends selected to attend her.

Steam had quit spurting from Joseph's ears late yesterday afternoon, and he'd forgiven Victoria for her outrageous stunt of taking Heidi; he'd discovered after little more than a half mile of tracking that the two had not left at the same time, and no others had gone their way.

He also knew Victoria too well to believe she had written that note.

For instance, why would she suddenly decide to take Heidi when she'd been so adamant before that she had to carry out her plans alone? She was far too wise to attempt such a dangerous stunt. Heidi, deep in grief, and determined to remain with Victoria no matter what, had packed her animals and followed. It was the only thing that made sense to him.

Yesterday morning before dawn, all he'd heard was the typical bray of Heidi's donkey and the clatter of a pot—which he'd determined to be someone getting up to start breakfast.

He'd determined wrong. Never in his life had he second-guessed his decisions so heartily. Victoria was the most headstrong woman west of the Appalachians, and he couldn't keep her out of his mind.

His fingers still itched to wring her neck as he glanced toward the village, scanning for Boaz. Instead, he froze when he caught sight of the reddest horse he'd ever seen, hitched at the post in front of the dram shop, down a ways from the mill and distillery.

He scanned the dirt streets of the town, but no other horse stood out. Only the one red animal. Thames?

"Victoria, what have you gotten us into?" he muttered.

Waving his arm in the air, he signaled the wagons to settle into the well-worn circle used by many another wagon train in the past. Time to prepare for camp. A loud whoop echoed from the end of the train where Buster Johnston jumped from his horse and danced a jig, stirring up dust. Joseph hoped the young troublemaker didn't stir up any more than dust while they were here. Granted, he'd shown his skills with any kind of shooting instrument in their makeshift tournament the other evening, but did he have the good judgment about when to use them and when to stay hidden?

"Folks," Joseph called as he gestured for the other adults to gather round, "remember why we're here. If anyone asks, we're looking for land and slaves. No one has to know that the land we're looking for is in Kansas and the slaves we're looking for aren't for purchase."

He studied the grim faces and curt nods. Everyone, from the most seasoned traveler to the youngest of the children, was aware of the danger they could be in if they spoke the wrong words to the wrong people, especially this close to the border.

"I have urgent business in town," he said.

"That's right," Audy Reich said. "We've got to make sure Dr. Fenway and Heidi arrived safely."

"And Deacon," said the man's wife.

Joseph nodded. "He knows the way."

"I could go searching for him."

"Wait a bit. If they got lost, he would've followed their trail and found them. I think the man we've been tracking is at the dram shop."

"Thames?" Mrs. Reich cried. "Here?"

"Want me to go find out for sure?" Buster asked.

"I want you to lie low," Joseph said. "I've seen no sign of the animals our doctor and Heidi took with them, but we can't take any chances if Thames or his friends are in town." He nodded to Mrs. Reich. "Would you take someone with you to the mercantile?" He pointed her in the right direction. "Find out where the Frasiers live. They're Dr. Fenway's friends. Everyone knows everyone here, so you shouldn't have much trouble."

"Will do, Captain," Mrs. Reich said. "If we all spread

out around the village we'll find our lost ones more quickly that way."

"The missus will go with some ladies," Reich said. "I can talk to the others."

"Just be sure to—"

"Don't worry, Captain, we know how to keep our noses long and our lips closed." Reich returned to his wagon, where his wife had gone ahead to unhitch the horses. They held a murmured conference for a moment.

Joseph found himself praying silently that Audy Reich would find the Frasiers and that Victoria and Heidi would already be there. Something made him feel it wouldn't be that easy.

No time to worry about that. Joseph had a visit to make at the dram shop, and he'd decided to trust Gray Johnston to check the livery for any familiar horses. Instead of unsaddling the mare he'd exchanged with McDonald so Victoria's Sadie wouldn't be recognized, Joseph rode into the center of town, past the mill and distillery along Capps Creek. He couldn't prevent himself from studying the lay of the land and praying to find his horse, Boaz, and that noisy little runt of a donkey that Heidi loved so much.

The scent of fresh water and mud, the aroma of budding flowers and trees lent a perfume to the place that truly did give credence to the village's nickname—Jolly. Coming through here in the flowers of springtime definitely beat riding through early spring storms or autumn rain or the heat of midsummer.

He led the mare, Countess, to the front of the dram shop and looped her reins to the post. The big buckskin nuzzled his neck as he walked past, reminding him of a habit McDonald had begun with her years ago—she always received a splash of whatever McDonald carried when he purchased alcohol for medicine.

He rubbed her ears. "Don't worry, Countess, you'll get your share."

When he stepped through the heavy wooden door, the scent of smoke and a mixture of whiskey, rum and ale hit him in the face, but what caused him to misstep was the sight of a man standing at the bar, as tall as he was, with shoulders as broad as a barn, long, silver-gray hair in tangles down his back.

It took all Joseph had to walk through that door as if he hadn't just caught sight of a snake in the guise of Broderick Thames without his braid. The man's eyes drooped, and his face was overly relaxed. He and a companion had apparently been here for quite some time, as their words and laughter echoed extra loud against the walls of the small shop, drawing the attention of four men puffing on pipes and cigars seated at a smoke-hazed table in the corner.

Thames drawled a string of coarse words to his partner. "…rash of runaway slaves in these parts," he was saying. "Boss sent me to round 'em up."

Joseph stepped to the bar adjacent to them and gestured to the bartender, still listening to their conversation without making eye contact.

"Heard tell there'sh a cave that goes from here all the way to a new sett'ment they're calling Plymouth." Thames had more liquor in his system than Joseph had guessed. "Nobody 'round here's talkin' 'bout it. Guess I'll have to smash some heads together. Maybe raid this place and show 'em who's got the power in this state."

The other man gave a low murmur of agreement, then snorted with laughter.

When the bald bartender approached Joseph, he cast

a slit-eyed glare at the two men at the bar. The last thing Joseph needed was to get involved in a local fight. He quickly ordered a fifth each of rum and whiskey.

The bartender lowered his head and peered over his glasses. "You do know this is a dram shop."

"Sure do."

"If you're lookin' for bulk, you might get it cheaper at the distillery."

"I figure you wouldn't mind selling a couple of full bottles."

The man hesitated, shrugged. "It's your money." He turned to fill the order and silence reigned in the room, punctuated by the sweet scent of smoke and a fine hint of freshly sawed wood. The place was just being built last time Joseph came through.

One of the men in the far corner at the table leaned back in his chair and glared at Thames and his pal. "You think the two of you could take on our town, do you?"

Without turning to look toward the table, Thames stared into his drink and gave it a dark grin. "I heard talk about you folks. I hear you don't approve of slavin'."

"We got slaves here, and they'd fight right alongside us if our town was threatened. No use in you or any of your kind bushwhacking a peaceful settlement."

Thames's companion snorted again. "Town. This place here's a hovel. Maybe it wouldn't feel threatened if it had a few real men in it."

"We've got plenty of real men, just no raiders forcing their views down the throats of innocent folks," called another man from the table.

Thames glanced at his buddy. "You know what, Thad? We could take the mill over and pack in the money for our cause."

"You're not stealing our mill and forcing your will on

innocent strangers," called another. "You got an army out there in the woods somewhere?" This man looked familiar, probably someone Joseph had spoken with on his way through here in the past.

Joseph gave the hostile fellow a quick, warning shake of his head and caught his gaze. Surprise slithered up his backbone. He knew this man, but not from these parts. Quinn. Adam Quinn. An abolitionist from Illinois. What was he doing here?

Quinn sat back in his seat and muttered to the others, his voice too soft for Joseph to make out his words.

When the bartender arrived with Joseph's order, he uncorked the rum at Joseph's request, then screwed up his face in confusion as Joseph replaced the cork gently, paid and walked out. A tiny splash of the liquor in the palm satisfied Countess, and Joseph recorked the bottle and slid them both into his saddlebags. For a moment he'd expected Thames and friend to show a bit of curiosity about why he'd chosen to pay more for his bottles, but they'd already had enough alcohol to sink their wits.

Either Thames hadn't seen Victoria in town yet, or he hadn't recognized her, because Joseph had a clench in his gut that told him Thames, in his rantings to his buddy, would have likely mentioned her if he knew she was here. So where was she?

Another concern trailed Joseph like the dust on the street, sweeping up and hovering around his head. If Thames recognized Quinn, there could be an explosion of violence on the streets of this tiny village. But the man's presence here gave Joseph a sense of relief. Others were taking up the fight. He and his small band of wagoneers might not be so alone.

Despite the long trek Countess had already endured today, Joseph urged her into a trot and covered the streets and the byways that led out into the country. Nary a sign of any of the three animals or two humans he sought, nor even an indentation of familiar footprints in the dust on the streets. He met up with Mr. Reich and the two of them covered the roads again, out past the edges of town. Nothing.

By the time Joseph returned to camp, Countess was irritable and jerking on her bridle bit, jumping sideways to unseat him every few moments, and in every way possible letting him know she was tired and ready for some dinner—what she typically did when starting off in the morning.

Joseph's stomach continued to tighten into a knot of worry.

He slid from the buckskin with an apology to her and pulled the saddle from her back. Next time he'd ride bareback. These saddles were heavy.

Before he could lift the currycomb to cool down the mare, Gray Johnston stepped forward and grabbed the comb from him. "None of the ladies have seen hide nor hair of Victoria or Heidi, sir."

"Mrs. Reich and her posse are back already?"

"Yep. You'd think someone would've noticed a new woman and girl in town, especially two so pretty."

"This is a stopover town, Gray. All kinds of travelers come through here every week. We just need to keep looking."

"What you need's someone with a fresh horse, then," Gray said, taking over the currycomb and giving Countess a long sweep of tines. "I got me one at the livery stable, traded my horse for him, promised to do some shoeing tomorrow to pay it back. Thought I might ride out and see if I can find them."

"Good idea, but do you know the trail they took?"

"No, sir."

"Then I'm going to need your fresh horse, son." Joseph nearly smiled when he saw the disappointment in Gray's eyes. The kid thought he was going to race out into the wilderness with no idea where he was going, find Heidi and Victoria and be their hero. "See those kids up there fishing in the mill pond?" He pointed toward the huge wooden gristmill. "Soon as you finish with Countess, take my fishing pole up there and do some sleuthing for me, find out what any of them know about a local cave. Don't be too obvious, and don't act too interested."

Some of the disappointment left Gray's face. "You'll let me use your fishing pole?"

"Sure will. But do more listening than talking *or* fishing, son." Joseph gave Gray a hard look. "You got that?"

"Got it, sir."

"And don't go near the cave if you find out about it, just go to Mr. Reich and let him know."

"Where will you be?"

"Backtracking as fast as I can." If he told Gray where he was going, the kid was half-likely to try tagging along after him. "And remember, anyone asks you about our wagon train, you know what to say."

"Yep. We're looking for land to settle and slaves for sale."

"But don't volunteer anything. Can you handle that?"

"Yessir."

"Then grab some grub and let's get moving."

Shadows of blue sky, green forest and the gray ears of Boaz spun in Victoria's sight. Pain etched its way down her legs, weakening her grip on the saddle. The spinning upset her stomach, so she closed her eyes.

This was what she'd brought herself to by raging at God. And why not? It wasn't as if she counted on Him. How could she have expected to bare her anger toward Him and live? And yet her rage increased.

The Bible said she was the clay and He the potter. He had the right to do anything He wished to her, as if she was some soulless, emotionless piece of dishware. As if He was a heartless being who enjoyed watching the tiny creatures on this earth squirm in agony. "I hope I'm providing You with some enjoyment now," she muttered.

She was going to pitch off this horse at any moment so weak had she become from blood loss, and they'd found nothing to stop the bleeding for good. For some reason, she believed the gelding could sense her struggle, because he walked with a smoother, swifter gait than any horse she'd ever ridden. A horse could be more gentle and merciful than God.

She knew that somehow her reasoning was off, that there was another side to that argument, but her mind didn't seem to be working properly...all she wanted to do was sleep.

Heidi's short-legged donkey, Pudding, gave a bray of complaint that jerked Victoria awake once more.

"That thing don't stop his squalling I'll cut him loose," Heidi muttered.

"We need him."

"We need to get you to help. You suppose the captain's reached the mill town yet?"

"I can't be sure he went that way."

"He would have."

Victoria breathed deeply of the cool forest scents. Both she and Heidi had neglected to pack the ginger root that was so good for nausea, and so Victoria focused on breathing in deeply through the nose. Hold. Exhale quickly. In again. Hold. This she had learned in another country…couldn't remember where.

She focused on the splash of water in the creek beside them, but the bright sunlight blended with shade of the trees against her closed eyelids and made the spinning start again. Her stomach heaved and churned. The dizzy-feeling vibration in her head extended into her limbs.

Before she could grab the saddle horn, she felt herself float away from her grip on Boaz. She heard a scream that started with piercing strength and then distanced itself, as if caught on a bird flying away from her.

Something slammed into her body and pressed the breath from her. Blackness surrounded her, along with that scream that refused to stop.

For some length of time—though she could not tell how much—she thought she was floating upward, as if perhaps she was going to join her husband in heaven. Though what reason would God have to give her that honor? She'd treated Him like the enemy these past months.

Soft hands embraced her cheeks, and she blinked up to see Heidi's pale, tear-filled eyes, feel her hands shaking, hear her sobs.

"Another mile or so, maybe less," she was barely able to whisper. "Then head east. Follow the creek."

"No." Heidi's voice grew firm. "I'm not leaving you here!"

"You'd better think about that again, or you could die with me here."

Chapter Twelve

Joseph was just getting the hang of the cantankerous horse Gray had borrowed from the stables when he reached the spot where Capps Creek emptied into the larger Shoal Creek. One more thing the kid needed to learn was that a man got what he paid for, and he'd sure paid little enough for this nag—or the stableman was a new one Joseph had never met before, and he was crooked.

The nag perked her ears forward and her chest rumbled about the same time another sound reached Joseph—a scream, high and light, like a young girl's cry. The sound chilled him to the core, and the nag found new energy when she received the smack of his hand on her rump.

The rocks were bad in this section. A horse could have fallen. Snakes were numerous. He forced himself to stop thinking of every catastrophe that could have befallen Victoria and Heidi and focused on getting to them in once piece.

One thought wouldn't stop pestering him, though. Where was Deacon? He was a good tracker, and with Heidi's little donkey braying—yes, there it was now, as obnoxious as ever—how could he not have caught up with them? Surely there couldn't have been some kind of ambush when no one even knew they were here.

A rocky cliff forced Joseph to ride the horse into the middle of the water, where sand and mud, amazingly, made for easier travel. When he rounded a bend in the creek, he saw Victoria lying on the bank with Heidi kneeling beside her.

He slapped his mount on the rump again. Water and sand flew all around him. He was off the horse and kneeling beside Victoria in seconds, shocked by the blood on her breeches. "How much has she lost?" he asked Heidi.

"Too much." The girl's voice shook like she was riding over rocks in a wagon. "It just keeps seepin', and she's hot now."

Joseph rubbed the backs of his fingers down the side of Victoria's face. He'd felt many a face with this same kind of heat. "What's she been drinking?"

"Fresh water from every spring we've come to, but she can't keep it down. I've done everything I can think of, but I'm no doctor, and she's not aware enough to tell me what to do most times. I can't even find any yarrow—"

He turned to Heidi and took her frail hand. "What happened? That doesn't look like a gunshot wound on her leg."

"Panther got her. My fault. All my fault. I drew his attention and then like a crazy woman, started running away. Doc got between us and he got her."

"And then?"

"I shot him."

Joseph felt the muscles of his jaw clench in horror, but Heidi didn't need to be more upset than she already was. "Looks like you did a good job with what you had, too." He could smell the whiskey they'd obviously used to clean Victoria's wound. He felt a stirring of humility. Embarrassment, even. He'd been so self-righteous about this beautiful woman's ability to take care of herself, and here she'd saved Heidi's life. And then Heidi had saved hers. Courageous women, both of them. But now it was time to get busy, not brood about allowing Victoria to get past his defenses—both in his heart and in his job.

"Guess you were right." Victoria's voice reached him, cracked and weak, barely there over the trickle of the stream, and he looked down to find her eyes the color of the sky-fed water staring up at him—pale blue, reflecting her weakness.

"Guess I was wrong," he said. "You're close to the village, and now you have an escort."

The relief in her face, of course, forced him to release any and all resentment that might have been hiding anywhere in him. Later, when he knew she'd be okay, he could teach her a few things about listening to a man with experience...but he suspected she might have already learned that. In fact, he knew she hadn't wanted to carry out this stunt in the first place. She'd merely done what she thought was right.

"Let's get you up from here." He reached down to lift her and she cried out. He held her closer. "Heidi, got any whiskey left?"

"Ran out. I poured it all into that gouge in her leg."

"Get a bottle out of my right front saddlebag." Alcohol was good for a lot of things, but apparently it hadn't worked for Victoria. Still, the alcohol in it could cool her hot skin better than water.

While Heidi did as he said, he asked Victoria, "What all have you used to try to stop the bleeding?"

"Heidi packed it with cloth, with sassafras and soaked it with whiskey. Had a tight bandage."

"I brought something just on a whim. You know how the ladies like to dry their herbs and such hanging inside the wagon during the day? I gathered some potato." He reached into his pocket and pulled out some ground dried starch from the inside of some of the potatoes Mrs. Reich had dried after a foray through the field some weeks ago.

"I remember. How dry?"

"I think it'll do the job."

"Had to come from last year's crop." Victoria's voice sounded weaker.

"Whoever planted it must have moved on, don't you think?"

"What if it's already too late?" Her eyelids fluttered. "I think the Almighty wants me dead, and I don't think I'll be following Matthew to heaven."

"I think you're delirious." He laid her into a soft mound of grass just as Heidi returned. "Miss Ladue, I'm no doctor, nor am I a woman. You need to do this procedure. I can guide you."

Heidi frowned at him and handed him the bottle. "Me? I've almost killed her already." Her voice cracked. "You know what you're doing. You do it."

"You're learning quickly. I daresay she's taught you a lot just on this trip, and it's more proper for a lady to treat a lady."

"Oh, for the love of King David," Victoria said with a soft rasp, "someone just do something before my blood turns the creek red."

"I'd rather get you back to the village first," Joseph said, "but I don't want to take the time." He could see the position of the wound clearly. He pulled a knife from his belt, glad he'd taken time to sharpen it.

Proper etiquette in this season's society not only said a man was never to touch a woman where Joseph was about to touch Victoria, but it also said he wasn't supposed to acknowledge she had a thigh. He'd never been one for those kinds of societal rules, which was why he'd taken to the trail so quickly. Women couldn't afford to be picky when their lives depended on common horse sense.

"Heidi, pour some of my whiskey, please, then give me the bottle."

As the young woman did as he asked, he used the last few drops from the other bottle Victoria must have dropped and cleaned his knife, glad he'd been frustrated enough on this trip to spend time sharpening the blade.

He could feel both women watching him. "I've done this procedure before, Victoria."

"W-with a knife?" Heidi asked. "How're you going to stop the bleeding with a blade like that?"

He noted that Heidi had apparently cut a slit in the breeches Victoria wore and tied strips of buckskin to either side of the slit, obviously so she could treat the wound more easily.

He untied the strips and pulled them back, then gently unwound the cloth covering the wound. What he saw made his blood chill. "Doctor, how many panther-claw wounds have you treated?" He looked up at her and saw her face pale further.

"We didn't get any of those. Are you going to teach me another thing or two?"

"They lick themselves, and they eat a lot of things—"

She raised a hand, her movements graceful even

under these circumstances. "That's enough information for me. My stomach is already weak."

Doing as Matthew had once done with him, Joseph doused his hands with whiskey and reached for the wound. He felt Victoria stiffen, but when he looked down into her eyes they held trust and determination.

"Holler if you have to," he said. "I need to get these shavings out, and I might have to cut out some bad flesh. I promise what I have will be more comfortable than shavings. Heidi, I brought more supplies. You'll find some clean cloths in the right saddlebag."

He was reaching for the wound to pull out the packing when the clatter of horse hooves along the creek bed echoed from behind. One horse. "Heidi, get behind a tree. Quickly!"

She did as she was told while he leaned over Victoria to cover her body with his. There was no time to go for his rifle.

But there was no need. He recognized Deacon Fritz's piebald mare as she raced into sight from the creek bend, splattering through the water. Deacon's hat was pulled down low over his head.

He was avoiding a trail. Joseph didn't like the looks of this.

The mare was winded when Deacon pulled her to a stop, but he didn't get off. "You two ladies are hard to follow."

"Meant to be," Heidi said.

"That's a good thing, but you can't stop now. Doctor, how bad are you hurt?"

"She's not good, Deacon," Joseph said.

"Can she keep traveling? We've got us four men on horseback coming this way. I found some locals who told me they've seen rough riders patrolling the road through Jolly Mill for wagon trains headed to Kansas. We were right. There's bad blood."

"How far back are the riders?" Joseph asked.

"Not sure. I've been leading 'em on a maze. You know how hard it is to follow one trail and leave a different one? I'd say they're at least a mile back."

"You think they're bushwhackers?" Unable to wait any longer, Joseph covered Victoria's mouth with one hand and used the old bandage to ease out as much of the packing as he could. When Victoria groaned, he apologized and kept working.

"This bleeding has to stop now for her to survive, Deacon. We can't leave yet. Take Heidi and the animals and follow the creek."

"You think I'm going to leave you two behind?" Deacon shook his head.

"No!" Heidi pulled the bandages from Joseph's saddlebag and ran to Victoria. "We'll hurry. We'll get this wrapped and take you with us."

"No time," Joseph said. He took the cloths from Heidi and laid a hand on her arm. "You did a good job, child, but I have other work for you now. Deacon can lead my borrowed horse and I'll take Boaz into the woods with Victoria. My horse knows how to be quiet, and if you make the tracks obvious, those men will track you instead of us."

"I think we can stay ahead of them," Deacon said.

"No, please." Heidi's face puckered and tears trickled down her cheeks. "I can't leave her. I can help. I'll do anything you tell me to."

"Then divert the riders," Joseph said. "Keep them off our trail. That's what we need most from you right now. You could be saving her life."

"Directions?" Deacon asked.

"You'll reach Capps Creek in a mile or so. It feeds into this one. Follow Capps upstream a mile and you'll reach Jolly Mill. If you move fast enough, you'll reach town before they can catch up." He hastily cleaned the wound with whiskey and pulled out fresh bandages. "You'd better get the wagons out of sight as soon as you get there. Tell the others to pull out as if they're headed east. They'll encounter less resistance if they're perceived to be leaving Kansas instead of entering. Then have them circle around and camp in the forest above the creek. No fires. No noise.

"Got it, Captain. Anybody find the doc's friends?"

"Not before I left, but if they have I daresay Buck and Francine will know what to do to help you, show you where to hide. They'd be prepared."

Deacon nodded. "Let's get on up the way, girl. And muzzle that donkey of yours. We'll keep a pace so fast he won't be able to run and breathe at the same time. We've got to warn the others."

"Let him bray," Joseph said. "You can muzzle him later, once the riders are past us."

Deacon and Heidi prepared to leave as Heidi's arguments echoed from the rock ledge above the creek, but she did as she was told.

Joseph wrapped the bandage as tightly as he could. But even then, there was no groan. As Deacon and Heidi rushed the animals up Shoal Creek, Victoria went limp in his arms.

The sound of birdsong reached Victoria just before she heard the rumble of male voices in the distance. The words were unclear, and she soon realized this was because everything around her was indistinct except for the faint fishy smell of nearby rushing water, the scent of wood smoke and wild mint that often characterized Joseph's presence and the comforting aroma of horse.

She recalled Joseph stuffing her mouth with cloth and going to work on her leg right there on the creek bank. She recalled the warning they'd received from Deacon before she lost the mental coordination she needed to digest his message. Danger. They could be in danger. Or they already were. What had happened?

Her leg ached, but not as sharply as it had hurt all day. The scent of clove oil engulfed her. Comfort. After the initial pain, the mild disinfectant had lessened the pain. She opened her eyes and found herself being held firmly in Joseph's arms. When she tried to move, his arms tightened around her and his hand came over her mouth. His mouth found her ear, and he shushed her.

Confused, she shivered despite the situation. She was far too affected by Joseph Rickard, but she didn't have a choice. Not in her condition. She tried to pull away and ask what was happening, but he answered before she could ask. "Wait," he whispered. "Wait until the men are gone, and pray they follow the right trail."

Her chest squeezed and she found herself praying, despite the fact that less than—what, an hour ago?— she'd been near to taking her life into her own hands by berating Him again. He would not answer her prayers, but she continued to pray. After all these months of silence, she'd not forgotten how to pray, but the words that continued to sound in her heart were, "Forgive me. Please forgive me."

What would the Almighty think of a person who only came to Him when told to do so? She'd not called on Him after the panther attack, only when reminded by Joseph to pray.

She prayed a few seconds longer and then she

stopped. He'd mentioned a trail. She opened her eyes and studied the forest around them but she saw no trail, only juniper and pine trees surrounding them. She looked up to see Boaz hovering nearby, head lowered as if he, too, was praying. As she watched, the horse lowered himself to his knees and then lay on the ground.

Joseph leaned forward again, lips against Victoria's ear, and once again she felt a shiver that had nothing to do with any physical danger, nor with the fever that heated her skin.

"The bleeding's stopped," he said.

She closed her eyes and took a deep breath, surprised. What was this? An answer to prayer? "You're sure?"

"Nothing more has come through the potato starch."

Could she trust it? Of course, she wasn't out of danger yet. None of them were. "What will happen to Deacon and Heidi if those men catch up with them?"

"You don't know how long you've been out, do you?"

She blinked up into his dark eyes, made darker still by the shadow of his hat low over his forehead. "Couldn't have been long."

"Those loud-mouthed men know nothing about tracking and seem to be slow about their business of pillaging, raiding and burning those not of their political persuasion."

Victoria heard the contempt in Joseph's voice through the roaring in her ears. She glanced upward and silently apologized once again for her mistreatment of the Almighty. She needed to beg Him for mercy, not ostracize Him with her anger.

Joseph touched her hair and brushed it back from her face. "Are you feeling ill?"

She nodded. She also felt terrified, ashamed, overwhelmed. She needed distraction. "The men are gone?"

"They aren't within hearing now. They're tracking Deacon and Heidi. If they're lost, though, they could come back this way. I'm waiting until I know for sure they're gone."

"I'm sorry for dragging you into this."

"I dragged myself into it."

"I didn't mean for you to." She swallowed and closed her eyes but she opened them again quickly, because the dizziness affected her stomach.

"I know."

"I knew when Heidi showed up that you wouldn't leave without her."

"I wouldn't have left without you." He peered through the trees toward the creek. "How could I, Victoria? I love you."

Her breath caught and held. "You seem able to say those words with ease." She was beginning to believe, after all this time and all the doubts she'd experienced, that he truly meant what he said. Though if he didn't, life would have been less complicated.

"I said the same words the day I left you in St. Louis. I meant them." He turned to glance at her for a few seconds before returning to his study of the creek. "Maybe not as much as I mean them now."

She tried to sit up, but her stomach churned. "We've danced around the subject for five weeks, and there's never seemed to be time to talk."

"I had the impression you didn't want to talk."

She took a deep breath through her nose and tried to calm her stomach. Must not make any sudden movements. "I've wanted answers for a decade, but when you showed up I wasn't sure I still wanted them."

"Do you now?"

"The way I feel right now, I'm not sure I would remember what we said." She paused to breathe slowly. "When I heard about your engagement, I felt you simply loved me less than you loved your father's ambitions for you. Or…that you truly loved the woman you were called upon to marry." She said it lightly, but her heart seemed to beat through every word. He mattered far too much to her, and even though she knew her words were those of a desperate woman, and not something she would say if she were completely in control, she needed to say them. What if she didn't survive this? He should know the truth, shouldn't he? She felt ashamed to feel so in need of Joseph's reassurance. Ashamed and vulnerable. It was an awful feeling.

"I can't believe you have doubts now, after all this time," he told her gently. "Why do you think I avoided seeing you and Matthew together?"

"What about those letters I never received? What… did you write to me?"

"I explained that no matter what you might hear, I was not going to marry Sara Jane, my lifelong neighbor and childhood friend."

"You cared for her?"

"She was like a sister."

"So you wouldn't…you wouldn't have married her even if she'd lived?" Her head pounded and she swallowed back the nausea again. Now was not the time for this conversation.

He turned to look at her, frowning. "Victoria?" He touched her forehead. "Your skin's getting hotter."

"I know. Tell me about Sara Jane. I need to be distracted right now."

He moistened a cloth and placed it over her face. "It was always you." His voice was tender, filled with compassion. "I never loved anyone else the way I love you. I would never have married Sara Jane. My father was ill. He made the announcement of our engagement without consulting either of us. He and Sara Jane's father made the plans without us. The first I heard of it was when Sara Jane came riding like wildfire to the house to beg me to put a stop to it. That's when she told me she was secretly engaged to a man in Atlanta." Joseph studied the terrain past the trees again. "The announcement Matthew received about my engagement was from my father, not from me."

"She was going to be married." For some reason, tears burned Victoria's eyes. "She was in love?"

"With a good man, but not with me."

"And then she died." Victoria never cried over sad stories like this. But the tears dripped down her face. She dabbed at them, sniffed. She had never felt so awful in her life.

Joseph held her hair away from her face, lifting it from her shoulders. "You're overwrought because of your fever. We need to cool you down."

"I wondered why you wrote to Matthew and not to me," she said.

"I know. I sent you letters as well, many more than I sent to Matthew. At the time, I believed you never wrote back because you no longer cared. All I received from you was silence."

"If I'd only known."

Chapter Thirteen

Frustration slammed through Joseph like the kick of a mule. He had suspected for many years that Matthew had somehow intercepted the letters to Victoria so she would believe she'd been abandoned by the man she loved. But even as he'd suspected, he'd known Matthew too well to truly believe it.

"I picked up the clinic mail most days," Victoria said, her words a little slurred by the effects of fever. And the tears. "What else did you tell me in the letters?"

Memories combined like burrs under a saddle for a long moment. "Everything."

She leaned forward and buried her face in her hands. "Oh," she said on a sigh.

"I asked you to wait. I told you all about Sara Jane and our childhood friendship and the trick our fathers pulled on us. I told you when she died and how I grieved her death."

"You loved her as a sister."

"I was devastated when she died, but never because I wanted to marry her. I wanted her to marry her beau and pull out from under her overbearing father's fat, greedy thumb. Her death was only one incident that helped me decide to leave the family plantation for good. I told my father I was going to marry you."

"Did you tell Matthew about any of this?"

"No. I knew how he felt and I didn't want to rub salt in his wounds. He knew you and I were in love."

"How could the letters have been lost? It isn't as if you sent them all at the same time." She looked up at him. "Where *did* you send them from?"

Joseph held her feverish gaze for a moment, then closed his eyes. Now that he knew the truth—that Matthew had not intercepted the letters and Victoria had never received them—he realized who had sabotaged their delivery. "Cleophas Rickard."

"Your father?"

"He was a man accustomed to getting his way."

"You posted your letters with him?"

"I didn't think about it at the time, but yes. Or rather, I might just as well have." Joseph fought back frustrated resentment as the reality of his loss settled into him.

"I suppose he had servants...slaves...do that."

"My father had a young houseboy, Robert, who was at his beck and call all hours of the day and night. He slept at the foot of my father's bed. I often left to post my own mail and poor Robert would be told to race to catch up with me and do the mailing for me. I would have preferred to send him away to play at the creek with friends, but I knew he might receive punishment for that, so I allowed him to stay busy."

"You think your father had your letters destroyed."

Joseph had been brought up not to speak ill of the dead, especially not his father. But anger held him captive. "I was wrong not to suspect something was up when you didn't at least return greetings to me when I wrote to you, but I thought you were angry."

"If I had received those letters…" She shook her head. The tears had stopped falling. "I'd have thought you and Matthew would communicate better."

"I didn't write to Matthew about you, and he seldom mentioned you in his letters. His posts were all about some new medical technique he had learned or a new medicine he'd begun to use on patients."

"We both thought you had settled in Georgia for good."

Joseph knew it must have been very difficult for Matthew to resist Victoria, especially when she wasn't receiving word from the man she loved. "I regret to say that I held much resentment against Matthew for so many years."

But the end result was that his love for her had been preserved, and right now he didn't care why. God worked in amazing ways, and who was to say that God's work, this time, had been as successful as always to bring about His will in the lives of His people.

"I knew of your frustration with family expectations," Victoria said. Her voice was hoarse and her face had grown crimson.

Joseph picked up the wet cloth and remoistened it with whiskey. "I think you're dehydrated. You need to drink."

She took the cloth from him and used it to moisten her neck. "I don't think I could hold any water in my stomach. When can we leave? The men haven't come back this way."

He desperately wanted to leave. He wanted to pick Victoria up and carry her to the creek and douse her to lower her temperature. "Not yet. I want to get you out of here as soon as possible, but we can't take the chance yet."

She sighed. "I trust your judgment. Tell me, then, when your father deeded the plantation to your brother."

He recalled his father's fury with him, and then his death. After all that, to learn that Matthew and Victoria had married...it was like a stake in his heart. After all he'd gone through, his greatest wish was denied him, but if not for the past ten years of struggle, would he be the man he was now?

"He changed the deed when I told him I was going to marry an abolitionist."

"I did write to you, Joseph. I take it you never received the letters."

"Of course not. After my father died I was angry to the bone and sick of life. I took a wagon train West to get away from the world I'd always known."

"Why didn't you ask me about the letters long ago?"

"When you were already married? A man doesn't get that personal with the wife of another man. The only conclusion I could draw was that you had chosen security over love. How could I blame you? I didn't realize how much I'd hurt you when I left."

"You mean you didn't know how much I loved you?" she asked.

"I thought that if you loved me enough, you would have gone with me."

"But I didn't—"

He touched her lips with his fingers. "I know better now. You are a woman of strong principles. You were wise enough to know you couldn't have withstood watching slavery in action in every part of your life. I blamed myself for forcing you to choose a loveless marriage because of my need to obey my father's dying wish."

"My marriage wasn't loveless."

Her words stung, and yet he was glad, for her sake, that she'd not been lonely. "Can you tell me it was anything like the love we would have shared?"

Victoria looked up and held his gaze for a long moment, her eyes bright, face still flushed from the fever, and he felt like a brute. Why was he doing this now?

She shook her head, then leaned back against Boaz. "I think I'm the kind of woman who can only truly have a deep connection to one person my whole life. That spot was already taken. Matthew knew that." The words fell softly, almost as if she felt guilty for speaking them.

Joseph held Victoria's clear gaze. It was the same gaze that had always had the power to scramble his thoughts to the point that he was unable to hold an intelligent conversation. He felt her studying him.

"Now we know," he said, feeling weak with regret, thinking about what might have been. "I've wanted to ask you about what happened for the past five weeks, but—"

"But you're a gentleman, and we had to get to know one another again." She could read his mind. She knew him so well.

"I wasn't able to tell you before," he said. "But all those nights on the trail, you were the one I dreamed about, and the guilt of dreaming of another man's wife came close to driving me crazy. I was guilty of the sin of coveting my friend's wife, and I fought it by keeping busy, by joining the cause you and Matthew started me on in the first place."

"I'm so sorry you endured those years." Victoria's voice weakened. "I never lacked for gentle company or interesting work. But you built a town in Kansas. God blessed your attempts to flee from your temptation."

"I think it was necessary for us to go our separate

ways for a season," he said. "Your skills will be vital in Kansas Territory, and I would never have gained knowledge of the wilderness and been able to lead other wagon trains to the Territory had I not been forced from your side. Do you remember the day your brother found me lying in the street?"

He got the response he wanted when she smiled. "I remember," she said. "Albert carried you to the clinic where I had taken a job working for Matthew, an old family friend."

"You chose to work in a dangerous part of town."

"And you chose to interfere when you saw a man beating his wife." Her smile widened. "You always were the interfering sort. Albert and Matthew took to you immediately."

"And you?"

"What woman wouldn't take to a man like you?"

He liked that. He recalled looking up from the cot where broad-shouldered, red-haired Albert had placed him and seeing Victoria at the far end of the room folding bandages. The vision of her had burned into his heart that very first time. Only in the weeks and months later had her depth and character burned into his soul.

She took a breath and let it out slowly, as if trying to settle the pain in her thigh. "I believe Matthew intended to ask me to make a marriage/business partnership with him before you came along. He'd already begun to teach me minor skills."

That was something Joseph hadn't known. "Matthew was the one who suggested I propose to you. He was like a fond uncle expressing his approval. He even seemed angry when I told him I was returning to Georgia."

"Of course. He doted on me. He always wanted me to be happy."

Joseph thought he heard something. He stiffened and held his hand up for her to be quiet, but when he peered through the screen of trees, he saw a doe drinking at the creek. He shook his head and tried to relax.

"I once told Sara Jane that she shouldn't be traded off like some prized pig," he said.

Victoria found the energy to chuckle at him. "Prized pig?"

"She was a lovely young lady and deserved to marry for something besides money, which could be eaten by moths, destroyed by war or famine or theft."

An expression of wonder entered Victoria's blue eyes. Her shapely lips parted with a chuckle. "Spoken like a true gentleman…except for the prized pig part."

"The two of you could have been friends."

"For a while, I hated the woman I thought you'd left me for, but how could I blame her for loving you?"

Joseph frowned at the increased color that had begun to stain Victoria's face and neck. He touched her face. "Your fever is rising."

She nodded. "My eyes are burning. I can always tell."

He moved closer to her. "We need to get you out of here as soon as it's safe."

She stared up at him with eyes that had haunted him ever since he'd left, especially after receiving word of Matthew's death. Those eyes had lingered in his dreams for his whole adult life.

Joseph took her hand. It was cold. He took both of her hands in his and tried to instill some warmth in them. "You have permission to sock me in the mouth for all my poor behavior as soon as you're well enough."

She gave a weak chuckle. "You could serve as my target stand when I practice my shooting."

"I'm all yours." He halfway meant it. Sometimes he

wondered if he hadn't behaved more like Buster Johnston than he could admit to himself.

She laid her head against Boaz's side. "Do you really think those men are coming back?"

"I wish I knew, but we can't take a chance yet."

"If they're coming, I wish they would hurry." Her eyes slowly closed.

He knew she was feeling worse and he prayed silently for something he could do to help her, distract her. "You know those arguments we had about slavery when we were falling in love? Your words only underscored what I'd come to believe. When I returned to Georgia, I felt as if I was returning to undertake a battle. I had even decided, at one time, to free all the slaves in the plantation."

Her lids fluttered open. "You did?"

"It wasn't until I arrived there that I realized I couldn't do that. Not only would it endanger my family, but it would have endangered the slaves who had served my family for so many years. My younger brother, Edwin, shared many of my convictions, and together we made plans for greatly increased care for the slaves, increasingly better food and sanitation, better homes, shorter working hours. Since my father had already improved their living conditions a great deal after his father died, other plantations in the area improved the standards of living."

"It was a start," she said as her eyes closed again. "I never knew."

"No. I wrote to you about it."

"I don't care what your family says. You were a good son. Now," she said, pressing her fingers to her forehead, "I think I'm going to be sick."

He rushed to help her lean forward and held her hair

back as she retched into the weeds, her whole body trembling. When she finished, he drew her back and dabbed her forehead with a damp cloth, helped her wash and gave her a sip of water.

"Mint leaves?" he asked. "Did you pack any?"

She shook her head.

"Even if we dared try to return to town, you can't ride in your condition," he said.

She moaned. Then her eyes widened as she went still and silent, nodding toward the creek.

He heard what she had. More movement. Were the men coming back, or were more deer joining the doe at the water?

Victoria breathed quietly while Joseph picked up her Colt and stepped with easy stealth through the thick growth of briars and trees. Good thing it was later spring and the brush covered them completely. He would prefer a cave, but their little hiding place would serve.

He caught sight of one of what sounded like four riders along the creek. They were talking more softly this time, all wearing hats except one. That one…something familiar about him. And then he spoke, and for a moment Joseph could not breathe.

Buster Johnston. He was riding with Silver Tail—Broderick Thames—who had apparently sobered up since Joseph had seen him a few hours ago.

"You say you thought they were following this creek?" Thames asked Buster.

"They sure were. Don't know how many came this way, but if you ask me, they've got a lot of shooting skills."

Victoria's trembling hand found its way to Joseph's arm and she squeezed tightly. Her hand was as hot as her face appeared. He nodded and patted her hand with reassurance. What was the kid up to now?

"You say they were men from the wagon train?" Thames asked.

"Sure. Slave traders going to Kansas Territory. Bet I could get them to join your army, every one of them."

Joseph caught his breath again and felt a nigh-irresistible desire to burst out of the brush and grab Buster by the scruff of the neck. He was going to get them all killed.

"Hold up, men!" Thames called, his voice louder. Much more sober than he'd been in the dram shop. Perhaps his behavior in town had been an act.

There was the sound of boots landing on the rocky edge of the creek bed. "I thought you said that wagon train was settling around these parts."

"Not if we can't find…land or…slaves to buy." Buster's voice sounded as if his throat had closed up on him.

"Boss, got some blood here," called one of the other men. "Got a lot of it."

Buster jumped from his horse and bent over. "Whoa! Lots of blood. Your men said they saw somebody coming this way. Think they got a shot at somebody?"

"If they did, I wasn't told," Thames growled.

"But why would they shoot at slave traders?" Buster demanded. "Don't your men need all the help they can get?"

Thames straightened and looked at Buster for a long moment, but the kid was still looking down at the blood on the rocks.

"Looks like more than one person got shot," Buster said. "See this here? And there's some over there. What could cause this much blood loss?"

As Joseph continued watching and Buster continued

to study the ground, Thames reached for his pistol and nodded to the other two men.

Joseph slowly cocked his weapon, making no sound, but suddenly aware that he wasn't alone. The barrel of a rifle eased forward to his right. He didn't have time to turn and look, but he knew Victoria was backing him up.

At the creek bank, Buster finally looked up to see the weapons aimed at him. He froze. "What are you doing?" he cried. "I thought you said you were looking for men to join your raiders!"

"I thought I caught the scent of an abolitionist," Thames drawled. "You shouldn't have changed your story." Thames nodded to one of his men, who cocked his rifle. "Get up, kid."

Buster didn't move. "Nope. If I stay here, you might not be so quick to shoot me. Bullets can ricochet from rocks, you know. Want to take the chance you'll end up shooting yourself?"

"Shoot him!" Thames told his rifleman.

Before Joseph could aim, a deafening blast caught him beside his right ear. The would-be shooter tumbled to the rocks beside Buster. Thames and his remaining cohort pivoted toward the trees where Joseph and Victoria stood camouflaged behind thick brush. The cohort raised his rifle.

Joseph caught the other man in the chest while Buster jumped to his feet and hauled a pistol out of his back pocket. It belonged to Deacon Fritz. What was Deacon thinking? The kid aimed his pistol at Thames and walked toward him, pointing the barrel directly into Thames's face.

"Try to hurt my friends, *slaver,* and you won't have a face for your murdering posse to recognize." The gun in his hand shook, and rage turned his face red. "You know what? I think I'll just get rid of one more bush-whacker, save a few helpless Africans."

"Buster!" Joseph called. "No, don't do it."

At the sound of Joseph's voice, Thames raised his weapon. Victoria shot the man in the forehead before Joseph could stop her. Buster jumped backward with a yelp, tripped over a rock and fell on his hind end. "Captain? Tell me that's you!"

The rifle stock aimed upward. Joseph turned in time to see Victoria lose her grip on the barrel and stumble.

"I shot him," she whispered.

Joseph caught both Victoria and her rifle at the same time and eased her onto the blanket beside Boaz. Though alert and slightly wide-eyed, the gelding hadn't moved from his spot.

Victoria trembled violently, lips parted, eyes wide in shock. "I sh-shot him," she whispered.

"I know. It wasn't as simple as you expected it to be, was it?" Joseph glanced toward the creek. "Buster, bring us some water from the creek," he called out. "I think we're safe for now, but if you ever pull a prank like that again you'll wish you'd been shot, because I know a lot more painful ways for a man to leave this world."

He returned his attention to Victoria. "Are you okay?"

Tears filled her eyes. "I…really…shot them."

Carefully, Joseph drew her into his arms and held her against his chest. His first thought was that her fever had worsened and he needed to break it. His second thought that this was likely the first time she'd killed a human being, much less two at one time, and she was in shock.

"You killed Matthew's murderer, Victoria. He can't hurt your friends now."

"What if he's already hurt Buck and Francine?"

"That kind of thinking will do you no good." Joseph pressed his lips into her hair and continued to hold her. He didn't want to let go, not ever. He wanted to stay beside her and protect her for the rest of their lives, and he didn't care how many people thought he was being irreverent or inappropriate. This woman, this brilliant and caring doctor, needed someone to stand beside her always, to protect her so she could continue to heal and help others. He intended to be that person.

Before he could say anything to her, she closed her eyes and her head fell back against Boaz.

Chapter Fourteen

Victoria awakened to the spatter of rushing water and the sound of raised voices. Her leg screamed with pain and she gritted her teeth so hard she was afraid she might break some of them, but it was better than crying out. She opened her eyes to find Joseph and Buster Johnston, of all people, hovering over her. The smell of dried fish eggs, water, whiskey and the reassuring scent of horse reminded her where she was.

Had she really just shot two men? To save the life of this annoying upstart? What was he doing here? And why was he pretending to be a slaver?

But wasn't one of the men she'd shot the very monster she'd chased through Missouri to seek revenge for her husband's murder? And now she had her revenge. Why did it nauseate her?

She needn't ask Buster any questions because Joseph was doing an admirable job of grilling him.

"Captain," Buster whined, "I didn't have a choice. Deacon Fritz and Heidi Ladue came riding into the camp like their horses' tails were afire. Said the doctor was hurt bad and they were trying to lure the border ruffians away from her while you hid her."

"So Fritz sent you alone with those men to follow their tracks?" Joseph leaned over Victoria with a cloth of icy-cold water from a spring that fed the creek.

"Well, no, but what was I supposed to do? Four men came riding into town along that same creek a little later, their horses all sweaty and slathering, and they went barging into the dram shop. A couple of minutes later they came out, all mad and glaring because that guy with the braid was shouting so loud his voice echoed from the cliffs across the creek."

"And you thought that would be a good time to join them?"

"Pa always said when folks was all riled up was the best time to convince them you're part of their crowd. I waited until the other fellas took their lathered-up horses to the stables and did what you told us to, asked Thames if they knew of any land or slaves for sale. Then I told them I'd seen someone I thought was looking for land and slaves go riding down Capps Creek, and I thought I knew where they were going."

"And he let you ride with them, just like that?"

"Sure did. I told you, those men were all het up. Fella wasn't thinking straight."

"Then you forgot your original story and told them we were headed for Kansas Territory. Not much of a liar, are you, son?"

Buster kicked at a rock. "I guess I got kind of caught up in the excitement. It slipped out."

Joseph groaned. "You took it upon yourself to join their gang and spy on them? You thought that was a smart thing to do when you didn't know anything about them?"

"It's what you'd've done, Captain. You wouldn't've let them get to the doctor."

"That's right, and you should have trusted I was doing just that—keeping them away from her by hiding her where they couldn't find her. But now the trail is so obvious a three-year-old could find it, so I have to get her out of here."

"How could I know that?" Buster spread his hands. "How was I supposed to know you were prepared?"

"When's the last time you saw me unprepared?" The tone of Joseph's voice deepened. "Except, perhaps, when you and your brother convinced Claude Ladue to help you cross the flooded river."

There was an unhappy sigh from Buster. "I know, Captain. It's all I think about. I'm doing all I can to make things better."

"I'll tell you what you can do," Joseph said. "You need to push the bodies of those border attackers into the middle of the creek and hope they keep on floating southeast."

Buster swallowed so loudly that Victoria heard it over the rush of the creek. "I...I can do that."

"You sure?"

"No burial or nothing?"

"I'm here to keep Victoria alive, not bury killers. Do you have a shovel? Can you dig the graves and carry those bodies to their graves and cover them up before someone comes looking for them?"

"I'll get 'em into the water."

"Good. Then you need to gather their horses and ride as fast and far as you can against the wind."

"Huh?"

"West. The weather usually comes from the west. Then you unsaddle the horses, set them free and then hightail it back to Jolly Mill before their friends realize what's up and peg you as the culprit. Did anyone see you leaving with them?"

"Don't think so."

"You don't *think* so?"

"The four men who rode after Deacon and Heidi took their horses to the stables before I went to talk to Thames, but I don't know who else might've been with their crowd. It's kind of quiet and watchful in town, you know."

Joseph closed his eyes and shook his head. "As soon as you get back to town, tell Fritz and Reich what's happening here, but don't tell another soul." Joseph stopped dabbing the water across Victoria's face and gave the kid a hard look. "And if you do tell another soul, I will come after you myself. I have a good aim. Don't you go risking still more lives so you can play hero."

"Okay, okay, I'm going." Buster sounded like a petulant child, but he did as he was told and crashed his way through the brush toward the horses.

"Lead the animals through the creek until you can get to a rocky ridge where their footsteps won't be noticeable," Joseph called after him. "I can't move Victoria quickly and I don't need all those tracks leading more men back to us."

Victoria pushed herself up on her elbows. "I can ride."

"No, you can't. You can barely move right now, and you're in shock," Joseph said. "Buster Johnston, just go, now!"

Victoria was pretty sure she would die soon. She suddenly felt like it. Rallying her strength to back up Joseph had taken the last of her energy.

There were some loud splashes when Buster gave

the dead men a water burial. Next came a major scuffle while the kid herded horses and apparently got tangled in four sets of bridles. If the kid was as awkward with the rest of his mission as he always had been, he would lead other ruffians directly to their hideout.

Joseph placed another cloth of icy water over her face, touched her neck and arms, brushed her hair back. She wished she felt well enough to enjoy his attention.

"Victoria, lie still. I'm going to search for some of those plants you had Heidi and Mrs. Reich gathering the other day."

"Has the bleeding truly stopped?"

"I've seen no more blood come through the packing I've placed there. I think the potato starch has done the trick." Joseph moved Victoria away from Boaz and urged the horse to his feet. He reached into one of the saddlebags and pulled out a hatchet. "I think we'll do this a different way."

"What?" She looked askance at the tool he held as he reached for a sapling.

"Boaz has pulled a litter before. It'll take longer to get you to town this way, but we need to get you away from here."

"Is Buster gone?" She heard no more splashing.

"He finally figured out how to lead all those horses downstream and out the other side."

"He was trying to help," she admitted.

"He did us no good stirring up the rocks along the creek with all the horse tracks."

"Those men might have found us if not for Buster distracting them." She couldn't believe she was defending the boy.

Joseph chopped two matching saplings—sassafras, by the smell of them—and knelt beside Victoria. He gave her some sassafras chips. "These may help settle your stomach if you hold one in your mouth."

He placed one on her tongue and gave her more for later. "How are you feeling?"

"Like a mouse that's been chewed on by a cat."

"Rest while I work." He felt her forehead again. "I don't think you're any warmer, but we still need to get your fever down."

"I didn't pack the feverfew."

"Then we need to get you to Heidi and her wagon."

Joseph spread out a blanket and helped her onto it so she could rest while he built the litter. He had come prepared for everything, and after weaving some vines back and forth between the cut saplings, he tied the ends to either side of the saddle with leather strips and laid his coat across the woven vines.

With gentle movements, he lifted her and the blanket from the ground and laid her onto the litter. "I'll lead Boaz and find the smoothest route, but we'll have to avoid the creek. That seems to have become a regular road today, with too much traffic."

He gave her a few sips of water from a wineskin and then left it beside her on the litter. "You know the drill, Doctor. A few sips at a time. Don't overdo it, but keep drinking as much as you can. If you start to feel worse, let me know and we can stop."

She looked up into Joseph's worry-lined face. Hot tears filled her eyes and dripped down the sides of her cheeks. It seemed she could do nothing today but cry. "All I feel right now is grateful."

"Good, go with that feeling and keep drinking the water."

She gazed up at him and the sky spun above his head. She closed her eyes. "So grateful."

"Victoria?"

She opened her eyes again, and he knelt beside her. He touched her face tenderly and adjusted the blanket beneath her. "I'll take care of you. I'm not losing you again."

Fighting darkness and dizziness, she couldn't help smiling. "I love you, too."

His movements stopped. "Try telling me that when you're not delirious with fever."

"I will. I promise." She closed her eyes again, and the darkness settled around his image—that image of a man who loved her and who would never let her go. The image lasted as she felt herself moving and heard Joseph talking to Boaz. It lasted even into her dark dreams. His imprint on her mind stayed and fought off the evil of the nightmares that haunted her of a man with a braided tail of silver whose evil killed a kind and gentle doctor…and of the horror she'd felt when she killed the man. Revenge. Somehow, she had expected it to be much more satisfying. All she felt was broken, as if she would never be the same again.

She was a physician. She healed people. She didn't kill them.

As Joseph continued to lead Boaz forward through the soft grasses, Victoria's eyes dripped with tears as she relived the awfulness of taking a human life.

After an hour of travel over the softest ground Joseph could find, he heard the rustle of brush to his left, near where a spring bubbled up and trailed a tiny stream toward the creek. He reached for his rifle and swung around, and his gelding stopped.

He saw long, golden-white strands of hair tangled in

a tree, then he heard a grunt and saw a tow-headed boy untangle the strands. It was Gray and Heidi.

Of all the undisciplined… "What are you two doing here?"

"Buster just got back and told us to—"

"Buster? He's already back in Jolly Mill? What about the horses?"

"What horses? He was on his horse."

Joseph sucked in a deep breath and slowly let it out. He wished he'd been more specific about how far Buster should lead those animals. The kid had probably led them barely a mile away and released them. No telling which way they would go or how soon they would turn up.

And what had he just told Buster earlier? To get to town and stay there. To tell no one but the men where they were. "It appears we're doing the dirty work for the ruffians, breaking ground for them to follow." Buster. As soon as he got his hands on that boy—

"I'm sorry," Heidi said. "Buster said you didn't want us here, but I couldn't do what you asked." She rushed to the traveling pallet behind Boaz, fell to her knees and burst into tears. "Please, Captain, tell me she's not—"

"She isn't dead," Joseph assured the girl. Why couldn't any of these young ones do as they were asked? What was happening with children these days? "Heidi, you could be placing us in danger. I need you and Gray to return to Jolly Mill. And take a different route, if you don't mind."

"Can't, Captain," Gray said. "I know." He raised his hands as if to ward off a blow. "I know you didn't want me to listen to Buster, but this time I think he's right. Besides, even Mr. Fritz said we needed to come. He's back at our new camp up on the hill making sure nobody follows us. Heidi brought medicines from the wagon and Mrs. Reich found the doctor's friends. Everything's going to be okay."

"Okay?" It was an effort for Joseph to control his temper. "Did your brother not tell you we killed three of the ruffians?"

"Yessir, but—"

"We could be bringing war down on our heads and on the wagon train because Buster couldn't keep his mouth shut and do what he was told."

"No choice," Gray said. "Buster said he saw those men leave the dram shop and head down Capps Creek. They'd've found you for sure."

"Unlike your brother, I left no tracks for them to find." Joseph flung down the lead rope, knowing Boaz would stay where he was. "But now if someone else rides that way they're going to see the blood of three dead slavers. Who do you think they'll blame?"

"Buster?"

"Abolitionists. Most likely, the whole wagon train. Or even strangers traveling through. They'll blame whoever suits their need for bloodlust."

"Buster said he caught a smell of whiskey where they stopped. Don't ya think they'd've caught a whiff and gone looking for the source?" He sniffed toward Victoria. "That's what you're using for medicine, right?"

Joseph gritted his teeth and looked down at Victoria, who was having a quiet conversation with a tearful Heidi.

"Buster's back there cleaning everything up now," Gray said. "Mr. Reich came with us after Buster told us what happened."

Joseph closed his eyes for a moment, relieved despite his anger. Reich. The voice of wisdom. Thank the Lord this would be the final journey for Joseph. Thirty wasn't old, but he suddenly felt as if he'd aged too much, riding back and forth from St. Louis to Kansas Territory these past few years, sometimes twice.

For some reason, Joseph had softened on this trip. He blamed Victoria's influence completely. Something about her had gentled the hardness that had grown within him, and he no longer kept the firm control over those in his charge the way he had before.

"I brought laudanum." Heidi's soft, tentative voice turned him from his musings. "Mrs. Frasier gave me some. She's a nice lady, but she had some scary news. Did you know she and Buck are hiding thirty people who were slaves?"

Joseph knelt beside the litter, partly because his legs gave way. "I was told they had two." He looked into Victoria's heavy-lidded eyes and saw the anguish there. Bad men were closing in, hungry for the kill, and now there was a whole crowd of vulnerable victims instead of just two.

"I was coming for Naaman and Josetta," she said hoarsely.

"Who's going to get the rest of them out of town?" He looked up at Heidi, who hovered at Victoria's other side, blocking the sun.

"That's what Mrs. Frasier wanted to know," Heidi said. "She told Mrs. Reich they've got a good hiding place, but sooner or later, what with all the ruffians scouring the town, they could find the whole bunch."

"Did she say where they're from?" Joseph asked.

"From up near the Missouri River." Heidi poured laudanum from a vial into the corner of Victoria's mouth.

Victoria swallowed and closed her eyes, her face flushed with fever. Joseph stared at the woman he loved and prayed with more intensity than he'd ever put into a prayer that she would heal from the abuse her poor body had taken.

"Some man named Duncan killed their owner," Gray said, interrupting Joseph's silent beseeching. "That means nobody owns them now, doesn't it?"

"That's what it should mean, yes."

"So shouldn't we take them all with us to Kansas Territory so they can be free?" Heidi gave Victoria another dose of laudanum, capped the vial and held up a different one. "This is feverfew."

"I'm glad you brought it." Bless the young woman for her wisdom, despite her willful companions.

Heidi gently touched Victoria's face. "She feels hot to me. I'll give her a little extra dose, okay?"

Joseph nodded his approval.

"Dr. Fenway brought it back to America from England," Heidi said. "It should help with the fever."

Heidi gave Victoria the next dose of medicine, slowly, so as not to choke her. "Gray was fishing with some of the other boys along Capps Creek and heard them talking about Africans. Tell him, Gray." In her excitement, she nearly dropped the vial she'd been using.

Joseph gently took it from her and recapped it, then patted her shoulder. "Well done, Heidi." He turned to Gray. "Tell me."

Gray hesitated, as if afraid Joseph might become angry with him again. "One of the boys was a son of a slaver who's been camping out at the edge of town. He talked a lot. The rest just kind of stayed away from him. I don't think many of the folks around here like the ruffians. They're slavers with a killing streak."

"I don't like them, either," Joseph said. "But since so many travelers stop at Jolly Mill to camp and resupply on their way to Kansas and Indian Territories, that's where the rabble-rousers hang out. They cause trouble for the travelers."

"How're we going to sneak thirty Africans across the border?" Heidi asked.

"Who says we are?" Joseph gently lifted Victoria and settled her more comfortably on the pallet.

"Francine says we have to, Captain," Heidi said. "We can't let the border ruffians find them and force them back into slavery."

Joseph tried not to grimace. If Duncan had anything to say about it, slavery might not be his plan at all. "We don't even have enough wagons with us to carry them." Now he wished he'd been less eager to send McDonald south with so many of their people. If they'd brought more wagons with them, they might have been able to pull this off. As it was, Heidi was right to be concerned.

"There's a cavern across the creek from the town," Gray said. "Several of the other fishermen told me they think the Africans hide there, but people have had accidents and died down there, so most folks keep away."

"You mean they're living in the cave?"

"Well, they sure don't live in town," Heidi said. "But they don't live in the cave, either. At least, not most of them. Buck and Francine had a full-time job keeping them fed at first, but then they made friends in the area and others started helping. The Africans knew how to dig roots and trap their own food."

"One of the boys told me that cavern goes all the way to a settlement called Plymouth," Gray said. "So if they have to escape, they can get out that way."

"That's less than ten miles from here, and from what I've overheard, Duncan's men know about that hiding place." Joseph studied Victoria's pale lids against the redness of her face. This was her mission they were discussing. She couldn't have handled it herself. In her efforts to protect others from danger, she'd volunteered herself for a mission of death.

Or had she? He'd learned long ago that Victoria had the heart of a gentle warrior. Or perhaps a prophet.

"I think we can do something," Gray said.

Joseph looked up at him. The boy had a mind of his own when his brother wasn't busy influencing him— and it was a good mind.

"Well, see, the wagons are all set higher so they could travel over the rough trails we've had since St. Louis, but if we follow the road from here, we won't have such rough trails."

"You're thinking about a refit of the wagons?" Joseph asked.

"We might be able to build carriers on the undersides of the wagons, make them big enough to fit a whole passel of people."

"Where are we going to find weathered wood to match the wagons?" Heidi asked. "Too obvious, and we won't have enough time."

"Well, you got any better ideas?" Gray frowned at her.

"We'll figure something out." Joseph helped Heidi to her feet. "Did anyone say whether or not the border ruffians have threatened the Frasiers?"

"Francine and Buck told me two of the men have been snooping around their house, questioning the Africans who live with them, Josetta and Naaman." Heidi shuddered. "That man with the white braid?"

"You're talking about Thames?" Joseph asked.

Heidi nodded. "He'd been threatening Buck and Francine that some man named Otto Duncan and a posse of his men and dogs are on their way to Jolly Mill to claim his property. What's he talking about?"

Joseph's heart ached for young Heidi, alone in the world, grieving the loss of her whole family, and now forced into this hotbed of murder and danger. She should already be living far out in Kansas Territory, working alongside Victoria, surrounded by the loving people of their wagon train and healing from her tragedies. Instead, she was facing yet more horror. One had to wonder if she would ever completely recover.

"Come here, you two," Joseph held out his arms as the last of his annoyance melted away.

Heidi stepped into his hug and clung to him as if she desperately needed reassurance. Even Gray hesitated for less than a few seconds until he joined them. Joseph gathered Heidi against him and laid an arm of comfort across Gray's shoulders, wishing he could instill strength into them, give them hope in what seemed to be a hopeless situation.

"Duncan seems to think he's going to get away with his evil ways forever," Joseph said. "He thinks he should own those Africans."

"He doesn't own them." Gray pulled away and spat on the ground with some force.

"In the end we know evil doesn't win. That's why we're fighting."

"It's up to us," Heidi said, her voice muffled from his chest.

"No, the results of the fight aren't up to us. Our actions are our only responsibility," Joseph told her. "In the end, Duncan won't get away with what he's doing, but we have to look higher than ourselves and seek God. Our job is to do the right thing now, and God will see to the end, whenever it may be. We might not see it right away."

Heidi lowered her gaze. "I don't think Dr. Fenway believes in God's righteousness."

"She's suffered a great loss, as you have, Heidi. Sometimes when that happens, our faith is tested. But God will hold on to her as she struggles. He is a loving Father who doesn't leave us. He isn't going to die."

"Will He hold on to me?" Heidi asked.

Joseph tightened his grip on her. "He has you surrounded."

"I've seen bad men get away with their evil," Gray said.

"As I said, you haven't seen the end of the story, son. I believe Kansas will be a state soon, and you might well be the state's future." He placed a gentle kiss on the top of Heidi's head. "I think that someday you'll be a doctor working alongside Dr. Fenway, surrounded by patients who depend on you. You'll probably marry and have children and a home of your own."

He patted Gray on the shoulder. "You have a fine mind and the ability to make good judgments and sift through necessary information for the truth. You could be a judge or a senator or even the president."

"Not if we don't get out of this situation," Gray muttered.

"That's the kind of thinking you're going to have to change. Your brother has heroic qualities, but he needs you to anchor him with your common sense. It's going to take courage to stand up to him. We're on this journey for you and for the children of the wagon train. This is for the future of our country."

Joseph gave Heidi a final hug and released her, studying Victoria's face. He knelt and touched her skin and nodded to Heidi. "I know Buster told you that Thames is dead, but that doesn't mean we're clear of his influence. I don't know if Thames was lying about Duncan or not, but we've got to be vigilant. If he comes, he won't be alone, and we must be prepared."

"We've got to get those people out of here and hightail it to Kansas," Gray said. "Hopefully before that Duncan fella gets here."

"But how can our wagon train possibly move all those people out of Missouri?" Heidi asked. "There's no time to refit the wagons.

"The wagon train needs to load up and leave," Joseph said. "Today. They'll attract too much attention if they stay. Tell Fritz and Reich not to wait on us, not to finish setting up camp, but to head out toward Neosho to wait for McDonald."

"No!" Heidi cried. "We can't leave you alone. I need to stay with you and treat Victoria."

"And I need you safely away from here before Duncan and his men show up and start a war with Jolly Mill."

"I don't care about safety, Captain." She touched his arm and gazed up at him with winsome eyes. "I have to stay with Dr. Fenway. Please. I can help."

He sighed. This one was also going to be a handful. "There's something you can do to help. I need you to go through Dr. Fenway's things in your wagon and find a stack of blank sale bills. They're used for livestock and slaves. Leave the papers with Francine and Buck, and have two of them filled out for Naaman and Josetta Brown, but tell them to use different names. They must travel with the wagon train posing as slaves. You stay with Gray and the Reichs."

"Captain—"

"We'll need your help on the wagon train, especially with the doctor unable to manage right now." He reached into Boaz's saddlebag and pulled out Victoria's Colt revolver. "Gray, keep this with you. I know you can shoot."

"Yessir."

"Take care of Heidi."

"I will, sir."

"Whatever else you do, make sure Heidi and the children stay out of danger."

Heidi crossed her arms, her delicate chin jutting out, eyes narrowing.

Joseph bit his tongue to keep from smiling. She appeared to be growing into the image of her mentor and friend, stubbornness and all.

"Miss Ladue," he said quietly, "your help is needed with the wagon train. I was given to believe you had been prepared by Dr. Fenway to care for our people in our doctor's absence. If she's failed to teach you what you need to know—"

"She hasn't failed anything."

"I'm sorry you're being forced to take on a grown woman's role, but the adults on our wagon train know to follow their captain. As your captain, I'm telling you that your best place now is with our people."

Heidi's shoulders began to slump. She stiffened them again for a moment, but then tears filled her eyes. She bent over and picked up the bag she'd brought. "Here. If her fever doesn't go down, she'll need another dose of this feverfew extract, and if she's hurting, more laudanum, but don't let her choke."

"When you get back to town," Gray said, "you'll find Buck and Francine's cabin across the creek, built in against a rock cliff. There's a spring beside the house, and I thought I could hear something like water falling behind the house, like maybe there was a cave opening there, but I couldn't find it, and they weren't too quick to answer questions."

"If you could hear it, then others can, too," Joseph said. "The doctor warned me that Buck and Francine would trust only her. Even after they trusted Mrs. Reich, I can see why they're concerned about strangers, especially after all of today's activities." He slung the medicine bag over his shoulder. "I'll take good care of her, Miss Ladue," he said gently. "She's going to be fine. I have enough alcohol to keep her wound clean, and we'll follow behind you, but don't wait for us. You might ask Mrs. Fritz or Mrs. Reich to purchase more whiskey for the road before the wagons head out. Now, both of you go."

They did as he told them, disappearing into the brush as quietly as they'd arrived. He heard no sound of footsteps once they had time to reach the creek. Maybe they were lighter on their feet than he had feared.

They would need more talents than light feet to keep them out of danger for the next few days. May God have mercy, and blind the eyes of the enemy in time to save them all.

Chapter Fifteen

Victoria lay on the moving pallet with her eyes closed against the sun's glare. She felt so much better than she had…what…an hour ago? Probably the effect of the laudanum. Joseph had stopped once and dribbled some into the side of her mouth between her cheek and her teeth, then worked her throat with his fingers as she swallowed.

She hadn't even opened her eyes. Actually, hadn't been able to because her eyelids felt so heavy. She had, however, felt the light touch of his lips on her forehead and heard his whispered words of prayer and of love.

Echoes of his words to Heidi and Gray remained in her memory, almost as if she had dreamed the conversation. His gentle voice had somehow pierced the darkness where she'd been wandering…his observations about God holding her as she doubted…as if he knew what she'd been thinking, even more than she'd realized.

Was it true? While her faith wavered, was God holding on to her, as He would hold on to Heidi while she struggled with her grief? A more intriguing question—was the Almighty using Joseph's words to reassure her and erase her doubts?

A new determination filled her as she lay there, exercising trust that Joseph would take tender care of her and that Boaz wouldn't take off running through briars or over rocks. Joseph would have called her new determination a reaffirmation of her faith. She wasn't sure what it was, only that she had never doubted God's presence. She'd doubted His kindness, maybe, and His mercy, because she knew from reading through her Bible that nothing happened without His permission. But God was God. His ways were not her ways, and being His child she had to accept that He had control of her future.

She opened her eyes slowly, squinting against the brightness of the sun that shone in the longest day she had ever endured.

Judging by the cooler air, the daylight would be gone within two or three hours, and if she'd truly overheard Joseph telling Heidi and Gray to send the wagon train away, they should be gone.

"Joseph?" Victoria's voice was so hoarse she could barely hear herself.

Immediately, Boaz stopped. She expected to see Joseph rushing to her side, but instead he urged Boaz to move on. The faithful animal rumbled deep in his chest and remained where he was. Victoria smiled. That gelding had excellent hearing. Joseph was probably still half-deaf from the loud report of her rifle in his ear today.

"Joseph," she called more loudly.

He appeared almost immediately, relief filling his dark eyes as he dropped to his knees beside her and pulled the medicine bag from his shoulder. He touched her cheek, his eyes filled with such tenderness that she once again felt her chest swell with love for him. How she relished his every touch, his expression when he held her gaze, the words of love he'd shared so freely.

"My fever's going down." Her voice was still hoarse but getting better. "My eyes aren't burning as they were." In other words, she wasn't delirious with fever or pain, and yet she retained all the sweet caring she'd felt toward him when she was at her worst.

"Are you cold?"

"I feel warm enough. My vision's blurred, though. How much laudanum did you give me?" Maybe that was what caused these tranquil, tender emotions.

"Enough to make you comfortable. I didn't want you hurting." His voice still held only compassion, no sense of urgency or distress. It was as if their time together blocked out all other thought for him.

"Oh, I'm not hurting." She smiled up at him.

He chuckled.

She loved the sound of his amusement, even if it did come from her predicament. Laudanum was better than she'd thought for discomfort of all kinds.

In all the years she'd treated her patients with the medicine, she'd never felt the effects of it. Now she could understand why addictions were so common with this concoction. "I heard you sent the wagon train on."

"They should be out of sight of the village by the time we arrive."

"Out of danger?"

"Nothing's certain so near the border. If they took Naaman and Josetta and filled out the bills of sale, they should make it to Neosho without trouble. We will do all we can to be there by the time the other wagons arrive from Elk River, but if we don't make it, McDonald knows the way."

"We'll be a large target with twenty-five wagons."

"I don't plan to take the main roads. I know some trails that are familiar only to the locals. If we can avoid detection for a few days, we should get past the danger spots and into Indian Territory, then ride far enough west to slip into Kansas Territory undetected."

Victoria attempted to sit up, but she was too dizzy to remain upright. Joseph helped her lie back down, his touch gentle and lingering, as if he couldn't quite bring himself to release her.

"How far are we from the village?" she asked.

"It's just past the trees ahead. Rest a little longer and we'll get you more comfortable."

"I wish I could ride in."

"You can't even sit up."

"I don't want to draw more attention than we already have. Pulling me through town on a litter is bound to cause a stir."

"I'm not taking you through town. Buck and Francine live across the creek, and there's a log bridge south of town for travelers. We'll go that way." He touched her forehead, rested his palm on her cheek, leaned close, as if he might press his lips against her skin. He didn't. She felt a stirring of disappointment.

"You're cooling down," he said. "That medicine works. Now, lie still and I'll get you there without anyone being the wiser."

Joseph found Buck and Francine Frasier's cabin as Gray had described it, complete with a bubbling spring and the sound of splashing water that seemed to come from behind the rocky cliff against which the cabin was built. But the cabin was more like a mansion, with a second story and a porch around the three exposed sides of the house.

Before Joseph could step onto the porch to call to the house, the front door opened and a very familiar fourteen-year-old girl with white-gold hair came rushing out in a fresh, pink-and-white calico dress.

"Please don't be mad, Captain." She skittered to the edge of the porch and touched his arm with charming entreaty. "We couldn't leave with the others knowing Dr. Fenway was still sick and not knowing if she'd heal up, and what with the help you'll need—"

"We?" He nearly groaned aloud. Who else had stayed behind? "Who has your wagon?"

"Mrs. Reich is driving it and dragging Bacon and Pudding along behind." She jumped from the porch and ran past Joseph to the pallet where Victoria lay. "Doctor, I'm so glad you're awake! How are you feeling? Do you need anything? Your skin feels better. Do you need more medicine?"

Victoria chuckled softly and reassured the girl.

The door opened again and two more frighteningly familiar figures edged onto the solid porch flooring, hands in their pockets, heads bowed as if braced for a tongue-lashing. The "we" Heidi had referred to were the Johnston brothers. How could Reich and Fritz have allowed this?

Joseph didn't have a chance to take a breath before the door opened again and two more people stepped out the door. Finally, unfamiliar faces.

The broad-shouldered man had the bulk of an ox, and Joseph could see a woman, with gentle features and bright, curly red hair, peering from behind her husband.

"I take it you're the Frasiers?" Joseph asked.

"Buck and Francine." The young, brown-haired man held out a beefy hand to shake with Joseph. "We've been hearing a lot about y'all from the young 'uns." His grip was firm but not brutal.

"Been so worried about Victoria." Francine stepped

out from behind her husband, her bright curls bouncing from beneath a bonnet that matched Heidi's dress. She appeared to be expecting a child within the next few hours. She rushed down the steps of the porch with a swiftness that belied her size and made her way to Victoria. Buck joined her.

During a tearful reunion between Victoria and her old friends, Joseph sidled over to Buster and Gray. "I'd like to know how you convinced Fritz and Reich to let you stay behind."

"Who said we did?" Buster raised his chin and straightened his shoulders like a banty rooster trying to intimidate a horse. "I'm old enough to make my own decisions."

Gray jabbed his brother in the ribs and gave him a warning look. "Mr. Fritz gave us a good talking to, didn't he, Buster?"

Older brother glared at younger for a few seconds, then shrugged. "Like I told them, we can keep watch, and we can shoot if we have to. What with the doctor all stove up and Mrs. Frasier not moving around too good right now, they need more help."

"The doctor didn't do too badly this afternoon when Thames tried to shoot your head off," Joseph said.

"That was her that shot him?" Buster blinked and looked toward the litter, where Buck had lifted Victoria into his muscular arms and turned to carry her toward the house.

"You two take care of Boaz," Joseph told the brothers. "Then stand guard on the porch, but don't let it look like you're standing guard."

"How're we supposed to do that?" Buster asked.

"I don't know, just sit and whittle and talk like you're visiting relatives. Think you can do that?"

"Never visited relatives."

"We can figure it out," Gray said quickly, nudging Buster with his elbow.

"And make sure no one happens by and overhears us inside," Joseph said. "Watch the top of the cliffs, as well."

He expected an argument from Buster, but he got none. Still, with the brothers' tendencies to forget what they'd been told, he knew he'd be checking on them every few minutes throughout the evening.

Buck and Francine ushered Joseph and Heidi into their expansive log cabin and settled Victoria into a soft bed in a plainly furnished bedroom on the ground floor. They left Heidi to tend to Victoria's injury.

"Y'all've got to be starvin'," Francine said, stepping to a fragrant-smelling kitchen open to the rest of the large front room. "I've cooked us up a roast with potatoes and carrots canned from last year's crop, plus wilted lettuce salad."

Buck stepped around the kitchen and front room closing windows and curtains, lighting lanterns. Joseph glanced out the front door and saw that Boaz had disappeared. Buster sat on the steps, keeping watch with serious focus, his head turning at every sound. Far too stiff and guardlike.

"We keep our animals in a shed built across a break in the cliffs," Buck said. He nodded toward the abundance of food stacked along the kitchen counter. "You folks oughta stay a few days so Victoria can heal up, and we've got plenty to feed you."

Francine lifted a roasting pan from the top of a black cook stove. "We have a lot of friends." She cast Joseph a pointed look.

"The slaves from Missouri River area?"

She nodded. "They have their own gardens back in the hills, and they know how to hunt and forage. When they discovered we'd be startin' a family soon, they took it upon themselves to feed us." She stepped back so Buck could take the heavy pan from her. "They're hidin', what with all the activity around town lately." She sank down onto the chair beside Joseph. "They've heard the stories about that Duncan fella and his dogs coming here to hunt them." Fire shot from her amber eyes when she looked up at him. "Captain, things are gonna be bad here. It's only a matter of time before a slaver catches one of our friends and raises a ruckus."

"If they'll trust me, I believe I can lead them past the danger spots, but we'll need to gather them and prepare them for some hard travel to Kansas Territory."

Francine's eyes widened and her lips parted. "You really mean that, Captain Rickard? Buster said you could move mountains with your faith, but you think you can get all those folks to safety?"

Joseph could not contain his surprise. Buster said that? He glanced out the window toward the steps where the ornery kid perched. "I think we will do all we can and then trust the Lord for the outcome."

Buck placed the large roasting pot on the table and added plates with eating utensils. "Like sassafras tea?"

"Sure do." Joseph got up to help set the table. "Mind if I take some of this food out to the boys? I asked them to keep watch."

"Give them extra helpings," Francine said. "I heard they've had a busy day."

"That they have," Joseph said over his shoulder as he carried the two plates out the front door.

Gray had finished his duties and joined his brother, mimicking Buster's guardlike stiffness. When Joseph delivered the food, the boys thanked him then tucked into it with dirty hands.

"When do you think that Duncan fella's gonna show?" Gray asked.

"We don't know that he will," his brother replied, talking with his mouth full. "You know how rumors spread like wildfire."

"Shouldn't take any chances. Maybe we oughta sleep out here tonight."

"It looks to me as if there's plenty of room inside," Joseph said. "Someone might think it's odd if they see you sleeping on the porch when there's a big, two-story house behind you. You look odd enough already."

"Oh, him?" Buster said, opening his mouth, filled with potatoes, as he pointed a thumb at his brother. "He always looks odd." He cackled and choked on his food.

Gray shook his head and sighed. "We'll be in after you folks make your plans. I just hope your plans don't include hightailing it out of town without us."

"Keep your heads down and your mouths shut around the locals, and I'll see if there'll be room for you to ride with us," Joseph teased.

"Ride?" Gray asked. "There aren't enough horses for thirty-five people to ride."

"That's something else we'll work on." Joseph stepped back inside the house and closed the door behind him, once again admiring the size and beauty of the cabin.

"Nice place, ain't it?" Buck asked.

Joseph nodded. "You have some amazing woodworking skills."

"Not me. That was Naaman's doing. About six of the Africans helped me with the house. They were so grateful to us for keeping them from being discovered and for seeing to their needs when we first found them, they haven't stopped trying to repay us. That food's from them, the woodwork, the upstairs…they built that soon as they saw we were in the family way, saying we should have a lot of children."

"How could they have remained hidden from the townsfolk?" Joseph asked.

Buck grinned and waved his hand. "Most everybody in town's seen Naaman and Josetta, and they think we own them, of course. Not all of them approve, but we don't dare tell them any different. To most folks, black skin is black skin. They don't pay much attention past that. So if Clement and his wife, Miriam, are seen working on the house or helping me with the horses, no one seems to notice the difference between them and Naaman and Josetta. It's like they don't have faces."

Francine beckoned both men to the table. "Joseph, come and keep Buck company while Heidi and I make sure Victoria eats and gets cleaned up. We've already blessed the food."

Buck helped his wife carry a tray for Victoria, then returned to the table across from Joseph and dug into the food. Joseph followed his lead and tasted the best bite of beef that had ever crossed his teeth.

Buck was watching his face, and he gave a huge grin. "Good, isn't it? My wife learned how to cook when we got here, and was I ever glad. I was afraid we'd go broke finding a place to eat out every night, the way we did in St. Louis. Turns out Miss Cora Lou, the pastor's wife, has the only eatin' place in the village, and she was being run over with work when the wagon trains came through. I told Francine maybe it'd be neighborly to help her out, and maybe learn a little about her recipes."

"How'd that work for you?" Joseph asked, relishing the tender roast.

"Like that," Buck said with wide, friendly eyes as he pointed at Joseph's fork. "My woman's a fast learner. Then she decided to teach me. Said we'd have us a passel of kids someday and it was about time I trained for it now."

"You're truly a blessed man. Victoria seems to think it's because you and Francine bless others so well."

"Did she also tell you how she found us?" The smile—which had until now appeared to be a fixture on Buck's broad, friendly face—eased away slowly until his expression was grim. "Francine and I took some cattle to the sale barn one day a few years ago. Cattle were selling well and we were going to have us a good meal before catching the ferry back across the Mississippi."

"You lived in Illinois, as well?"

Buck nodded. "You?"

"I had a ranch there once. What happened to you that day?"

"Big man held a gun on us and tried to rob us of the money from our cattle. I fought and shouldn't have. He shot me in the gut, near killed me, left me unable to protect my wife. Had his big ol' nasty paws on my Francine, was hitting her and manhandling her to the ground when a freedman attacked him and dragged him off Francine. Poor man was shot by Otto Duncan for his troubles."

"Otto Duncan, the blackheart," Joseph muttered.

Buck put his fork down and leaned forward. "You heard Otto Duncan murdered his neighbor last year? The one who owned the folks we've got in hiding?"

"I heard."

"You ever hear why he did it?" Buck's expression had darkened with remembered anger.

"I understand he enjoys killing."

"He hated his neighbor for freeing slaves. That neighbor of his, he'd purchase slaves at the market like the rest of his cohorts, but once his slaves worked for him for seven years, he released 'em. Freed 'em. In fact, most of the folks working for him were freed slaves who chose to stay on for pay so's they could have their own place someday."

"That's why he was murdered?" Joseph thought about his brother in Georgia. What if one of their neighbors took exception to the way Blake handled the plantation slaves, teaching them to read and write, building them a church, making sure they had time with their families?

"That freedman, he probably saved Francine's life when I couldn't," Buck said. "Our attacker got away."

"Where were the police?"

"Where they always are when violence breaks out— somewhere else. Then this tall doctor comes out and tries to save the life of the freedman, but it was too late. So he practically carried Francine and me to his clinic, where his wife was already setting up to treat our wounds. Francine was crushed after what she'd seen, and scared for me, what with the blood and all. Victoria held her and let her cry, treated her wounds, prayed with her and helped comfort the deeper wounds that didn't show with the blood and cuts. They made us stay with them long enough for us both to heal." Buck's calm, deep voice was a soothing balm through the huge room.

"Matthew and Victoria were friends of mine as well, with pretty much the same story," Joseph said. "Are you still running cattle?"

"Nope." Buck picked up his fork again, scraped his

plate clean and pushed away from the table. "I kind of took after Matthew, hung around his place, studied how I might make some of his medicines and surgeries work for my cattle, keep them from sickening so often. So now I'm the town doc for humans and animals alike." He reached into the stove and pulled out a pan of something that smelled spicy-sweet. "Granted, I'm nothing when it comes to Victoria's knowledge, but we get by here. Lots of travelers come through, and they always seem to need medicines for man or beast."

"So that's why Heidi was able to find feverfew and laudanum."

"That's right. We get wagons with supplies through here every so often. Cake?" He held up a bowl and spoon. "My own recipe, spicy black walnut apple cake. Sorry we don't have topping for it. I used the last of our black walnut apple jam to celebrate the coming of our first young'un."

"I'd love some, but if you dish it out I'll take it to the ladies first, then the boys. How did you manage to hide the Africans all the way across Missouri?"

Buck deftly filled bowls with the cake and plopped a spoon into each. "I had some scouting experience in the eastern part of the state. We took pretty much the same route you did, only deeper in the trees."

"On foot? No animals?"

Buck nodded. "That's where we all had to forage and hunt. They arrived with us here in the dead of night and lodged in the cave. Not a lot of folks in these parts go down into the cave because too many folks've had accidents down there. A couple have died. Bad footing."

"How do your friends keep from falling?"

"I grew up near here and knew about another entrance, a sinkhole on the other side of the mountain.

Then when we built this place, we cut into the side of the cliff and made another entry."

"So your friends in the field can come and go without being seen."

"That's right."

"No one else in town knows about the friends?"

Buck shook his head. "The fewer who know a secret, the safer you are with that secret. The problem is, now that Naaman and Josetta left openly with your wagon train this afternoon, it'll be harder to explain any of our friends."

"Unless we take them with us." Joseph gathered the bowls and headed toward the bedroom where he could hear the women laughing and talking.

He knocked softly. "Mind if I interrupt with dessert?"

The door swung open and Heidi's eyes widened when she saw the bowls. "Captain, you realize we'll have to stay here awhile, don't you?" She took the bowls and passed them around, gathered the plates and flatware. "The doctor can't travel like this, and we don't even have a wagon she can ride in now."

"I'll be able to ride by tomorrow," Victoria said.

"No need," Joseph said. "McDonald hasn't had time to gather the others from down south. He has several stops to make."

Victoria closed her eyes and rested her head against her pillow. "I've discovered I don't make a good patient."

Joseph chuckled. "You're just now finding that out? I could have told you what a horrible patient you would make." And how beautiful she was in spite of her illness.

Heidi and Francine giggled. Victoria made a face at him.

"You're independent and you don't like to put others out," he said. "You try to carry the whole world on your shoulders so no one else will have to worry about it." How he loved that in her.

The women stopped giggling. Heidi sighed softly. Victoria's eyes widened.

"So for now," he said, "you need to practice being a good patient so you'll be healed by the time we leave. I'm going to need Buck's help figuring out a way to get their friends to Neosho without being caught."

"You aren't forgetting Duncan, are you?" Victoria asked. "Francine told me he likes to range far and wide with his hunting dogs, and what about the posse Thames mentioned?"

"Duncan comes from north of the Missouri River. That's a long ride. Thames might even have been bluffing. Remember, Silver Tail won't be getting word to anyone about anything now."

"You should plan for Duncan, just in case," Francine said. "You know the kind of man he is. If he's caught word about our friends, you can be sure he'll head this way, even if only for some wicked sport."

"We won't underestimate him," Joseph assured her. "I think he may be underestimating our knowledge of this area, especially Buck's. For the time being, Victoria, you focus on healing. Let Buck and me work on other things."

He gave her a long, reassuring look, and then he turned toward the door as his assurance slipped away. Too much could go wrong. Too many lives were at stake. He desperately sought help from God as he closed the door behind him.

Chapter Sixteen

Three mornings after arriving at the Frasier home, Victoria decided she was ready to travel. Between Francine's abundant trays of food and Heidi and Buck trying different concoctions on her wound to heal the infection in her body, she figured if she didn't ride out of town sometime today they would kill her with kindness.

She dressed the aching wound on her thigh and bound it tightly. Much of the worst pain was gone. Must've been the salve Buck gave her yesterday. He used it on cattle, horses and goats, and the thought of that made her chuckle to herself.

Not only was her wound healing, but the sharp edge of pain in her heart was easing. Yes, she'd killed two men. She had once vowed to never take a human life, even if it meant losing her own. How young and naive she'd been then.

Taking the life of murderers to save the life of a man who was still half boy had been instinctive. With a battle heating up outside the front door of the Frasier home, she faced the fact that she might have to do more shooting, take more lives to protect the innocent. No matter how much she wanted to remain untouched by death, she was already in the middle of it and there was no way out.

Heidi was also steeped in death, and the heaviness of her spirit haunted her face, darkened her smile. Francine's loving grace and Buck's playful kindness had kept the young woman occupied so that the shock of her loss wasn't as obvious. For now. Later she would suffer. Victoria mustn't leave her alone.

Someone knocked on the door lightly. "May I come in?" It was Joseph.

She slid her skirt down and stood to walk to the door. Barely a limp. "I'm up." She opened the door to find him hovering in the doorway holding a mug of coffee. He looked better to her than the coffee or any of the delicious meals or desserts he'd delivered to her these past days.

"It's your favorite." He held the mug out for her. "Fresh cream, skimmed off the top."

"You remembered how I liked it." She thanked him and took the mug, then walked beside him to join the others who were already working around the breakfast table. "I can't remember how long it's been since I've had my coffee this way. At least since before we left St. Louis."

Joseph held a chair out for her and helped her seat herself. "I always loved to see your eyes light up when you were enjoying your coffee."

She looked up at him and sustained his gaze, recalling the mornings he'd met her for breakfast at her brother's house in St. Louis before the day's work began. How different he'd seemed then. Younger, of course, though burdened with responsibility—especially after their arguments began about his need to follow his father's wishes and return to Georgia. These days he carried a greater load on his shoulders with much more confidence and less angst.

"Just wait," Francine said, turning from the stove, "until you taste your coddled eggs and bacon. Heidi cooked the potatoes and onions good and crisp, the way we like 'em here."

"Absolutely." Victoria was aware Joseph's attention was still on her. "Heidi has gained a reputation as an excellent cook."

How good it felt to spend time with Buck and Francine. Their home offered a spirit of healing balm for anyone who stopped through the doors. Perhaps that was why the claw wound was less painful than expected.

Buster and Gray came clomping down the stairs with slow deliberation. Buster picked up a pot to scrub, silent for once. Gray gathered plates to set at the table, as quiet as his brother, gloom heavy in his expression.

"Is everything okay?" Victoria asked.

"Buster heard some news down at the stables this morning," Joseph said.

"Not something that will be fretted over at breakfast," Francine warned.

"That murderer's on his way." Buster scrubbed at an extra tough spot on the cast-iron skillet.

"I see." Victoria took another sip of her coffee and refused to let the news squelch her enjoyment. "I'm sure we'll be prepared by the time he arrives."

"We don't have everything ready yet." Gray slid a plate and fork beside her mug. "Enoch and Bart and Samuel worked all night on their flat bottoms."

Victoria blinked at him, hesitant to ask.

"Boats," Gray explained. "The creeks are high, and even though it'd be a roundabout way to get to Neosho, Shoal Creek will take us where we need to go. Buster and I've been keeping watch while everyone else works on the flat-bottom boats, but the poles aren't ready, and we need good poles because we'll be pushing our way up the creek."

"When did you last speak to the men?" Joseph asked.

"Couple hours ago," Buster said.

"It shouldn't take much time to cut some good poles," Joseph said. "Buck found the horses you released on Tuesday. He got their saddles, bridles and all, and since their owners will no longer have use for them, some of the ladies can double up on them."

Victoria returned to her perusal of the man she admired more than any other and was startled by the sudden direction of her thoughts; he would make an excellent father. Why hadn't she noticed this sooner? His patience with the younger ones impressed her.

"The guy who rode into the stables said there's got to be at least four or five dogs with that killer and his pals," Buster said.

"Did he say how long he thinks it'll take for them to arrive here?" Joseph asked.

"Maybe a few hours. I don't know what he meant by a few." Buster finished the pot, wiped it off and sank onto a chair.

"The horses are ready," Joseph said. "Food's packed, medical supplies aplenty. We have enough weapons and ammunition to fight off a dozen men, maybe more."

"I'd hate shooting dogs," Gray said.

Victoria took a heartening swallow of her coffee. "I don't believe dogs are typically vicious, especially if they're well fed."

"They won't be," Joseph said. "Dogs are usually starved just before a hunt so they'll have an appetite for their kill."

"I can almost hear the hounds now," Buster said.

The front door slammed open and Buck came stomping inside with chunks of wood for the cookstove, buffing the soles of his shoes on the front mat. "Y'all aren't waiting for me to eat, are you?"

"You're worth waiting for," Francine said playfully. "No better time than the present to gather together and say our prayers. These boys are likely to blow steam from their ears if they aren't given something to keep them busy."

"Duncan's coming," Joseph warned Buck.

"Well, then, that does give us reason for prayer." He seated himself at the head of the table as the others took their chairs. He held his hand out to his wife and indicated with a nod that all were to do the same. Victoria grasped Heidi's slender hand with a quick pat of reassurance and then felt the warmth of Joseph's strength as Buck beseeched the Almighty to protect them from Duncan, the killer of slaves and neighbors alike.

Victoria had been in other situations where friends beseeched God for protection. She'd felt this kind of camaraderie and love before with Francine and Buck, but always before, Matthew had been present. She peeked sideways at Joseph and saw him watching her. He gave her a slow nod of encouragement, squeezed her hand and closed his eyes.

By the time Buck was finished, her appetite was back, and she dug into her coddled eggs and bacon, fried potatoes and coffee, French toast with butter and honey. At least they would be filled if they had to leave in a hurry, though as the boys and men continued to murmur and mutter at the west end of the table about their plans for leaving, they also filled and refilled their plates with the abundant food, and Victoria felt empathy for the poor beasts that would be carrying their burdens.

"Francine," she said quietly to her friend, who sat next to Heidi, "have you and Buck considered coming with us?"

"It's all we've talked about." Francine indicated her huge stomach, glanced toward the men and blushed. One didn't speak aloud about such things in proper society, and Victoria knew Francine had been taught proper etiquette in her well-to-do home back East. "The little one's on its way any day," she whispered.

"Yes. I've already seen the signs." That was what Victoria had feared. "I've wondered if, perhaps, it might be sooner than a few days."

Francine patted her arm and chuckled. "Don't fret yourself, my dear. Women have been doing this since Genesis. I figure I'm fit for the task."

Victoria noted that there was no denial in her friend's answer. She watched Francine's movements closely, and she caught Heidi's look of blue-eyed innocence. If word got out that Buck and Francine had been aiding so-called runaways, their lives, and the life of their baby, could be at risk.

Joseph stood watching out the window after a farewell meal at the noon hour with the Africans in the large upper chamber of Buck and Francine's home. The morning had sped by far too quickly. He could feel the tension of impending battle loom over the town. Buster or Gray returned to the house every hour or so with news about the boat building, and he wanted to be there helping. He couldn't. He had to keep watch. Anything could go wrong.

He spotted Victoria on the bench at the side of the

house, her head bowed, her soft hair fluttering in the breeze. How he wanted to be a world away with her, running his hands through that beautiful hair, raining abundant kisses on that delicate face, sharing all the love he'd held inside for her all these years. Instead, they were here in sight of danger.

He settled onto the bench beside her, and he could almost feel her anxiety impact the air that surrounded her. "You know, there are a lot of hunting dogs in Missouri," he said. "What if that person Buster overheard this morning was mistaken? Those dogs they mentioned could have belonged to anyone." He reached out and touched her arm. It felt as he had known it would feel—like silken sunshine.

She took a shaky breath. "Or perhaps to the man at the stables, 'a few' means six hours, or even eight to ten hours, instead of four or five."

He slid his hand down to hers. She grasped it, held on tightly. The warmth flooded him. For her, with her, he could do anything.

"Or Duncan might not be in such a big hurry after all," he said, returning the pressure. "He might have stopped along the way to rest."

"Or to visit." Her hand lost its grip.

He glanced at the suddenly grim shape of her profile, the clenching of her jaws, and he hated the ominous sound of her voice. "What do you mean?"

"Do you remember I told you John Brown believed Otto Duncan was a member of the Knights of the Golden Circle?"

"I remember."

She nodded, eyes closing as her lips pressed together until they were white.

"You think he's rounding up some friends to help him hunt?" Joseph asked.

"If he believes John or one of his sons could be in the vicinity, a killer like Duncan would do anything to stop them, and he'll take all the help he can get." She leaned her head back against a smoothly hewn log. "I've been thinking. How likely is it that no one at all in this town has noticed the other Africans?"

"You're worried for Buck and Francine."

"I wish they'd come with us, but Francine can't travel now." Victoria stood slowly, as if in pain, and released his hand. He felt as if the sky dimmed.

"Is your wound hurting you?"

"It's stiff. I need to be ready to move."

"You need more laudanum." He stood with her.

"No, I need my wits about me." She walked across the porch and back. "The men should have everything ready to go by now."

"Buster knows where I am. He said I'd know when they were ready for us." Francine had been insistent on sharing today's noon meal with all their friends as a farewell, and though many had chafed at the delay, they'd had to agree that they needed a good meal in their stomachs. Buck, the boys, Heidi and several of the African women had done the work while Francine supervised. At Victoria's insistence, Francine remained seated with her feet up.

Before Joseph could comment again on Victoria's concern for her friend's health, he heard a sound that chilled him to his core. It was the baying of hounds.

Victoria sucked in her breath so hard she felt woozy. "Joseph!"

He stepped to her side and took her hand. "Remember what we said? It could be anyone's dogs."

"I think we were wrong."

"Settle yourself. We're almost ready to leave. We need to stick to the plan."

She squeezed his hand until she saw him wince.

"You've got a mighty firm grip for such a gentle woman," he murmured.

"Sorry. I feel as if the earth is moving from beneath us."

He took her arm. "No time to allow the food to settle. We're going. Our people need to get down to the cave now, and Buck and Francine need to hide the entrance."

"I still hate leaving them."

"So do I, but our getting as far away as possible without alerting anyone will be their best protection."

"The dogs can smell their way to a cave entrance if they know what they're hunting," she said.

"Then we'd better hope we can get out the other side before they arrive."

Victoria reached for the door and looked over her shoulder to see three men on horses following four hounds trotting down the main street of town. To her relief, they weren't coming toward the house, but their attention was drawn to the west.

Joseph groaned. "What's Buster doing now?"

The raw-boned young man stood a couple of hundred feet away from them, not far from the outside entry to the cave—the one Buck had said was dangerous. Buster held a large package covered in sackcloth. He tossed it into the air and caught it, kicked a couple of rocks so hard they splashed into the creek below. He appeared not to notice the approaching group and seemed deaf to the loud baying of the hounds.

Victoria thought she heard him chuckle. Loudly. She caught her breath. "He's taunting them. That kid's going to get himself and the rest of us killed."

The dogs picked up speed, followed by the horses and riders.

"They're following him, sure enough," Joseph said.

"Why? What interest would those men have in Buster?"

"He's using something to scatter a scent to draw the dogs. See how he's tossing that sack? Those men no longer have control. The hounds do."

"But they're headed for the cave. Is he crazy?"

"Get inside. I'm sure he has a plan, and Gray must be in on it."

"That doesn't mean it's a good plan."

Joseph held the door and urged her forward.

The house greeted them with a silence so eerie Victoria nearly stepped back, wondering if this was the same building where thirty-five people had completed a meal together less than fifteen minutes ago. Joseph helped her up the stairs to what Francine affectionately called her "ballroom." It was empty.

Someone had taken the time to clear out the food and eating utensils, obviously because they believed the house might be entered by the incoming attackers. The Africans had learned to become shadows over the winter.

"They must have heard the dogs," Victoria said. She walked across the room to peer out the only window, which was curtained heavily. It was high in the wall, built for parties such as the one they'd enjoyed today, with no place for snoops to look inside and see who was there. She could imagine them entering this room on cold nights and settling onto comfortable pallets for the night.

Joseph put a hand on her shoulder. "Let's go. They'll need our help."

She allowed him to lead her out the door and toward the stairs, but she caught a sound that chilled her. A cry. A stifled whimper. Someone was in pain. What kind of trouble...?

"Victoria?" The feminine voice, muffled by the closed door to Francine and Buck's room, held an edge of anxiety.

Victoria looked up at Joseph. "Something's wrong." No. This couldn't be happening. But of course it was. Francine had nearly blurted the truth at breakfast this morning. How long had she been in labor?

Joseph placed an arm across her shoulders. "What is it?"

"I can't leave right now. You go on and do what you have to."

"I'm not leaving you here."

"Francine needs me, and Buck's with the others."

Joseph frowned, then glanced toward the door of the bedroom as comprehension dawned. "Now?"

"You think she has a choice?"

She saw the struggle take place in his expression. They had to go. Lives were at stake, possibly their own, but she couldn't leave Francine yet.

His dark eyes grew black. "Can she be moved?"

"Of course not, but you have to go, Joseph. Save those people. You know I can take care of myself."

He didn't seem to agree. "I'll be back to get you as soon as they're out of danger."

Victoria followed him down the hallway to the stairwell, but he stopped at the second step.

He hesitated and turned back. "You'll be careful?"

"You're the one entering a danger zone, Joseph. I'm doing what I've done for years."

"Buck knows how to take care of her."

"I know, and as soon as he arrives I'll be able to leave, but she obviously needs me now."

He came back up the steps. "Victoria…"

She straightened to her full height. "Yes, Captain?"

Another cry reached them from behind the door where she stood. She started to turn, but Joseph took her gently by the arm and turned her back. "I can't lose you."

She felt his touch hum through her entire being. "Perhaps you should exercise some of that faith you seem to have in such abundant supply."

"You won't know where we'll be."

"How can I miss lanterns in the caverns or twenty-five covered wagons on the trail?"

"We won't be in sight."

"Then watch for me. Perhaps…perhaps my heart will find its way there." She attempted to pull away, but he held onto her arm.

"You are the most stubborn woman—"

"And you're the most bullheaded—"

He pulled her to him until he captured her lips with gentle pressure. His hand slid up to her shoulder and he drew her closer. His other hand caught her against him. He raised his head for but a second. "I've missed this," he said before lowering his head once again.

She had, too. As the tingle of warmth spread through her, she realized how much she'd missed this.

The kiss was timeless as they held each other, but there was no time for them. Not now. Too many lives depended on them.

He pulled away with patent reluctance. "Do you remember what you told me when you were delirious with fever?"

"I'm supposed to remember what I did when I was

out of my mind?" She reached up to draw his head down for one more kiss.

He evaded her grasp. "You promised."

"Don't hold me to it."

"You seemed to think it was important enough to recall."

She walked to a window to look for Buster up on the cliff. But he was gone. She had no doubt he'd disappeared down into that dangerous cave, because the dogs and men were gone and the horses were tethered to nearby trees.

"Would you be so gracious as to give me a hint?" she asked, suppressing a smile as she turned back to Joseph.

His shoulders slumped. "Only someone in love would remember such a statement."

She bit her tongue. How could she be such a heartless tease at a time like this? And yet the tension was so thick she could cut it apart with her scalpel. "And someone with a gracious heart would understand delirium. That was a very difficult day, and I couldn't tell whether I was thinking aloud or to myself. Whatever it was, I know how grateful I was for you."

Joseph took her hand, raised it to his lips and kissed it. "You told me you loved me."

Buck and Francine's bedroom door opened, and Heidi Ladue stuck her head out. Her glance immediately went to Victoria's raised hand. "Um, excuse me, Doctor. Mrs. Frasier's...well, Buck went down with the others into the cave, and I never done this before." Another low moan reached them through the door.

"Tell her I'm coming." As Heidi vanished behind the door, blushing furiously, Victoria withdrew her hand from Joseph's and touched his cheek, loving the feel of the soft beard against her fingertips and for some reason recalling Heidi's comparison of love to mashed goose liver. Whoever had told her that was wrong. This was so much more substantial than goose liver. "Don't worry. I'll be sure to recall what I said when the time is right."

Chapter Seventeen

Victoria's gentle voice followed Joseph down the stairs and into the back parlor. He couldn't bear to leave her unprotected in the house, but he knew where the hunters had gone. Time to take care of them. Later they could prepare for others who might be coming.

He slid aside a beautifully carved wooden chest that sat against the back wall. Had he not known, he would have never guessed the wood plank floor rested against a trapdoor. He pushed inward at the corner and the wall gave way just enough for him to get a grip on the edge of the floor and pull upward.

Only then did he pause long enough to light one of his torches. He lowered himself down the solid ladder Buck had built and landed in a second springhouse, where sides of venison and beef hung from the ceiling. Barrels of brine held fish, fermented cabbage and cucumber pickles, and dried fruits lined the shelving. This was the room where the Frasiers kept stores for their friends, so visitors wouldn't wonder why a married couple with no children would need so much food.

The shelves holding the dried fruit were nailed to a backboard that slid to the left, and Joseph stepped through to the other side where he caught the immediate scent of smoking lantern oil. It smelled new and thick, as he would expect it to smell with more than thirty people finding their way around columns and formations along uneven walkways and crawl spaces.

Deep inside the cavern, the scent grew stronger, and he held his torch high. There were no footprints, as this part of the cavern was pure rock. He followed the scent of lantern smoke across the width of the cavern and downhill on the other side. Several lights moved upward ahead of him through the darkness like stars floating toward the sky; the floor of the cavern extended into a gentle grade after he reached the lowest part of the cavern floor. Buster and Gray had, of course, spent a great deal of time down here when they didn't have chores, especially after the building of the flat-bottom boats had ended for the day. Joseph always seemed to have too many other things on his mind to pay much attention to their activities. He still did.

Victoria. The imprint of her hand had burned itself so truly into his flesh that he'd begun to wonder if his beard had been scorched. He grinned at the thought and reached up to feel his face. No scorching, no blisters. He couldn't get her out of his thoughts. But that was nothing new to him. She'd been burned into his heart since he'd first met her eleven years ago. He had to keep her safe for her sake, but also for his, because if anything happened to her now he would be destroyed, as well.

The echo of a baying hound arrested his attention. He stopped to listen along the length of the cavern. More hounds joined the first until the echoes became disorienting. He knew Gray had planned to go with the Africans toward the hidden entrance at the far western part of the cavern about two miles away in the direction where the lights floated upward.

If Buster led Duncan and his dogs a different way, the Africans would be safe, but what about Buster? Had he even given thought to his own safety? And what was in that sack he carried? Was it powerful enough to continue luring the dogs from the prey they'd been trained to hunt?

The sound of more than two-dozen whispers echoed against the stalagmites and stalactites, mingling with the splash of a waterfall nearby. The baying grew louder, and Joseph passed the intersection where the shorter arms of the cave crossed the system of caverns that was said to reach Plymouth. What did Buster plan to do, lead his pursuers all the way to Plymouth?

Otto Duncan and his men were vastly outnumbered. Either the hunter had more people coming behind him, or he was simply a madman.

Who but a mad killer would force his slaves out onto the land they worked and then force them to run from his dogs and his weapon? A madman. What those poor people must have suffered, knowing death could claim them at any moment. But not today.

The whispers grew louder when Joseph reached the top of a slippery wet slope. He found Gray and their thirty friends waiting for him, four men and Gray aiming pistols and rifles on him.

Joseph smiled. "You're prepared."

Gray heaved a sigh of relief as he and the others lowered their weapons.

"What's Buster up to?" Joseph asked.

"He has a deer hindquarter that he left out in the sun yesterday and today. Where's the doc?"

"Bringing a child into the world."

Gray's face seemed to pale in the low light. "What? How?"

Joseph hid his amusement. "I don't think that's our problem right now. We have people to protect."

"Heidi insisted on going to tell you and Victoria where we were. She said she'd be right back."

"Change of plans," Joseph said. "Believe me, it's necessary."

"But we've gotta get out of here, and we can't leave Victoria and Heidi."

"We can't leave little baby Frasier, either."

Gray's widening eyes pressed his brows farther up on his forehead.

"Think past your nose, son," Joseph growled. "Our situation isn't the only one brewing right now, and if we're careful, we can make sure this new development could impact the future of everyone we care for."

"You mean—"

"Victoria knows where we are but she can't leave her patient alone, and neither can Heidi. Where is Buck now?"

Gray recovered with admirable alacrity. His face flushed with excitement. "He was guarding the boats. Now he's circled around to the open cave mouth to see if more hooligans are riding into town. But, Captain, we have to get the doc and Heidi out of the house before others come."

"Then I suggest *you* be the one to go back to the house and tell Dr. Fenway she has to come with us."

"What if Buck sees more men coming?" There was a definite whine in Gray's voice now.

"Then he'll need help. We'll get the doctor and Heidi to safety, but I'd like to get the Frasiers out, too, if it's possible. You need to learn patience."

"I've lived with Buster for sixteen years. You think I don't have patience?"

"I think you haven't even begun to learn the meaning of the word, but you're about to start."

Gray let out a long expulsion of air that put to the test most men's deep store of patience. Joseph, however, grinned in the darkness. "Aren't you concerned about saving lives?"

Gray looked down and scuffed the toe of his boot against the cave floor. "Yessir."

"Don't you think it's important to save all the lives we can?"

"Well, yeah, but the Frasiers have that house and all those furnishings. Why would they want to leave?"

"You left your father's home and all the cattle and horses and furnishings. Are you sorry you left?"

Gray looked up and met Joseph's gaze. "Sometimes. Would you want to take off into the unknown with Buster?"

"I think as soon as our doctor makes sure her patients are safely in Buck's hands, she and Heidi will be right along. The Frasiers will have to decide for themselves if they can come or not."

The baying of the hounds started up again, silencing everyone. Buster was swift footed, but he would likely slow his steps enough to give the animals a good whiff of the venison so they would keep following him.

When the baying reached the intersection, Joseph motioned for the others to duck behind stalagmites. Everyone moved silently, most with bare feet. No one spoke. When Buster's noisy footsteps reached the intersection, their dark faces were bracketed by lantern light and outlined with fear, but a ridge blocked them all from sight.

Joseph didn't realize he was clenching his jaw until the dogs and their masters passed the intersection and continued to follow their original quarry. So far, everyone appeared safe except Buster, but the kid would need help, and soon.

Victoria gritted her teeth at the sound of Francine's shallow breathing. She was in extreme and constant pain. Something was terribly wrong.

A door opened and slammed shut downstairs. Heidi gasped, her face paling in the bright light coming in from the window. One set of footsteps echoed through the house.

"Those are Buck's footsteps," Francine said, her voice roughened by tension and pain.

Victoria nodded to Heidi. "You should go down and let him know he's about to become a father, and be ready to skitter out of the way if he swoons." She looked at Francine. "I can't believe you didn't even tell your husband you were in labor."

Francine had another pain as Heidi slipped out the bedroom door. Victoria held her beloved friend's hands as the grip nearly took her fingers off. The amount of pain frightened her. Even more so when the pain ended and Francine lost consciousness. Victoria took the opportunity to check the baby's progress, and she went weak.

The baby had turned, and now a tiny foot jutted from the birth canal. One foot only. This was always dangerous.

Heavy footsteps came clomping up the stairway, followed by Heidi's light, birdlike stride. There was a firm knock on the door.

Victoria was covering Francine with a sheet when she awakened from her faint and moaned again.

Another knock hit the door. "Francine? Dr. Fenway?"

"We're here, Buck," Victoria said. "We're making way for your new baby to arrive." She tried to instill cheer in her voice.

The door opened and Buck strode in. His mouth dropped open when he saw Francine. He went to his wife's other side and took her hand, turning pale at the sight of Francine's agony. "What's wrong here, Victoria?"

"It's a breach. I'll need to stay and help. Heidi, would you please go through my bag and find the laudanum Buck gave me? Bring it as quickly as you can." She listened until Heidi's footsteps skittered away. "Buck, you're the town doctor. I know this would shock polite society, but you should be in here with us for the birthing."

"I'm not leaving."

Victoria stepped over to the washstand and scrubbed her hands while Buck murmured comforting words into his wife's ear and dried her tears, mopping her forehead with a cloth. He kissed her cheek.

There was no missing the relief that spread through Francine seconds before her next contraction.

Heidi came running in with the laudanum and stopped at the threshold as if she'd rammed into the door, her eyes widening with distress, face reddening with obvious embarrassment.

"Heidi," Victoria said quietly, "if you wish to become a doctor—"

"I do."

Victoria smiled. "Then you should expect to find

yourself in some very personal situations. You will need to separate yourself from the fancy rules of the social set and learn about caring for patients, with all the living blood and pain and beauty. In this room we have two patients who need us."

Heidi closed the door behind her and crossed to the other side of the bed, obviously unable to look at Buck.

"Please give Mrs. Frasier a good dose of laudanum, Heidi. Is the birthing tea brewing?"

"Yes, ma'am. It's steeped and ready."

"Then place a cool, wet cloth over her forehead."

Buck cleared his throat. "Honey," he said softly to his wife, "when did you start having pains?"

"Last…night," she said between breaths.

"Why didn't you tell me then?"

"I knew it'd be a while." Francine's voice was weak. "Victoria once told me that first births often take longer." She grimaced and squeezed her eyes shut. "That's proved true with cows, so I figured I'd be the same."

"Yes, but you didn't need to endure the pain in silence," Victoria told her. "I could have given you some tea to help you feel better. You've been in labor for more than fourteen hours, and you've been suffering without support."

"But it hasn't been too bad until now."

"That's because your body's trying to give birth and the baby isn't cooperating."

Francine laid her head back into the pillow and closed her eyes. Tears dripped down the sides of her face and into the cloth beneath her. When she reached up to wipe them away, her hand was shaking. "Please don't tell me my baby's going to die. We've waited so long to have this little one."

"I just know it's a good thing I was still here. Buck

has big hands. Mine are slender." Victoria nodded to Heidi. "We'll be turning the baby. Buck, you know what I'm talking about."

"I've done it on cows, but I couldn't bear to hurt Francine."

"No, but you'll need to watch and learn, because hurting them now will be a lot better than the pain they'll endure if you don't do this. Besides," she said, indicating Francine's glazing eyes as the laudanum took hold, "I don't think this will be quite as traumatic as it would have been."

"My hands are smaller than yours, Dr. Fenway," Heidi said. "Maybe I should do it."

"Someday I'll teach you, but not on Francine. Not today. You need to help her cope when it hurts."

"I'll do that," Buck said.

"I'll bring the tea if you wish," Heidi said.

"Please, but make it quick."

As Heidi rose and went to the door, Francine caught Victoria's hands in her own. "I know you can do this."

"Yes, my friend, I can. And your baby has been active and kicking, so there's no reason to worry. It's just going to hurt more than usual. I'm so glad we had laudanum on hand."

Heidi came back into the room holding the cup of tea she'd prepared. She sniffed it and wrinkled her nose. "What is this stuff?"

"Some herbs I've gathered and experimented with in the past. It has willow bark, which tends to make the blood too thin with something like this, so I use crushed kale that slows the blood loss, and valerian root, which calms. Some nice sugar makes it go down easily enough. Help her sip it, please."

With Heidi on one side of Francine, helping her sip

the brew, and Buck on the other side, not looking the least bit embarrassed by his presence in a place where women ruled, Francine had another pain.

"I'm praying for you, my friend," Victoria said, surprising herself. And yet it was the truth. In her heart she was entreating the Lord to cover this family with peace and healing, that He would protect their friends in the cave and that she would be able to do what needed to be done.

She couldn't have told when she'd begun speaking to the Lord again or why it had taken her so long to do so. She also couldn't have predicted the peace that suddenly flowed over her with the reconnection she felt. She'd lost her dearest friend only to find Him again.

"What I'm going to do is reach for that little one and find out what position I need to change so the birthing will go smoothly." Victoria glanced at Heidi's flushed cheeks, at Buck's grim demeanor as he held his wife's arm and kissed her hand. "I believe I'll need to pull one little leg around so the baby can slide out without any problem. We can do this."

The tea had begun to mingle with the laudanum, and Francine broke into a wobbly smile. "I know. And I thank you for it. Okay, Doctor," she said, grabbing Buck's hands with both of hers. "Do what you do best."

Joseph carried his rifle down toward the main cavern, though he knew better than to fire a weapon in a cave. He held his torch low behind him to keep the light from reflecting against the white cave walls ahead. The men were at least thirty feet ahead of him, and their attention was all on the dogs and what they followed. In another situation it would've been comical, but this was a tense afternoon and the darkness seemed to hover around him like impending death.

When he arrived at the center of the intersection, the baying of the dogs grew silent for less than a second, but it was long enough for him to hear the moaning of a woman in the distance. Francine. He hesitated where he stood. A man with wooly white hair turned around.

"Hey, you there. What're you doing here?" He raised his rifle.

The dogs hushed again, and once more Francine's cry reached the cave. Joseph pretended not to hear her. How could her voice carry through a rock wall?

Joseph locked stares with Wooly. "In case you hadn't noticed, I'm not game."

"Ain't sure about that."

"Your dogs seem to be. You want to lower that thing? Anybody with a lick of sense knows it isn't safe to hunt in a cave."

The man didn't budge. "What's your business here?"

"I belong here. Friends with the townsfolk." He tried to ignore the rifle aimed at him as he remembered Buck telling him about a small vent he had opened between their bedroom's back wall and the cave against which the home was built. Their room was always cool in the summertime and never froze in the winter. It was why Francine's voice was carrying so well. He wondered how long before he heard a baby squall.

The hungry-looking dogs took up their baying once more and rushed after Buster, but the men turned their attention to Joseph. The other two raised their rifles.

"I'm trying to tell you it isn't a good idea to go hunting in a cave."

"I noticed you're armed," Wooly said.

"Did you also notice I'm not aiming? I might ask

what your business is here, since I'm the one with the local friends, and it's obvious you're from out of town."

"This is where the dogs led us," said the man on Wooly's right. "Think they caught a whiff of you? Or maybe you got others down here."

Judging by the lantern light, Joseph thought he had a good shot at all three of the men, but he wouldn't risk it with Buster on the other side of them. He, however, had a wall of white cave rock behind him, and he braced himself to fall to the floor if they took aim.

The dogs stopped baying, and growling commenced. Joseph chuckled. "I think your animals have found their prey. I take it they like venison?"

The tallest of the men raised his lantern and saw what the dogs had, then turned his rifle on Joseph. "We followed some of my runaway slaves down here. Heard they was hiding out in this cave."

"I don't know who'd tell you anything like that," Joseph said. But he wished he knew. He needed to get word back to Buck and Francine that not all of their neighbors had overlooked new faces. Not everyone passing through Jolly Mill was jolly. Not everyone they knew believed in their cause.

The tall man kept his aim on Joseph and walked toward him. "You'd be surprised who might tell me things."

"You know, I believe I must have been wrong. I think I do know who you are, after all. Are you that fella, Otto Duncan, who uses his dogs to hunt his slaves for sport? I can guarantee you won't find any sport in Jolly Mill today."

"Why's that?"

"Because there are no slaves here."

The man took three long-legged strides closer, his

face scrunched into lines shot with long-held rancor. "We know what a slave looks like."

Joseph's hand tightened on his rifle stock. He leaned down with slow caution to place his torch on the ground. "How can you?" With the same wary movements, he straightened again. "Most folks don't even look them in the face long enough to tell one person from another. Are you telling me you brought proof of ownership?"

Duncan cocked his rifle. "All I need's the law behind me."

"Whose law? You have a hill of sale?"

Duncan took aim and Joseph prepared to drop to the ground. He thought he could detect a gleam of insanity in the man's eyes this deep into the darkness. In fact, darkness was where he belonged.

Duncan squeezed the trigger and shot. Joseph dropped to the ground as he heard the bullet whiz over his head and ricochet from the wall behind him, echoing through the cavern with a deafening roar. The man cocked the rifle again, took aim and Joseph rolled behind a boulder. Another shot ricocheted, then another.

Someone bellowed and hit the ground with a crash of a lantern. The cavern grew darker as one torch went cold.

Joseph peered out from around the boulder and saw that Duncan's bullet had caught one of his cohorts, a neck shot.

A low whimper marked the man's death as he slumped over, his rifle sliding across the uneven stone floor. Joseph tried to see past the circle of light created by his torch and the two remaining lanterns, but he couldn't catch a glimpse of Buster.

Wooly dropped to his knees beside the dead man. "Everett?" He shook the body. "Everett?" He straightened and glared up at Duncan. "You shot my brother, you murdering—"

"I wasn't even aiming at him!"

Everett's brother didn't believe Otto Duncan. He raised his rifle and shot the slave hunter in the heart at point-blank range. Another lantern crashed to the ground and light swarmed through the cavern as the oil spread over the floor.

Racing footsteps echoed from the cavern walls and Buster emerged from the darkness where the dogs feasted and fought over their venison. He grabbed the rifle from Everett's brother.

Wooly shouted in protest.

"Sorry, fella," Buster said, "but I need this." He scampered out of the way when the man grabbed for him.

Joseph raised his rifle. "I wouldn't try it. Haven't you lost enough today?"

Wooly looked up at Joseph, and it was obvious in his drooping eyes and lined forehead that the fight had gone out of him. He returned to his brother and sank onto a slab of rock, burying his face in his hands.

"Don't worry," Buster said over his shoulder to the man. "Your dogs can lead you out the same way they led you down here."

"Not so fast," Joseph said. "Maybe not. Are there more of your Golden Circle friends coming?" he asked the grieving man.

Wooly looked up at him. "We know who you are, Rickard, and we know the people who live here. This town's doomed."

"I think that answers my question." Joseph joined Buster as he gathered the other rifles. "How far have you followed this cavern, son?"

"Miles up the way." Buster wrapped his arm around the rifles. "Couldn't help myself."

"Any other openings?"

"Sure are."

The snarling hounds fought over their venison as Joseph studied the wild-haired man. "Think you could escort this man out closer to Plymouth?"

Buster selected a rifle from those he held and gave the others to Joseph. "Be glad to. What about the Frasiers?"

"One thing's certain. They can't stay here."

With as much gentleness as she could muster, Victoria helped the strapping little boy into the world while Heidi cut the cord under the watchful eyes of his father. The baby had strong lungs and looked pink and perfect.

Buck and Francine were bonding as a new family when Victoria thought she heard movement downstairs. She reached for the pistol in her pocket and warned the family to hush as much as was possible with a new infant. She gestured for Heidi to remain where she was and then stepped out into the hallway.

The man who came up the stairs had skin blacker than a cloudy midnight, with broad shoulders and muscles that rippled with health.

"Isaac, what are you doing here? It isn't safe for you. Is all well down in the cavern?"

"Yes'm. Two of the killers are dead. Kinda shot each other."

So those had been rifle shots she heard. "Is anyone else hurt?"

"No, all's good so far." He glanced toward the door behind her. "The baby?"

"He's strong and has good lungs."

A white grin brought out the handsome features of Isaac's face. "We gotta leave with them, Capt'n says. I come to help them with their furnishings and animals. I'll be goin' as their slave, along with some others."

"I don't think that'll go over too well with Francine or Buck."

"No'm, but if somebody's gonna pose as my master, I'd like it to be them."

"Of course, but why do they have to leave? Have you heard of more trouble?"

"Yes'm. Gotta get the family away. Trouble is coming to Jolly Mill. Heard it from one of Duncan's posse. We can't let our friends get hurt."

"Did he say who betrayed them?"

Isaac shook his head. "Ain't no telling. That young Johnston boy, he already rounded up the animals and they have the wagon and buggy at the other side of the mountain. We can build our friends furniture when we reach Kansas."

Another friend, Washington, joined Isaac and announced that others were on their way to help carry food and as many items as they could through the cavern. They had built an extra boat, and with the Frasiers' seven horses, they would have transportation.

Victoria prayed they could all escape this place in time so that promise would be realized.

Chapter Eighteen

Joseph climbed into the basement of the Frasier home to the sound of footsteps thumping across the wood floor above him. He frowned and took the stairs to the ground floor and found people. Everywhere. Most of them were dark skinned, but he caught sight of Audy Reich in the kitchen, packing foodstuffs.

With a grin, Joseph realized that Gray had carried out his hasty orders—the Frasiers must travel with them now that danger had arrived. But Mrs. Reich?

As if she'd heard his thoughts, the lady turned and gave him a sweet smile. "Captain, don't even ask me why, because I don't know for sure, but you know how the Lord works sometimes. I told the mister I just had to get back here and make sure everything was okay. So he brought me."

"You've seen the baby?"

"That's the first place I went, and do you know I wasn't the least bit surprised it was a boy and that he was here already? A woman doesn't have a brood of young'uns without learning a thing or two. The Frasiers' little'un's gonna get to know Auntie Audy mighty well on this trip."

"I appreciate your help, but it was dangerous for the two of you to travel that section of road."

"Not to worry, Captain. Deacon and Ellen Fritz traveled with us, and we both know Ellen could outshoot me if we were to enter a contest—not that I would do something so unladylike, of course, though I can't speak for Ellen. And that Ellen's as strong as a man, and well nigh as tall, not to mention her hands are—"

"I'm right here, Audy, I can hear you," came a querulous voice from behind the stairwell, where Mrs. Fritz was packing jars of food into a wooden box.

Mrs. Reich gave an ornery chuckle. "Captain, you'll want to see the baby, of course, but I'm sure you're looking for your…for our Victoria." An impetuous grin traveled across the intrepid lady's tanned face. "She's safe, watching the road from the front porch." She nodded to her left.

"Thank you, Mrs. Reich."

He could hear her humming softly to herself as he crossed to the front door. He opened it to find Victoria seated on the same carved bench she'd occupied earlier, watching over the town, eyes narrowed, arms crossed, shoulders straight as she held herself erect. Waiting for a battle, no doubt, or to raise the warning cry in case other men with evil intent should ride in with more dogs trained to hunt slaves. Joseph could easily see her as a warrior princess; she had a passion for righteousness. She also had beauty.

"Is everything packed, Audy?" she asked over her shoulder.

"Not yet."

She turned to him, eyes filled with relief. "No more trouble with that man?"

Joseph wanted to reassure her that all was fine, but

something about Wooly's silence as he'd walked away with Buster had suggested a dark and simmering hatred.

"Joseph?"

He grimaced. "We'll see. His last name is Phillips. He never told me his first name. I told Buster to walk him to one of the cavern entrances east of here and warned him that if he returned to harm anyone he would be shot."

"We need to leave as soon as the Frasiers can get their things together. I tried to help but Andy wouldn't allow it. Have you seen the baby?"

"I needed to see you." Joseph stepped up behind her and rested his hand on her shoulder. "Word has spread that you saved mother and child."

She looked up at him, her eyes so blue as they reflected the sky that he could easily lose himself in them. "We can't know what would have happened, but Buck and Heidi were excellent under pressure. Matthew Joseph is blessed with good parents, and we hope he will have many more brothers and sisters."

Joseph's hand tightened on her shoulder. "Matthew Joseph." He smiled and suddenly wanted to meet this newborn baby.

"I wish you'd come earlier. I had to resort to threats to convince Buck and Francine to leave their home for the safety of their baby and future family."

He sank down beside her on the bench. "Their lives could be in danger."

"That's what convinced Buck. He has to protect his family. Isaac said he's traveling with them as their slave, but do you think it's safe for anyone to travel on the open road right now?" She made a wide gesture with her arms.

Joseph took advantage of her flair for the dramatic

to collect her hand and grasp it in his. "No, I don't," he said. "I think we all need to travel through the backwoods, along the rivers as far as we can."

She turned to stare at him as if he'd just swallowed a toad. "All the way there?"

He squeezed her hand. He wanted her safe, no matter what it took. "All the way. If we travel openly, we may or may not be attacked by the slavers, but we could also be attacked by the abolitionists. Both are guarding the borders and both sides can be dangerous."

She squeezed his hand and pressed her forehead against his shoulder. "Will this nightmare never end?"

He kissed her hand and released it, then placed his arm around her. She eased into the embrace as if she knew she had always belonged there, and she did. How empty his arms had felt for so long. How tempting to make up for lost time by kissing her right here on the front porch in sight of the whole town.

But he heard a quiet movement at the window behind them and sensed someone looking out at them. He was pretty sure he heard a feminine chuckle.

"I managed to get Phillips to admit that more of the Golden Circle thugs were on their way here," he said. "Buck and Francine are apparently well-known in that group, proving it's impossible for two white people to travel through Missouri with a large group of Africans without word spreading."

"Then why did it take so long for them to be found after they settled?"

"Because most of their neighbors are honorable people who wouldn't betray them."

"But so much traffic passes through here," she said. "With the atmosphere in this state, how can anyone feel safe?"

The door opened behind them. "The last thing I want to do is tear you two apart." Mrs. Reich's voice no longer held her characteristic humor. "We've packed as much as can be carried."

Joseph rose and helped Victoria to her feet. He gazed at the house Buck and Francine had built with their own hands. "This would be a difficult place to leave."

"What bothers me the most is who might decide they have a right to this place and just move in," Victoria said.

"Gray suggested emptying it and burning it down to keep that from happening," Mrs. Reich told them as she turned to go back inside. "But I think too much love went into building it to burn it down. I think it can withstand whatever happens here."

Joseph led the way through the front door and picked up Victoria's bag.

"I can carry that," she said.

"Don't forget you're still weak from your injury. Don't overdo it."

She narrowed her eyes at him. "Going to start bossing me again?"

"Protecting, my love." The word slipped out, spoken by the heart. He watched Victoria as her eyes widened, and he braced himself for rejection if he'd gone too far.

Perhaps it was merely power of suggestion, but Victoria's legs did feel somewhat weak all of a sudden as Joseph's endearment flowed through her like the warm nectar of honeysuckle. She wanted to step up to him and allow him to wrap her in his arms and kiss her until she couldn't breathe and murmur those words of love again.

"Joseph?" came Buck's voice from the back parlor

doorway. "Everyone's in the cave except the three of us and Buster."

"And where would he be right now?" Joseph asked.

"Right here, Captain," Buster called from the parlor. "Saw Phillips out of the cave. The dogs caught up with us and followed him out. I'm waiting for y'all to hightail it out, then I'll cover the floor so's no one can ever find this opening. And even if they do, they won't know about the one below."

He closed the trapdoor over them as they stepped into the moist cave.

"He's going to join us on the other side of the mountain, I suppose?" Victoria asked.

"That's his plan."

Buck turned to Joseph and Victoria. "I'm going to rush ahead and see about Francine and little Matthew. The women were taking care of her, and the men are using the litter I built you to carry her, but I just want to be sure."

"I wouldn't expect anything else." Joseph clapped him on the shoulder. "Matthew, is it?"

Buck turned back and held his new friend's gaze in the lantern light. "Matthew Joseph Frasier. I figure with those names, the boy can't lose." He turned away, whistling into the darkness, a man too happy about his newborn son to grieve the loss of his home.

Joseph chuckled and Victoria sighed with satisfaction. That was as it should be.

As the two of them walked alone through the darkness with only Joseph's lantern to light their way, Victoria felt many things fall into place. She loved being reunited with the Frasiers and was thrilled that they would be a part of her new life. She also felt her resentment against the two young Johnston scoundrels drift away. Buster might be impulsive and often arrogant, but he wasn't mean hearted.

"I love this place," she said.

"The cave system?"

She looked around. "Well, it's pretty nice, too. A little dark. I was talking about Jolly Mill. I can only pray the ruffians won't destroy it."

"You're right, we can only pray. I think you'll like our village in Kansas. It's in a hidden valley surrounded by fertile fields. You'll have a lot of patients to care for, but you'll have Heidi to help you, and Buck can learn more from you."

She smiled. "And you?"

"Hmm? What about me?" His tone was all innocence.

There was a skittering of rocks up ahead, which must mean they were drawing closer to the others.

"What's your life going to be like now?" she asked.

"No more wagon trains for me. The town will be a nice size once we arrive with this last group."

"You're a natural leader, though. Are you not even planning to take more wagon trains West?"

He walked beside her in silence for a moment, holding the lantern high as the sound of movement drew nearer. "If I did, would you go with me?"

"You said yourself that I'll have plenty of patients in Kansas."

"If you're staying, I'm staying."

Her steps faltered, and immediately Joseph slowed with her, bracing her arm with his hand.

"You need to rest."

"Later. Joseph, what did you mean about staying?"

He stopped and turned her to face him. "From now

on, I'm going to be wherever you are. If you decide to leave Kansas and return to St. Louis—"

"I'm not going to do that."

"If you do, I'm going with you."

She felt a jolt of hope, followed by the same hesitation she'd experienced several times with him on this trip. "You left me before, Joseph."

He raised his hand and cupped her cheek, gently, as if she might shatter. "When I was twenty, I had certain priorities. One of them was to honor my father."

"I seem to recall that you once promised to always love me."

"I kept that promise. I always loved you. And now my first priority is to not leave you unless you tell me to."

She couldn't break her gaze from his dark eyes and the assurance she saw in them. She watched until his face drew so close to hers that she closed her eyes. She was unprepared for the gentle force of his kiss, or the sense of vertigo, as if the two of them spun on the earth alone, with no one else but them.

The sound of footsteps brought her back to reality. She pulled away, still disoriented by the dark surroundings. Again, she stumbled.

"I'm sorry," he said. "You really do need to rest. You haven't recovered from your illness, or from the wound."

"I'll rest when we reach where we're going." She turned and continued along the path that had been carved into the cavern floor by countless footsteps, but her weakness betrayed her. The serenity she'd felt after delivering little Matthew dissipated as they walked through the darkness in silence. Her thigh ached, and she realized Joseph was right. She wasn't as strong as she wanted to think. That was true in many areas of her life.

"I think I should apologize about some of my comments in the past few weeks," she said.

"About?"

"Against our Maker. How dare I protest God's judgment?"

"Doesn't a child sometimes complain about his parents' judgments?"

Once again, something skittered quietly in the darkness, and this time it was behind them. Victoria peered over Joseph's shoulder.

"And yet they always loved you," he continued, obviously unaware of her distraction.

She shifted sideways to get a better view. Something jagged and white reflected against the glow from the lantern. It appeared to be a stalagmite, but it couldn't be. A stalagmite jutted upward from the cave floor, where minerals collected from dripping water. But no water dripped here. The formation jutted sideways, partially in the light, partially in the shadow. The formation looked fresh, white.

"He has a tight hold on you," Joseph continued.

She looked up at him and smiled, but out of the corner of her eye she saw the formation move. She gasped and grabbed his arm. "What is that?"

A pile of rocks shifted. A human shadow loomed, holding that formation like a bludgeon, its whiteness reflecting crazily in the lantern light.

A man with wild white hair raised the weapon. Joseph caught her in his arms and wrenched her away from the intruder as the stalagmite glanced off his shoulder.

He grunted in pain. "Get down," he told her. "Get away!"

The attacker drew his bludgeon back and turned it

around as if to use it as a sword. "Thieves, robbers!" he spat. "Stealing our property from under our noses. You won't get away with it." He lunged forward and jabbed at Joseph with his makeshift weapon.

Victoria reached into her skirt pocket for her pistol but the man kicked her sideways with his booted foot. She stumbled against a boulder as pain shot through her wounded thigh. The gun slid out of her reach.

Joseph grabbed for the man, but he stepped aside and stabbed at Joseph again, knocking him to his knees. Wooly raised the rock again, high above his head. Joseph lunged upward and caught the man's arms, shoving him away.

A loud war cry came at them from the shadows behind Wooly. Gray emerged, head low, shoulders hunched, and rammed the man from behind with a hoarse grunt.

Wooly stumbled. The rock fell to the ground with a clatter.

Victoria screamed as the wild-haired slaver fell forward, chest first, onto the lethal point of his own weapon. Joseph grabbed her hard against his chest and turned her away, shielding her eyes with his shoulder.

Gray gasped loudly, then moaned. He stumbled back into the shadows and retched.

For a long moment, all Victoria could do was cling to Joseph with her face pressed against him, needing the power of his arms around her as she listened to poor Gray burst into sobs behind a rock formation.

"Captain." Gray was trembling.

"It's okay, son." Joseph's voice rumbled in Victoria's ear. "You did the right thing."

Victoria pulled from Joseph's embrace and dropped to her knees beside the attacker, but she could tell before checking that he was already dead, his eyes open wide as he stared into the darkness.

Joseph drew her to her feet. "He's gone?"

She nodded, wordless.

"He tried to kill you, Captain," Gray said. "I heard him. He had to be following you for a long way. I thought I saw his shadow a couple of times in your lantern light." His voice broke. "I didn't…I wasn't thinking to kill him."

Joseph's arm tightened around Victoria "Gray, why were you following us?"

"I…well…I kept thinking about that man, thinking he could've followed you back inside, or if he'd get out and tell others and they'd catch up with us." He swallowed hard. "I couldn't let anybody hurt the doc."

Victoria turned to their young hero and recognized that expression. She'd felt the same way the day she'd shot Matthew's killer. "It's going to be okay, Gray. You saved lives today. You helped save a lot of lives. That's what you need to think about."

The boy's face turned red and his eyes brightened suspiciously. His jaw worked in silence as if he wanted to speak but couldn't find the words. She held her arms out to him. He stepped up to her and hugged her tightly, laying his head on her shoulder. She kissed him on the top of his head and released him. "You don't need to eavesdrop anymore, Gray. Go on ahead and help the others."

He looked up at her with a forced, watery-eyed grin. "So you can go ahead with your sparking."

"Gray," Joseph warned.

Gray sighed and walked on ahead, head bowed, dragging his steps.

"It's going to take him some time to recover," Joseph

said. He leaned over the body and studied it. "I think this man has his tomb right here."

"I feel badly for his family." She turned to follow Gray.

"So do I, but we have other families under our care. Your limp is worse."

"We'll be at the boats soon."

Before she could take another step, he handed her the lantern, picked her up in his arms as if she was no heavier than the new Frasier baby and held her closely to his chest.

She caught the scent of wild mint and felt the flexing of his muscles, and she relaxed as, once again, time folded in on itself. She laid her head against his shoulder. "Joseph?"

"Hmm?"

"You remember when I was delirious?"

"I'll never forget it."

"I told you that I loved you."

"Yes?"

"I do remember. I still mean it."

His steps slowed. "Are you sure you're not delirious?"

"I just witnessed a life leave this world less than an hour after I helped a life enter it. I've realized how precious life is. How precious time is."

"I don't think I'll ever tire of hearing those words."

"That I delivered a baby?"

"That you love me."

"Good, because I don't think I'm going to get tired of telling you."

"You are the only love of my life, Victoria. There's never been another. I don't know that I could live without knowing you're always lighting up your corner of the world."

"Then I suppose we should stay in the same corner together."

His arms tightened. "Are you proposing marriage to me?"

"No, sir. I wouldn't do that."

"Then I guess I'll have to ask the question that's been on my heart for over ten years. Victoria Fenway, will you marry me?"

"When?"

"What?"

"How soon?"

He chuckled. "There'll be a parson waiting for us when we get to Kansas."

"I think that's a wonderful idea."

They were sealing the pact with a kiss when a shout reached them from ahead. "We're here!" It was Gray again. "The boats are loaded and all's quiet. McDonald's here!"

"McDonald?"

"Made good time." It was the deep voice of the scout. "We've got us a full wagon train waiting for us north of Neosho. Everything's set and I've got a lead on a trail nobody else knows about. Good thing I went to Elk River."

They heard celebrating and laughter at the mouth of the cavern, and as they stepped out into the cool night air and onto the boats lined up along Shoal Creek, Victoria felt a stronger sense of hope for the future than she'd felt in many months. This was perfect.

Chapter Nineteen

Matthew Joseph Frasier was three weeks old when he rode into his new home, the Kansas Territory village that had been named Rickard in a town-hall meeting two weeks earlier. He made his presence known with the strongest set of lungs the citizens of Rickard had ever heard.

Of course, the village was young yet, having been founded by the man who carried that same name, Captain Joseph Rickard. Five wagon trains had been led by the captain to this hidden valley blessed with an abundance of trees on the southeastern side of the state, where hills and valleys and creeks and rivers nourished the newcomers. They were far enough away from the border wars that, for now, they felt safe enough to build and settle.

And build they did. The first sign anyone saw upon entering town was engraved with the town name. Folks here were proud of their founder and of the fact that they had the good sense to follow him to their haven of rest. They were a people strong in their convictions.

Joseph rode ahead of the twenty-six-wagon train beside his scout, McDonald, who kept his head down as the crowds on either side of the road raised flags and shouted and cheered the newcomers.

Victoria and Heidi rode in the Ladue wagon, and as always, Pudding brayed his heart out from behind the wagon while Heidi threatened to cook some donkey stew someday soon.

To Victoria's amazement, Joseph and McDonald led the train to a brand-new building with an engraved sign for the Rickard Clinic. Victoria could not suppress a smile.

She jumped down from the wagon and walked to stand by her fiancé. "Just how sure were you that I would agree to marry you?"

"I needed motivation to get you here. You didn't know I had more tricks up my sleeve if the proposal didn't work out."

"Captain," said a man who had obviously come from working in the field to greet them, "there's more. Follow us."

The man, whom Joseph introduced as Parson Freemont, led them on around the town square where a wood-carved mansion stood in all its glory.

Victoria gasped at the beauty of the handiwork.

"We all built this for our new mayor," the parson said, gesturing with muscular arms toward the townsfolk who surrounded them. "And who would be more appropriate to serve as the new town mayor than the man who has proven his ability to handle every difficulty any of the townsfolk threw his way?"

To Victoria's delight, in front of everyone who had come out to celebrate the arrival of their new mayor, Joseph drew her to his side and introduced her as his bride to be. Everyone cheered.

"Captain!" called Heidi, loudly enough for everyone

to hear. "That there's a parson? It's not just his name, like Deacon Fritz?"

"He's a real parson."

"Can he marry folks?"

Laughter grew as the travelers disembarked from their wagons and stretched their weary limbs to huddle around their beloved friends.

"I sure can," said Parson Freemont.

"Then what're we waiting for?" called Audy Reich. "These two young'uns have been courtin' on and off for over ten years. We need us some children to grow this town into a nice, big city."

The parson's white teeth split his coffee-black face. "Seeing as how we have us a great crowd of witnesses right here, and seeing as how you don't seem to mind a minister with some mud on his boots and black on his skin," he said, raising his mud-caked work shoes, "then I don't see why we can't do exactly that."

It lasted ten minutes, if that. Parson Freemont must have studied the vows well because he never had to look at a book. His deep, black eyes were filled with tears of joy by the time he had Joseph and Victoria clasp hands. He placed his big, work-worn palm over theirs, prayed to the Almighty for their lives to be filled with joy and with tears dripping down his face, he pronounced them man and wife.

The crowd cheered. Joseph pulled Victoria into his arms as if he couldn't bear to let her go even a few inches away from him. "Well, my love, we've proven our devotion to each other through grief and loss. Now it's time to prove it with a family, and with a long, happy life together."

Their travel these past three weeks had forced them to be apart for most of the time, and she cherished her time with him now. She knew she would always cherish his touch, his nearness, the expression in his eyes.

"Joseph," she whispered.

"Yes, my love?"

"Will you always look at me like that?"

"Like what?"

"Like I'm the most important person in your life."

"That, you can depend on." He captured her chin with his fingers and raised her face to kiss her. And kiss her. And kiss her. They ignored the good-hearted teasing that surrounded them. At that moment, all that mattered was the two of them. All else could take care of itself for the next day or two. Maybe even a week. They had a mansion to explore, and their own love to explore and enjoy.

Victoria had a strong hunch that they would figure out how to explore that to the best of their ability.

* * * * *

Dear Reader,

When I visited the privately owned park of Jolly Mill and studied its history, I knew I wanted to share it with you in the story. The mill you read about in these pages still exists. The village was once called the Village of Jollification, and locals believe that name rose in favor when the mill was a distillery for alcoholic beverages. More than a hundred and fifty years ago, Jolly Mill was a popular resting place for wagon trains traveling to the new frontier. If you find yourself in the southwestern corner of Missouri, you might want to find Jolly Mill and visit the park. I hope you enjoy it as much as I have.

Hannah Alexander

Questions for Discussion

1. *Keeping Faith* begins with Dr. Victoria Fenway working with her young assistant while secretly watching for her husband's murderer to sneak up on them. Have you ever had to continue living your life as if nothing was wrong when you felt as if calamity could strike at any time? How did that feel?

2. Out of concern for the emotional well-being of those around her, Victoria battles her heartache in silence and conceals most of the truth about her past love for Joseph. Do you think that was the best thing for her to do? If you were her, would you share the past with new friends?

3. Have you ever shared secrets with a friend and then found out they couldn't be trusted? If so, what did you do about it?

4. Joseph battles feelings of betrayal as well as guilt over the history he shares with Victoria. Should he have approached her sooner, when her husband was still alive, about why she had not replied to his many letters? Why?

5. The only reason Joseph allows the troublemaking Johnston brothers to continue traveling with the wagon train is because their father had once saved his life. Do you think he believed the boys could grow up to be good men like their father, or was he simply afraid they were so clumsy they could get killed if he'd sent them back home alone?

6. Did you ever act out as a teenager? How did that turn out for you? Have you seen young adults who were once wild grow into responsible adults?

7. Victoria works at a profession in a time in history when women aren't accepted as physicians, and even men don't often make enough to live on. Why, then, do you think she's taken Heidi on as an apprentice? Shouldn't she just encourage Heidi to find a good man to marry and have children?

8. When Victoria leaps between an attacking panther and Heidi to save Heidi's life, she is badly injured. She would likely have remained safe if Heidi hadn't disobeyed her orders to stay with the wagon train. How much trouble would you have forgiving someone whose willful disobedience nearly killed you?

9. Have you ever suffered from the poor judgment of others? How did you find the strength to forgive? Or have you been able to forgive?

10. Joseph is torn between responsibility and love when Victoria disappears into the forest in the middle of the night to travel to a village she knows is dangerous. He ends up splitting the wagon train in half and going after the woman he loves, while appointing someone else to lead the other half of travelers. Is he betraying those who have placed their trust in him? Why do you feel this way?

11. Have you ever broken a promise because of someone you loved?

12. Victoria knows she is entering a dangerous place when she leaves the wagon train to rescue people in need. Do you think she would do this if she was safely ensconced in a happy, stable marriage with Joseph? What would you do if you made a promise, and then the situation changed drastically?

13. Joseph and Victoria travel to Kansas Territory with many abolitionists in an effort to ensure freedom when Kansas becomes a state. They know there will be great turmoil, and possibly a war. Would you have gone to Kansas, or would you have continued on West to avoid the conflict?

14. If you were Heidi, which boy do you think would be best suited for you as a husband—William Reich, Buster Johnston or Gray Johnston? What would be the merits of each?

15. Victoria marries the love of her life less than a year after her husband's death. Do you think this will cause contention in the ranks of the new community Joseph has built? Would you wait for a more suitable time?

COMING NEXT MONTH
from Love Inspired® Historical
AVAILABLE OCTOBER 1, 2013

A FAMILY FOR CHRISTMAS
Texas Grooms
Winnie Griggs

Stranded in a small town after defending an orphan stowaway on the train, Eve Pickering decides Turnabout, Texas, may be just the place to start over with her new charge. Especially when a smooth-talking Texan rides to their rescue....

THE SECRET PRINCESS
Protecting the Crown
Rachelle McCalla

When Prince Luke rescued Evelyn from a life of servitude he never suspected she was the daughter of his greatest enemy. But this Cinderella must keep her royal blood secret lest she lose her heart—and her life.

TAMING THE TEXAS RANCHER
Rhonda Gibson

In a race to the altar to claim his inheritance, Daniel Westland thinks love is a luxury. But things change when he meets his beautiful mail-order bride....

AN UNLIKELY UNION
Shannon Farrington

Union doctor Evan Mackay has no tolerance for Southern sympathizers—no matter how lovely. As they work together to heal Baltimore's wounded soldiers, can Southern nurse Emily Davis soften his Yankee heart?

LIHCNM0913

SPECIAL EXCERPT FROM

Love Inspired

He was her high school crush, and now he's a single father of twins. Allison True just got a second chance at love.

Read on for a sneak preview of
STORYBOOK ROMANCE by Lissa Manley,
the exciting fifth book in
THE HEART OF MAIN STREET series,
available October 2013.

Something clunked from the back of the bookstore, drawing Allison True's ever-vigilant attention. Her ears perking up, she rounded the end of the front counter. Another clunk sounded, and then another. Allison decided the noise was coming from the Kids' Korner, so she picked up the pace and veered toward the back right part of the store, creasing her brow.

She arrived in the area set up for kids. Her gaze zeroed in on a dark-haired toddler dressed in jeans and a red shirt, slowly yet methodically yanking books off a shelf, one after the other. Each book fell to the floor with a heavy clunk, and in between each sound, the little guy laughed, clearly enjoying the sound of his relatively harmless yet messy play.

Allison rushed over, noting there was no adult in sight. "Hey, there, bud," she said. "Whatcha doing?"

He turned big brown eyes fringed with long, dark eyelashes toward her. He looked vaguely familiar even though she was certain she'd never met this little boy.

"Fun!" A chubby hand sent another book crashing to the floor. He giggled and stomped his feet on the floor in a little happy dance. "See?"

Carefully she reached out and stilled his marauding hands. "Whoa, there, little guy." She gently pulled him away. "The books are supposed to stay on the shelf." Holding on to him, she cast her gaze about the enclosed area set aside for kids, but her view was limited by the tall bookshelves lined up from the edge of the Kids' Korner to the front of the store. "Are you here with your mommy or daddy?"

The boy tugged. "Daddy!" he squealed.

"Nicky!" a deep masculine voice replied behind her. "Oh, man. Looks like you've been making a mess."

A nebulous sense of familiarity swept through her at the sound of that voice. Not breathing, still holding the boy's hand, Allison slowly turned around. Her whole body froze and her heart gave a little spasm then fell to her toes as she looked into deep brown eyes that matched Nicky's.

Sam Franklin. The only man Allison had ever loved.

*Pick up STORYBOOK ROMANCE
in October 2013 wherever Love Inspired® Books are sold.*

LIEXP0913